KV-010-072

SPECIAL MESSAGE TO READERS

This book is published under the auspices of

THE ULVERSCROFT FOUNDATION

(registered charity No. 264873 UK)

Established in 1972 to provide funds for research, diagnosis and treatment of eye diseases. Examples of contributions made are: —

A Children's Assessment Unit at Moorfield's Hospital, London.

•

Twin operating theatres at the Western Ophthalmic Hospital, London.

•

A Chair of Ophthalmology at the Royal Australian College of Ophthalmologists.

•

The Ulverscroft Children's Eye Unit at the Great Ormond Street Hospital For Sick Children, London.

You can help further the work of the Foundation by making a donation or leaving a legacy. Every contribution, no matter how small, is received with gratitude. Please write for details to:

**THE ULVERSCROFT FOUNDATION,
The Green, Bradgate Road, Anstey,
Leicester LE7 7FU, England.
Telephone: (0116) 236 4325**

**In Australia write to:
THE ULVERSCROFT FOUNDATION,
c/o The Royal Australian College of
Ophthalmologists,
27, Commonwealth Street, Sydney,
N.S.W. 2010.**

Linden Salter was born in London, has been a teacher and researcher in various countries including Nigeria and Papua New Guinea, and now lives in Australia's remote Northern Territory, in a small community that rejoices in the name of Humpty Doo. Linden Salter's first novel was *The Lady and the Luddite*.

AD 03509287

THE MAJOR'S MINION

Determined to prove her brother innocent of murder, Katherine sets out in male disguise to find the real criminal. The most likely suspect is Major Lancaster, a hero of the Peninsular War. After she saves the Major's life, he offers her a place in his household. He finds in this intelligent and sympathetic youth (as he believes) a person to whom he can unburden his soul, while she finds in him something very close to her ideal man. But as her love grows, so does her belief in his guilt, and she faces the agonizing choice of sending either him or her brother to the gallows.

Books by Linden Salter
Published by The House of Ulverscroft:

THE LADY AND THE LUDDITE

LINDEN SALTER

THE
MAJOR'S MINION

Complete and Unabridged

ULVERSCROFT
Leicester

First published in Great Britain in 2000 by
Robert Hale Limited
London

First Large Print Edition
published 2003
by arrangement with
Robert Hale Limited
London

The moral right of the author has been asserted

Copyright © 2000 by Linden Salter
All rights reserved

British Library CIP Data

Salter, Linden
 The major's minion.—Large print ed.—
 Ulverscroft large print series: romance
 1. England—Social life and customs—19th century
 —Fiction 2. Love stories 3. Large type books
 I. Title
 823.9′14 [F]

 ISBN 0–7089–4790–5

LINCOLNSHIRE
COUNTY COUNCIL

Published by
F. A. Thorpe (Publishing)
Anstey, Leicestershire

Set by Words & Graphics Ltd.
Anstey, Leicestershire
Printed and bound in Great Britain by
T. J. International Ltd., Padstow, Cornwall

This book is printed on acid-free paper

In memory of Michael Collins
who died too young
Kano, Nigeria, 1980

Acknowledgements

I thank everyone who has supported me in writing this, especially the members of the Republic of Pemberley at <http://www.pemberley.com> who have shared their knowledge of the period, the Northern Territory Department of Arts and Museums for a grant which helped the final stages of editing, and all those who read and commented on early drafts. The responsibility for any errors is mine.

1

On the evening that he was to be murdered, George Lancaster wandered into the wrong room.

The Rose and Crown was an old inn in this year of 1813, having been built in the Wars of the Roses when the original landlord was kept busy repainting the rose every time the crown changed hands. It had been improved and added to many times over the centuries, and the stairs and hallways were far from regular, which was why George Lancaster, who disdained directions, entered the room immediately above his own.

Most men, when faced with a young woman in her petticoat repairing a rip in her dress, would have muttered an embarrassed apology and retreated hastily. Not this man. The woman wasn't entirely to his taste, being much too tall, much too strongly featured, and much too slim. But she was young, barely clad, and alone: that was enough for him.

Her icy request for him to leave he ignored: he noticed only how she blushed at his invasion. 'Oh, come now, my charming girl,' he said, walking steadily towards her, smiling. 'Such a happy chance must be put to advantage.'

She did not scream for help: good. She stood up: good. But then to his surprise she took a stance more appropriate to a fencer than a seamstress, and brandished her three-inch needle like a foil. 'Get away from me,' she hissed, still holding her dress in her other hand.

His interest increased: this was something new. 'I don't think that will protect you, my dear,' he said, still approaching, his arms ready to capture her in an embrace.

Suddenly she whipped her dress into his face, blinding him for a moment, and he felt a stab in the back of his hand as she ripped the needle through his flesh. It wasn't enough to confuse him: he was under attack, and his instincts took over. His hand reached down to cover his groin, and the kick she landed there was only enough to hurt, not disable him.

'Bitch!' he cried, sucking the blood from his hand. It was no longer lust that drove him: it was revenge. He grabbed her in his arms, forcing his mouth on hers. But she took him unawares again as she bit his lip hard enough to draw blood, and he flinched away from her, allowing her to call out.

'Help!' she screamed. 'Harry! Help!'

His mouth was back on hers, stopping her voice; his hand was on her breast, squeezing it hard; his other arm was round her, pulling her so close to him she couldn't struggle. Though she kicked him again, her feet were bare and had little effect on him. He threw her to the floor and landed heavily on her, winding her. He forced his knee between her legs, ignoring her hands that tried to gouge his eyes out.

Then he felt a hand at the back of his collar, and he was pulled away from the woman. Quickly he rolled over and stood up, prepared to brazen it out; but he was given no chance as a fist landed squarely on his chin and sent him reeling.

The man who attacked him was no taller than the woman: perhaps six inches shorter than he. But both of them together he could not face, for the woman was getting up with fury in her face and reaching for a heavy brass candlestick, prepared to crash it on his skull. And now there were other faces appearing in the doorway, and both men were held to stop them fighting.

'Gentlemen, gentlemen!' It was the landlord. 'I must protest! Stop at once.'

'Get this pig away before I kill him,' panted the shorter man. The woman went over to her rescuer: they stood together accusingly.

3

George Lancaster tried to recover his dignity now he had an audience. 'How dare you!' he breathed heavily. 'D'you not know who I am?'

'You're the man who assaulted my sister!' snarled the other man. 'That's all I need to know.'

'Assault your sister? She loved every minute. Ask her how long it was before she cried for help!'

The brother would have attacked him again if he had not been restrained.

Now the landlord intervened. 'Mr Lancaster,' he said. 'Let me show you to your own room.' George Lancaster felt the grip of a sturdy inn-servant edge him towards the door; he did not resist, recognizing that this was the safest way out.

The landlord ushered him down the stairs into his own room. He was not to leave it alive.

* * *

Katherine Faulkner dipped her handkerchief into the water jug and wiped her face, trying to wash away the memory of a brutal mouth on hers. 'I'm glad you arrived, Harry. I was beginning to worry that I couldn't get rid of him.'

'Thank God I did, Kitty,' said her brother. He put his arm round her in comfort, and she rested her head briefly on his shoulder, glad not to pretend to be brave.

Neither of them liked to fuss. The young man's fiery red hair was at variance with his peaceable nature: he was roused to anger only by the most extreme circumstances — such as a man trying to rape his sister. She was naturally less placid, but she scorned exhibitions of sensibility and tried to appear as calm as her brother. Not that either of them needed to display much emotion when they were together: they were twins, and each knew what the other was thinking and feeling almost as readily as they knew their own minds.

They had always shared their joys and comforted each other in their griefs, from the time their mother had died when they were still small children. Their father had never remarried: though he was a handsome man, well-respected as the squire of Eastham, he'd never loved another woman. He'd left both his children to grow up pretty much as they wished to: and they wished to be together.

Katherine picked up her dress and examined it. 'Oh dear. It's even more torn than it was before,' she said, glad to talk of something mundane.

'Throw it away, then. Aunt Helen will fit you out with new clothes when we reach London.'

'I should,' she said, surveying the rip in a dress that had never been lovely. 'But I'm attached to it. I never realized that a dress could be a weapon of defence. Or a three-inch needle, come to that.'

'Is that how you were fighting him off?' Harry asked with a small laugh of disbelief. 'What a good thing you insisted on joining in my fencing lessons!'

'You remember how everyone was shocked and kept telling me to learn how to play the piano instead? I was in the right, it seems.' She laid the dress aside, recognizing that it was ruined past repair, and donned another from her portmanteau.

She was decently clad when the landlord returned, full of apologies, promising them the finest dinner that the Rose and Crown could provide. 'Do you wish to make charges, Mr Faulkner, Miss Faulkner?' he asked, his hope that they wouldn't plain on his face.

'Yes,' said Katherine.

'No,' said Harry.

'I'll leave you alone to discuss the matter,' said the landlord. 'But I must tell you that Mr Lancaster is a rich and powerful man, and well-connected. He made very sure to inform me that he's a close friend of the Prince Regent.' He apologized once again as he left.

'We can't let a man like that go free!' protested Katherine. 'God knows how many other women he's attacked: women who couldn't fight so well as I, or had no brothers as convenient as you.'

'Kitty, we can't,' said Harry quietly. 'Just think for a moment. You know what he'd say in court. He'll tell the world that you encouraged him. You should have called for help earlier.'

'I should,' she acknowledged. 'But I thought I could manage alone.'

'You always do think that,' he said. 'But sometimes you can't.'

'I know. I shan't make that mistake again.' She paced about the room, as if she could walk away her anger. 'But what are we going to do? I refuse to let him get away with it!'

'I'll challenge him,' Harry sighed with reluctance. 'That's the only thing to do.'

'No!' she cried, horrified. 'Why should you risk your life because he assaulted me?'

'Because if I don't, he'll brand you a wanton and me a coward. You heard what the landlord said — he's got powerful friends. Our reputations would be ruined.'

'Oh, bother our reputations! What do they matter?'

'Do you want to go through life with everyone thinking that you encouraged a man like that?'

'No, but — '

'And I certainly don't want to have everyone think that I dared not challenge a man who tried to rape my sister.'

'Oh, but not now!' she cried. 'Wait!'

'What for?'

She searched for an excuse. 'Wait until we get to London. You can't call him out now: you don't have any seconds.'

He gave a laugh. 'You could dress up as a man and act for me: he'd never notice.'

'That's not funny, Harry,' she reproved. 'Oh, at least — at least make him challenge you! That way you have choice of weapons. You're much better with a sword than a pistol.'

'Oh, I think I'd manage to hit him with a pistol,' he said with an air of ease that did not deceive her. 'He's a much bigger target than I am.'

Just then their dinner arrived. Katherine welcomed it, knowing that it would give her more time to try to dissuade her brother. But she was wasting her breath.

He had grown up so fast in the past few months since their father died. Until then she had always been the leader of the pair; but

8

when he became the squire of Eastham at twenty-one, the responsibilities made him suddenly much older. No longer could she lead him, and she knew that she should not even try.

That was the reason for this journey. She loved Harry, so she must leave him. When the invitation came from her fashionable aunt, Lady Fenton, to spend a Season in London, she accepted it gladly. Though it hadn't been stated, the aim was clear: to find her a husband.

Though Harry had insisted that she always had a place at Eastham, she knew that things must change. One day soon he would take a wife, and she didn't think she could bear giving way to another woman, a stranger, and fading into the small dignity of a maiden aunt.

Harry had been reluctant at first, until he had extracted a promise from her: she would not marry a man she did not love. She was perfectly willing to give it. She was a practical young woman, not given to high-flown romantic notions, but their parents' happy, loving marriage would not let her settle for anything less.

She didn't have to marry: her fortune of ten thousand pounds was enough to live on — infinitely preferable to living with a bad husband. But living with a good husband? That had its attractions. She'd felt a small pang when she and Harry set out from Eastham, but far greater was her anticipation of a season of pleasure. Though she had grown up a self-confessed tomboy, she was woman enough to enjoy the thought of fine dresses and fashionable routs. She would enjoy a few months of gaudy dissipation, even if she didn't find someone to catch her fancy.

There had never been anyone in Eastham — not since she was fourteen and the brawny village blacksmith had married a farmer's daughter. She knew she wasn't conventionally beautiful, but she also knew that her aunt's advice on dress and deportment would make her far from repulsive. She would not do for a man who wanted to marry a beautiful idiot, but then such a man would not do for her either. Surely there must be somebody who looked for companionship in a wife rather than mindless adoration and submission, and in London she might meet him.

But not if she was already marked as someone who would encourage the attentions of such a vile man as Mr Lancaster.

Dinner was over. Harry put down his glass and stood up. 'No sense in wasting any more time,' he said heavily.

'Harry, I — ' She didn't finish: she put her

arms round him, then let him go.

'I shan't be long,' he said, and then he left.

Alone, she leaned her elbows on the table, resting her head in her hands, her repugnance at the memory of Lancaster's assault vying in her mind with the sick fear she felt for Harry. What would she do if he were killed? It would be like losing half of herself. But perhaps that revolting man wouldn't accept a challenge: he might be brave enough only to attack a lone woman. He didn't seem to be any too skilled in fighting: she could have beaten him off if he'd not been much bigger and heavier than she.

So much for the tall, dark, handsome man she'd dreamed of meeting, who would cherish her and initiate her tenderly into the joys of love. Tall and dark, yes: perhaps she could even have thought him handsome in other circumstances. His was the first mouth that had kissed hers, his were the first hands that had felt her body. She wondered if she would ever obliterate the memory enough to welcome another man's kiss and embrace.

Perhaps that's why I didn't manage to stop Harry, she thought: I wasn't as opposed to his wish as I should have been. I want Lancaster dead.

Suddenly there was a sound from beneath her feet: it seemed alarmingly like a pistol shot.

The walls and doors of the old inn were very thick, and she could hear no more. Should she wait here? No: perhaps Harry needed her. She ran out of the room, down the stairs to the floor below. She could see that she was not the first to be attracted by the noise: a small crowd of inn-servants were gathered round an open doorway, and the landlord was running to join them from the other direction.

She too ran to the doorway: it had been broken open. Like the others, she looked inside the room. And there was Harry, kneeling down, holding a pistol in one hand, the other hand bloody from the gaping wound in the chest of the man who had once been George Lancaster.

'You shouldn't have done it,' she heard the landlord say. 'Oh, Mr Faulkner, you shouldn't have done it.'

★   ★   ★

Katherine's first instinct was to run after Harry protectively as he was frog-marched away by two big inn-servants, but she quelled it. She had other things to do.

She did not shake away the arm of the landlady who led her back to her room, though she refused the proffered smelling salts: she was not about to faint.

'Now you just sit down, Miss Faulkner,' the landlady was saying. 'You've had a nasty shock. Two nasty shocks, you poor thing. And in my inn, too. I can't tell you how sorry I am.'

'Where will they take Harry?'

'The lock-up. Constable Webb's there. He's a fair man: he won't let any harm come to your brother.' Until they hang him for murder, she did not say. 'I must say, I can't blame your brother too much for killing that dreadful man.'

'He didn't!' cried Katherine, hoping desperately that she was right. 'He's innocent!'

'Well, if that's right, then you've no need to worry, have you?' said the landlady with jovial insincerity. 'He'll get a fair trial.'

Katherine urgently needed time to be alone to think, so she got rid of the landlady, saying that she needed to lie down to recover from the shock. It was no lie: she was extremely shocked by the horrific events of the evening. But now she had to compose herself: she had a desperate task ahead of her.

Could Harry have killed George Lancaster in cold blood? That wasn't the sort of thing he would do: but he had been very angry. She dismissed her doubts: her preparations would have been just the same whatever her brother had done.

It didn't take long to get ready. Leaving the money for the night's accommodation on the mantelshelf to be found the next morning, she made her way to the local lock-up.

The lamps inside allowed her to see in through the window: there was a man there, presumably Constable Webb. She could see the bars of a cell, but it was too dark for her to make out whether Harry was inside. She quite deliberately allowed the horrors of the evening to flood through her so that tears came to her eyes. This was the time to look distraught, horrified, and, above all, harmless.

She burst into the lock-up, wailing in misery that was not entirely assumed. 'Oh, Harry!' she cried. Her brother's face appeared at the bars of the cell and she rushed up to him.

''Ere, miss,' said the constable: he was a little shorter than she was, but well-built, and his face was shrewd. 'No getting close to the prisoner, I'm afraid. That's agin' regulations.'

'But it's my brother!' she wailed.

The constable's voice softened. 'All right, miss, you can talk to him. But not too close. It's my job to make sure you ain't passing anything to him, you understand.'

'Oh, thank you, thank you,' she sobbed.

'I'm sorry to trouble you with my female weakness.'

'That's all right, young lady,' said the constable kindly. 'I'm used to the wailing of women in my job.'

'It's all right, Kitty,' Harry said, obviously alarmed at her unusual display of the vapours. 'I'm innocent. They won't hang an innocent man.' She wished he looked more confident of that statement.

'You are innocent, Harry?' she asked — though he was hardly likely to admit otherwise when the constable was so obviously listening to their every word.

'I'm innocent, Kitty. Word of a Faulkner.' The old childhood promise, never to be broken no matter how great the temptation.

That was it. All doubt fled from her mind. 'But what happened, then?'

Aware that the constable was listening, he told her. He had gone to the room belonging to George Lancaster prepared simply to enter, slap the man's face, and await his challenge. He had needed a few seconds to summon up his resolution, so he stood outside the door. 'And then I heard voices, Kitty,' he said. 'It seemed — well, it was dashed awkward, bursting in on him when there was someone with him.'

She reflected dryly on the etiquette that

would allow him to challenge a man to a duel to the death but not to interrupt a private conversation.

'Listen, Kitty,' Harry continued urgently. 'This is important. I heard Lancaster's voice quite distinctly. 'Killing Lord Bowland — it's a hanging matter,' that's what he said!'

'A hanging matter? Then — '

Harry didn't let her finish. 'Then the other man said something, and Lancaster shouted again: 'It's not too late for me to confess.' Then I heard the other man say something — the only words I could hear from him: 'On the contrary, George. It is much too late for you to do anything ever again.' Then I heard Lancaster cry out: 'No! Don't!' The next thing I heard was a pistol shot. I grabbed at the door handle and tried to turn it, but it was locked, so I kicked it open. Lancaster was on the floor, blood everywhere, and there was a pistol beside him.'

'What about the other man? Did you see him?'

'Yes. He was climbing out of the window — he must have heard me trying to break the door down. I chased after him, but I wasn't fast enough. Then I heard a groan from Lancaster, and I had to turn back to him to see if I could help him, but I couldn't — he died without saying anything. Then I looked

16

up, and there was everyone crowded round the doorway, and I realized what it must look like. I didn't kill him, Kitty; but God knows how I can prove it.'

She turned to Constable Webb as if he represented the opinion of the world. 'You see? He's innocent. Don't you believe him?'

'Don't make no difference whether I believe him or not, miss. My job's to look after him until the magistrate sees him. But I'll tell you this. Whether he did it or not, there's few that'll blame him for it, seeing as what that Mr Lancaster tried to do to you.'

'Will they — if he's found guilty — will they — I mean, you said people wouldn't blame him — will he be — '

'Will they hang him, you mean?'

She nodded.

'Oh, yes, they'll hang him all right, but there'll be a lot of people sorry to see him go.'

Her sobs, which had vanished while she was listening to Harry, burst out again with renewed force. 'Oh my brother!' she wailed with enough vigour to rattle the walls. 'My poor Harry!'

The constable came close to her to comfort her. 'There, now, miss, there, there,' he was saying, patting her on her shoulder.

'I'm sorry,' she managed to say, her hysterical cries abating. 'I have a handkerchief somewhere.' She fumbled in her reticule. 'Could you — would you get me a drink, please?'

The constable turned away from her towards a small barrel of beer that stood on his table. Now was her chance. She took a deep breath as she produced from her reticule, not a handkerchief, but a stocking filled with wet sand. She took the two paces necessary to reach the constable, raised her arm, and brought the stocking heavily down on the back of his head. He dropped instantly.

'Please, God, let me not have killed him,' she prayed as she knelt down beside him. To her relief he groaned as she fumbled inside his jacket and found the keys. Hastily she unlocked the door to Harry's cell, and her brother almost fell into her arms. There was time only for a quick murmur of thanks, and then they hurriedly turned to the constable, unconscious on the floor.

'Quick, tie him up,' she said ruthlessly.

'That seems hard on the poor man, Kitty.'

'The rope goes round his wrists or your neck.'

He argued no more, but grabbed a cord from the wall and proceeded to tie up Webb's wrists. There was another low moan and the man's eyes opened.

'Oh, miss,' he groaned. 'That was taking mean advantage of a man's good nature.'

Katherine helped Harry to sit him up against the wall. 'I'm frightfully sorry, Constable,' she said. 'But it's my brother's life, you see. That's more important to me than anything.'

Then brother and sister turned and fled into the night.

2

'Rich men may find it hard to enter the kingdom of heaven, but they have impressive funerals.' Major Richard Lancaster did not hide his cynical disgust. 'George lived abominably, and he died because he tried to rape someone. Now we bury him with full pomp and ceremony.'

'Pomp and ceremony have their uses, Richard,' said his cousin, the Earl of Bowland. 'In the eyes of the world, the Prince Regent's presence at the funeral will lessen the dishonour that your brother brought on our family.'

The major tried to recall just one occasion when George had shown any concern for his own or the family's honour, or just one moment in which he and George had felt any affection towards each other. There was nothing. Instead, he remembered the time — God, it was twenty years ago! — when he'd come upon his elder brother cutting the tails off a litter of kittens for sport. He had protested, and George had jeered at him for being unmanly.

The insult had stuck. From that moment

he was determined to show that George was wrong. He had to prove — to himself as much as anyone else — that manliness did not mean callousness. In his youth he believed that all he needed was chivalry. So he had fought any school bully bigger and older than himself, and found himself revered by the smaller boys as their protector. When he was grown, and there were no bullies left around him who were stronger than he was, he had taken on the strongest of them all, Napoleon, and joined the army.

It was then he learned that chivalry was a fraud. Yes, he had proved himself a man; the praise he had received for courage and cool-headedness began to convince even himself. After all, if Wellington had clapped him on the shoulder and called him a hero, who was he to disagree with his commanding officer? But he had become callous. He had seen friends shot down, and he had learned to turn away from them and rally the troops to fight on. Only during the nights as he tossed in his sleep could he hear the screams of the dying, feel the agony of the besieged cities, and see the broken human bodies.

That was over. He was out of the army now. He had returned to civilian life to discover that, while he was gaining a military reputation, his brother was gaining one for fashionable debauchery. In comfort, and in safety — as he'd thought. George had wealth and connections, and had escaped punishment for his vices and crimes — until now. George had had a quick, clean death: far, far better than he deserved.

Now here they were, burying him. The procession was long, the preacher was fashionable, and the coffin a triumph of expensive joinery. The hypocrisy of which he was part made the major's skin crawl, as if he were wearing a hair shirt instead of these impeccably tailored mourning clothes. He turned to his cousin. 'George's death was in keeping with his life: a disgrace. Nothing can cover that up.'

'You put it too strongly, Richard,' Lord Bowland replied.

'Consider this, Edward. There's some poor young woman who has had the privilege of being assaulted by George, seen her brother arrested for killing him, and been forced to flee from the law. My brother's last act was typically ruinous.'

'Before you get sentimental about her, recall that her brother shot your brother down in cold blood. Not at all the thing. Should have called him out.'

'He's likely to go to the gallows for that breach of etiquette — if he's caught, which I

22

sincerely hope he's not. I hope that the pair of them are in safety somewhere hundreds of miles away.'

'Indeed, I'd observed a certain lack of fervour in your quest for your brother's murderer.'

'What, have a man hanged for defending his sister's honour?'

'Yes, I gather that the young man's of good family; nephew of the delightful Lady Fenton, I believe.'

The major looked icily at his cousin. 'You mean that if he'd not been, you would have had him swallowing George's assault on his sister?'

'I don't mean that at all.' Bowland smiled. 'Come, Richard, let us not argue at the funeral: we have a coffin to carry. If it makes you happy, I'll wish the young man every success in staying hidden.'

'Perhaps that is best for him. But I'm far from happy about the sister; it's damned hard on her, to be forced into hiding because George tried to rape her. God help her, wherever she is.'

★   ★   ★

She was not hundreds of miles away, nor even hundreds of yards. Major Lancaster would have seen her if he'd looked at the loiterers outside the church instead of keeping his eyes straight ahead. But even if he had seen her, he wouldn't have known her for what she was.

A few days had turned Katherine Faulkner from the respectable daughter of a country squire on her way to her first Season into a fugitive in male disguise. She was far too tall a woman to escape notice, but in these old clothes of Harry's she could appear as a man of moderate height. After a fierce argument — brief, as they'd had no time to waste in their flight — Harry had agreed to go into hiding. Katherine alone would take on the task of proving his innocence. And the only way to do that was to find the man who really had shot George Lancaster.

Harry would recognize the man again, but he was not in a position to stroll the streets of London looking for him. Harry's bright red hair could easily be covered up with blacking, but the forces of the law would know that too and not be deceived by such a simple disguise.

But she had a good idea of the man she was looking for. A gentleman by his appearance, aged around thirty, and as tall as George Lancaster himself, Harry reckoned. He had grey eyes — Harry had seen them glinting in the lamplight as the man had stared at him for a second just before he'd climbed out of the window. He'd been wearing a ring: 'It looked like an heirloom, Kitty,' Harry had said. 'You know, one of those old-fashioned things. It was made of rubies, set in the form of a rose.' Presumably he wanted to kill someone called Lord Bowland: Katherine resolved to find this aristocrat as soon as she could. Finally, and most usefully, he had called his victim George. That meant a considerable degree of intimacy; anyone so intimate would almost certainly be at the funeral, because to miss it would cause comment.

Blessing her man's disguise, since women did not normally attend funerals, Katherine trusted that nobody would take any notice of her in her place among the idlers who were hanging around St George's in Hanover Square to watch the spectacle. Nobody knew her, and she knew none of those who arrived in the procession, except that she recognized the Prince Regent from his pictures.

Hastily she scanned the mourners entering the church. Too old, too short, she thought. She wasn't close enough to see the colour of their eyes, and they were all in black gloves so any ring was hidden, but surely there must be at least one tall gentleman of thirty among all these people? There were, as she realized when she looked at the pall-bearers. All six of them. Of course, she reflected: old men and small men couldn't carry the weight that had been George Lancaster.

She moved closer to study their faces and features, and to fix them into her mind. She didn't know who any of them were, but it shouldn't be hard to find out later. She could see the faces of only half of the pall-bearers, as the other three were obscured by the coffin as it rested on their shoulders. One by one she memorized the profiles of the men on her side of the aisle, making sure she could visualize each one before she studied the next.

There, that's three of them, she thought. I'll recognize them if I see them again. She sidled unobtrusively round the back of the church until she reached the other side and she could see the other pall-bearers. Again she studied them: the fourth man, the fifth.

Then the sixth.

To her it was as if everyone else in the church had suddenly faded away. There was no need for her to work at memorizing his features; they were stamped on her mind indelibly.

He was no taller than the rest, for they were all much of a height. No handsomer either, for they were all fine-looking men as befitted a fashionable funeral. He did nothing more than solemnly carry the coffin, one man among six, but everyone else — the Prince Regent, the preacher, the other pall-bearers — appeared as nothing more than shadows around him, as if he were the only living person among them.

What was it about him? Then she realized: it was the sheer manliness of the man. It made her feel how inadequate her clothes, her cropped hair, her assumed swagger and her deepened voice were to support her disguise. Whatever it is that he has, she thought, I wish he could give some of it to me.

★　★　★

Lady Fenton looked with disdain at the card that was presented to her on an elegant silver platter. It was a cheap card, printed rather than engraved, and the address was far from fashionable. The name — Mr Kit Jackson — was unfamiliar. She was about to tell her butler that she was not at home to this visitor, and to chide him for even thinking that she might be, but then Stewart said, 'The — er — gentleman says he wishes to see you about Mr Henry and Miss Katherine Faulkner.'

'Oh, very well, Stewart. Show him in.' Her

butler obviously knew the dreadful circumstances of her nephew and niece: but then, so did all England. The death of George Lancaster in such disreputable circumstances was a splendid item of gossip which Lady Fenton would have thoroughly enjoyed had her family not been involved.

Just a few days ago, she had faced only the task of marrying off her niece. A challenging task, she had admitted to herself, considering Katherine's height, her far from pretty features, her hoydenish tastes for reading and fencing, and her lamentable spirit of independence. But not an impossible one: the girl had an elegant figure, a respectable family, and an unusual charm of manner. The combined talents of Lady Fenton and her redoubtable maid would have made heads turn when Katherine walked into the room.

Now they would turn for a different reason: to see the sister of a murderer. Lady Fenton had no idea where her niece and nephew were, and she devoutly hoped she would stay in ignorance.

When Mr Jackson was ushered in, Lady Fenton's eyes opened in surprise. This was the image of her late brother-in-law, Jack Faulkner, all those years ago, when the young and handsome squire had stolen the hearts of half the ladies in London. The young Helen

28

had already been married off to the rich and elderly Lord Fenton, so she had been forced to subdue her envy of her sister.

If this is Jack's bastard son, as I believe he must be, Lady Fenton thought, perhaps there wasn't such a reason to envy her.

Mr Jackson's appearance confirmed her suspicion: the clothes were well made, but not for the present wearer. But the air of undoubted gentility, the irreproachable manner, and the pleasing tenor voice produced a favourable impression. 'It is good of you to receive me, Lady Fenton.'

When the necessary rituals of welcoming a stranger were over, Lady Fenton said, 'Now, what is your concern with my nephew and niece?'

'Henry Faulkner is innocent of murder,' said Mr Jackson bluntly. 'And I'm going to prove it.'

If that's true, thought Lady Fenton, it's the best news I've had for days. The young man is here to ask my help, I presume. It was all such a wretched business. What was she to do? Should she dismiss this young man and leave her nephew and niece to their fate? But the memory of her sister came to her, and Jack Faulkner's passionate brown eyes looked out from the young man's face. She couldn't abandon them; there would doubtless be even more of a scandal if she did. 'Mr Jackson,' she said resolutely, knowing that she would almost certainly regret it. 'If there is anything I can do to help you, you need only ask.'

To her amazement, Mr Jackson leapt off the chair and clasped her knees. 'Young man!' she said — not unkindly, for it was a very handsome face that looked up at her. 'Could you be a little less demonstrative in your gratitude?'

Mr Jackson laughed delightedly. 'Aunt Helen, do you really not know me?'

It was time for some plain speaking. 'Jack Faulkner may have been my brother-in-law, but that hardly gives his illegitimate son the right to call me aunt,' she said stiffly. 'You are Jack Faulkner's child, I presume?'

'Yes, I am Jack Faulkner's child, but I am neither illegitimate — nor his son.'

★ ★ ★

Richard Lancaster stripped off his mourning gloves and handed them to his steward. 'Send Gregory to me at once, McTavish. I won't wear these damned clothes another moment,' he said as he walked upstairs to his room.

Yet perhaps there is a cause for mourning, the major reflected as his valet helped him divest himself of his blacks. If only George and I had been more brotherly all these years since we were boys, if only he hadn't been so worthless, then he wouldn't have died, and I could have found in him a friend; and God knows, I need one now. *If only* — Ha! he thought in self-disgust. The most useless words in the English language.

When he was changed into his more usual coat and buckskins, he went down to dine in lonely splendour. He wasn't hungry, but he couldn't bear the reproachful but silent looks of his servants, and he wouldn't hurt the feelings of Mrs Rogers, his cook, so he would force down something from every dish that was placed before him.

Tomorrow he'd dine with his cousins Edward and Julia. He liked Edward, certainly more than he'd ever liked George, but there had always been a stiffness about him, one that had grown recently since he'd become Lord Bowland. But Julia was pleasant company, and easy on the eye. In their company the major would manage to get through another evening. But not tonight, he thought as he reached for the brandy. Tonight I'm fit for nobody's company but my own, much as I dislike it.

McTavish saw his master pour himself another glass, and couldn't repress a sorrowful shake of his head. 'You may go,

McTavish,' said the major coldly, having caught the tiny gesture.

Outside, the valet was waiting, grim-faced. 'He's going to make a bad night of it tonight, isn't he, Mr McTavish?' he said as he dragged the steward off into a room where they could talk privately.

'Aye, that he is, Mr Gregory, God help him.'

'It can't go on like this. Night after night he drinks himself into a stupor.'

'And if ye have a suggestion about what we're to do to stop him, I'll thank ye for letting me know,' replied the steward. 'I've been with him since he was a wee laddie, and I've not the slightest idea what to do.'

'I'll venture to suggest that I know him in some ways better than you do, Mr McTavish. You weren't with him in the Peninsula, and I was.'

'Ye think that the war has aught to do with the drinking?'

'Things happened there that could weigh on any man's mind; I speak from experience.'

'I dinna ken,' said McTavish doubtfully. 'He's not talked about it. But then he's not talked about aught that could be troubling him, and I wish he would.'

'A man doesn't talk about things like that, not to another man.'

'And to a woman?'

'No: some things are not fit for the ears of the gentler sex.'

'And as he's not the sort of man to confide in one of those who canna make up their minds what they are . . . '

'Good God, Mr McTavish, of course he's not: you quite shock me even to suggest it!'

'As ye say. But it leaves a fearful burden on the man that he canna share with another human soul.'

'So he's going to carry on like this, you think?'

'Och, no, Mr Gregory. He canna keep drinking like this. If he doesna stop, he'll not live another year.'

★　★　★

Desdemona, Lady Fenton's excellent if not always respectful lady's maid, was not amused when she entered the room to find her mistress in the embrace of a handsome young man and talking most companionably. 'Milady!' she scolded. 'Where anyone can walk in!'

Katherine — or Kit Jackson as we must now call her — saw that her aunt wasn't put out by her abigail's displeasure, nor offended by her rebuke: she knew that they had been together a long time. 'Desdemona, your timing is impeccable,' said Lady Fenton. 'Look closely at my guest and tell me what you think. If you can fool Desdemona, Mr Jackson, you can fool anyone.'

'Oh, there's some trick, is there, milady? All right, young sir, let's see if you can pull the wool over my eyes. You need a new set of clothes, for a start,' she began her review. 'Those weren't made to fit you, anyone can see that. Made for a much wider man. Stand up.'

Kit stood obediently. 'Thin, very thin,' Desdemona continued. 'Handsome face. Around how old? Say something, young sir.'

A quotation from shakespeare came to mind.

> ''Tis most easy
> The inclining Desdemona to subdue
> In any honest suit.'

'Clever,' the abigail approved. 'Good voice. Well educated. I still can't make out how old you are. Something says you're twenty, and something says you're twelve. Walk about a bit.'

Kit strolled backwards and forwards across the room, conscious of a penetrating stare. 'Ah-ha! Got it!' Desdemona's voice was triumphant. 'All right, you can sit down, miss.'

'Oh, bother,' said Kit. 'I thought my disguise was quite good.'

'So it is, miss — Miss Katherine, isn't it? You tricked me for a minute, and I knew there was a trick to be found.'

'I think you escape with some credit,' said Lady Fenton. 'Desdemona was an actress before she became my wonderful and loyal abigail; I couldn't do without her. She has the sharpest eyes in London — and the most discreet tongue, so you needn't worry that she'll betray you.'

'No, she's not bad,' Desdemona acknowledged. 'Sitting down she could fool anyone, and standing up, too. It's the walk that does it. Men and women just don't walk the same way, and there's no hiding it. With better fitting clothes it'd be even more obvious.'

'What can we do about it, Desdemona?'

'Wait a moment,' said the maid, and left the room without bothering to ask permission. She returned with a handful of small stones. 'Put these in your boot and then walk around.'

Kit obliged and took a few steps. 'Ow,' she complained. 'It hurts.'

'It's supposed to. Keep walking.'

After a few seconds Kit got the pebbles

into a new position under her foot. They were uncomfortable rather than painful, and she felt she could limp a few hundred yards without agony. 'But what's the point?'

'We must change that walk. When anyone sees you, they won't think *man*, and they won't think *woman*. They'll think *cripple*. See?'

Lady Fenton clapped her hands in appreciation of her maid's cleverness. 'Excellent, Desdemona. And it gives her an excuse to carry a stick. Bring me Lord Fenton's sword-stick; it's in the attic.' Desdemona left. 'It hasn't been used these twenty years, but it can be useful to you now, since you are putting yourself in a position of considerable danger. You are certain this masquerade is necessary?'

'What else can I do? I must find out who the real murderer is; it's the only way to save Harry. But how can I do it as Katherine Faulkner? Kit Jackson has much more freedom.'

'But are you — are you absolutely sure that — Oh, dear, don't be offended — Are you certain that Harry is telling the truth?'

'Yes,' Kit said simply. She could no more doubt her brother than she could doubt her own existence.

'Very well, I must accept your word,' said

her aunt, sighing. 'Where is Harry now? Ah! I know; he's escaped abroad. Now I think on it, that inn you stayed at is close to the river. He could easily have found a captain of a ship who'd be deafened by the chink of gold to take up a passenger.'

'He hasn't escaped abroad. He's gone to Eastham.'

'Eastham! That's the first place he'll be looked for.'

'And the last place he'll be found. He knows every rabbit-hole, and there's no one there who'll betray him.' Kit made her voice casual. 'Has he written?'

'Why should he write here?'

'That's how we agreed to keep each other informed. He'll write to me here, telling me how to write back to him once he's secure.'

'So you two presumed that I'd help before asking me?'

'Were we wrong?' Kit said, only slightly abashed.

'No, child, you weren't.'

★ ★ ★

Lady Fenton dined in private with her guest, but her servants were not unused to such an event. This scandal concerning her nephew and niece was certainly the worst scandal

Lady Fenton had ever faced; but she had faced a few others. A rich, beautiful and childless widow was the target of every fortune hunter in the kingdom, and she had spent her time as enjoyable as discretion would allow; sometimes, indeed, rather more enjoyably than that.

Once the last footman had gone, Kit completed her story, telling her aunt everything she knew (apart, that is, from her reaction to the man at the funeral, which she dismissed as irrelevant to the tale).

'We need more help,' Lady Fenton said decisively when Kit finished. 'You have enough to do without checking each man's — what's the word? — *alibi*. I shall enlist the services of Mr Latimer, my man of business. And — yes, Hamlet!'

'Hamlet?'

'Desdemona's brother, still an actor. I've done him some service in the past; he can repay me now. He and Mr Latimer between them should be able to find out a great deal about George Lancaster's acquaintance. I shall confide in them your mission, though not your sex. To them you will be Harry's bastard brother.'

'I'll keep watch on this Lord Bowland,' Kit said. 'George Lancaster and the murderer were obviously in a plot to kill him, so I shall just have to ensure one of them doesn't succeed now he's killed the other.'

'That description of Harry's: it fits too many men. And the ring — it's infuriating: I'm sure I've seen one like that, but I can't bring it to mind.'

'Let's try another approach,' Kit said. 'Do you know of a connection between Lord Bowland and George Lancaster?'

'Indeed I do. They are — were — cousins: Lord Bowland's name is Edward Lancaster. He has but newly come into the title, on the death of his grandfather. The old earl was one of the wickedest men I've ever had the misfortune to meet. His two sons and their wives are long since dead, doubtless tired of waiting for the old man to go, and you needn't concern yourself overmuch about them.' Kit smiled: her aunt was enjoying a legitimate excuse for relating gossip.

'Bowland is loaded with far more dignity than money, since his grandfather left the estate monstrously in debt. He is at present trying to restore the family greatness; the Lancasters claim they are an offshoot of the Royal House of Lancaster that fought in the Wars of the Roses, though not many people give the idea credence. The world assumes that Bowland will marry an heiress; he's the handsomest bachelor in the peerage, and he should have no difficulty in finding someone who will trade money for rank. He has been forced to let his estate, and he lives with his sister, Lady Julia, in their town house off Grosvenor Square.'

A house off Grosvenor Square was hardly grinding poverty, thought Kit, though an earl might see it differently.

'His sister has a chaperon, Maria Maitland. We came out together, and I shall renew the acquaintance. Julia is a very pretty girl; the belle of last season. Bowland and his cousin are her guardians.'

'George Lancaster guardian of a pretty girl? That's surely setting the fox to guard the chickens.'

'Not the abominable George; his younger brother. Their father chose a wife with more money than breeding, and her two sons inherited a huge fortune.'

'This younger brother; do I need to concern myself overmuch about him?'

'Oh, yes, you do,' said Lady Fenton, her voice full of meaning. 'You should know that he is aged about thirty, tall and grey-eyed. He acquired in the Peninsular War a considerable reputation for defying danger, he left active service in circumstances that nobody has ever explained, and since his return he's become known as a man who gives little heed to what other people think. Furthermore, the death of his older brother George makes him Lord Bowland's heir. Indeed, Mr Jackson, I believe that you should concern yourself a great deal about Major Richard Lancaster.'

3

It was long after midnight. Kit didn't know what she could achieve outside Lord Bowland's house in Grosvenor Street at that time, but she couldn't make up her mind to leave. She wouldn't sleep, so she might as well stay and watch to see if anything happened.

The lights were still burning in the house, so there was at least some activity going on. Would anyone leave at this hour? Would his lordship? Would he walk unknowingly into danger? There was nothing she could do to warn him, so she would have to guard him unseen.

She had no desire to return to her lodgings: small and cramped, and right at the top of several flights of stairs. But better rooms in fashionable London were far beyond the touch of the likes of Kit Jackson. She'd hoped to move into her aunt's house, but her ladyship had decided that her reputation wouldn't stand the gossip of having a very handsome young man staying with her.

There was still no word from Harry.

As so often in the past day and a half, Kit

tried to suppress the thought of the man at the funeral (as if there hadn't been any other men at the funeral, including five others who would bear investigation). She kept telling herself that she had more important matters on hand — like saving her brother's life.

She leaned against the wall and rested her foot. The stones in her boot were highly effective in disguising her walk, but they were also highly uncomfortable. *Damned* uncomfortable, she said to herself, practising in the privacy of her own mind the manly art of swearing. *Bloody* uncomfortable.

Suddenly she became aware of a movement in an alley across the road near to Bowland's house. Was anyone there? Had they seen her? She took a tighter grip of her stick, loosening the handle so the blade was ready for action. Otherwise she remained motionless.

The minutes stretched on. She made no move. The watchers in the other alley made no move. She began to doubt what she had seen. Had there really been anyone there? Other than herself and whoever might be on the other side of the road, there was no one about.

A lone dog strolled along the dimly lit road, concerned with nothing but itself. It ambled into the alleyway opposite; then came a sharp yelp, and it reappeared suddenly with the indignant expression of a dog that has been kicked when all it wanted to do was make friends. There *was* someone there!

Just then, the door of Lord Bowland's house opened. The oblong of light from inside framed the figure of a man, and the words, 'Can lock up,' floated across the street.

It was *him*, the man at the funeral. Could he be Lord Bowland himself? The familiarity he showed with the household seemed to indicate it.

The man turned left, towards the alley where the unknown watchers waited. He was clearly somewhat cup-shot, though he wasn't drunk enough to stagger. He reached the entry to the alley. Kit gripped the handle of the sword. The man passed the entry. Nothing happened. Kit began to relax. Too soon.

A man leapt out — and another — and two more. The walker heard them: he lifted his arm to ward off the attack. A cudgel was lifted and a knife blade glinted in the moonlight. Four of them against one unarmed man.

She was going to have to be brave. Stifling her fear, she ran across the road as fast as her limp would let her. For a second she thought her help would be unnecessary; the victim had floored one of his attackers and was just laying another low with a mighty fist. But as he did so, she saw that one of them was creeping unobserved behind him with a cudgel. 'Behind you!' she yelled.

The man whirled round, dodged the blow, and the cudgel only dazed him rather than smashed his skull. He tried to ward off the fourth man's knife attack with nothing more than his upraised hand. He didn't utter a sound as the knife viciously cut through the flesh: but for a second he was defenceless as he instinctively grabbed his wounded arm with his other hand. The cudgel rose again, and she heard the sickening thud as it crashed against his head. He slipped down onto the pavement and his attackers moved in.

'Stop!' she shouted. The attackers took little notice. Then she was across the road, the sword out. She leapt forward. One of the attackers turned to face her, his knife against her sword.

But the sword was longer, and she drove it into his body. With an oath he fell, clutching his chest. She jumped into the space he'd left. She stood astride the still form of the defenceless man, her sword out against the other cut-throat, the one with the cudgel. One of those who'd been knocked out staggered to his feet, cursing. Then another joined them.

For a second she stood facing the three of them, while the fourth, the one she'd stabbed, lay motionless on the pavement. Then at last doors began to open and windows began to be thrown up. Someone was running from Bowland's house. The attackers fled, and her fear left her as she could stop being brave.

She bent over the body of the man she'd defended, trying to see his face. He was still alive, for he groaned. Blood was streaming from his right arm and hand.

Another groan, this time from the man she'd driven her sword into, and then there were voices all around her. 'What happened?'

'Why, it's Major Lancaster,' said someone. 'Are you all right, sir?'

My God! she thought, as her fear returned in full force. Not Lord Bowland. Instead, it was the man who was most likely to be the murderer. What an enemy I've chosen; what a staggeringly formidable opponent!

She took a deep breath and forced herself into calmness. At least he doesn't know I'm his opponent, she reflected. Quite the opposite, indeed, since I've just saved him from almost certain death. The footpads had given her a marvellous opportunity. Saving his life was in any case an excellent way to get to know him and his relations; and in such a manly way to defend such a manly man! Nobody would suspect her now.

'Ah, you're alive,' said a well-bred voice, full of concern. 'Take my arm, Richard.'

'Oh, no, my lord,' said another voice. 'You'll get blood all over your clothes.'

'Damn my clothes,' said my lord — the real Lord Bowland. Kit recognized him as another of the pall-bearers. 'What about my cousin?'

'Your cousin will be better if you would all stop fussing about him,' said Lancaster, gripping his wounded arm with his left hand in a vain attempt to stem the flow of blood. He sat up and leaned against the railings; he looked at Kit and said, 'I think I owe my life to you.'

'I am glad that I could be of service,' replied Kit, returning his gaze. I will send you to the gallows if I must, she thought. If I can.

'What about this one?' said another man, kneeling over the attacker Kit had stabbed. 'He's still alive.'

'Good,' said Bowland, his voice filled with menace as he turned to the man who'd tried to kill his cousin. 'He'll get what he has earned for tonight's work.' He gave rapid orders. 'Slater, help me take the major into my house, and call the doctor. He can attend to this one,' indicating the fallen attacker, 'at the same time. I'd hate to lose him before we can question him. You two take him in and stand guard over him.' He turned to Kit and held out a hand. 'I'm Bowland.'

'Jackson, Kit Jackson.'

'You will return to my house tomorrow, so I may offer my thanks in the manner which your action tonight deserves,' said Bowland as though Kit had no views in the matter.

Kit, who had hoped to be invited inside, started to walk away. 'Stop a moment,' came the major's voice. 'I think I'm not the only one who needs assistance.' He looked at Kit. 'You're wounded too.'

'No, sir,' said Kit without hesitation. 'I escaped without a scratch.'

'Your leg.'

'I'm afraid that's an older hurt than yours, sir.' It was time for a manly swagger. 'However, it proved useful tonight, as otherwise I shouldn't have been so well-armed.' She wiped the blood off the sword, slid it back in the stick, and limped away.

★ ★ ★

It was fortunate that Slater, Lord Bowland's butler, recognized Kit the next morning, else there wouldn't have been the slightest chance that she would have been admitted. His face registered disdain for a second as Kit presented her cheap card, but a glance at the stick which she still used must have jogged the butler's memory, and she was ushered in with a smile.

Closer, and with more light than she had seen either of them in before, she noted the strong family likeness between Lord Bowland and Major Lancaster: and, on reflection, the unlamented George. The same towering height, the same colouring, almost the same face. But there were differences: it was as if there was one model of a man, which had been covered in fat in George Lancaster, smoothed and polished in Lord Bowland, and roughened in the major.

'The handsomest bachelor in the peerage,' her aunt had called Lord Bowland, and indeed he could have been the model for a Greek god were it not for the thinness of his lips. But the major's features were too harsh, his eyebrows were too bushy, and his jaw was too strong for him to deserve any such description: in fact, he was close to being downright ugly. Lord Bowland's nose was straight while the major's was broken; his skin was smooth and clear while the major's had been burnt by the sun; his fine jaw was clean-shaven while the major's still had yesterday's stubble; he was impeccably dressed from the folds of his starched white cravat to the soles of his shining boots, while the major was wearing a dressing gown that was obviously borrowed, since it was much too tight for his well-muscled body.

All the same, the major looked a deal better than she had last seen him; his right arm was in a sling and his hand was heavily bandaged, but he was clearly recovering. There was a drawn expression on his face, but the lines had been etched longer ago than the previous night. His welcoming smile at her made his craggy features more agreeable, and gave him some claim to good looks.

Lord Bowland, whose clothes must have taken an hour of dedicated work by his valet to don, gave a quick glance over her that made her aware that Kit Jackson had been judged and found wanting. 'Ah, Mr Jackson,' he murmured. 'Again we are in your debt for coming to pay us this visit. In the confusion of last night, I failed to take note of your address, and we would have been put to some trouble to find you again.'

Lord Bowland was manifestly not used to being put to any pains. 'I am glad that I could spare your lordship trouble,' Kit murmured dutifully, trying to conceal her inward smile. But the sharp glance that Major Lancaster gave her showed that she hadn't concealed it well enough from his lordship's shrewd cousin. I've got to be careful with this man, she told herself: he's awake on every suit. 'I am glad to see you looking better, sir,' she said to him.

'I must have looked uncommonly bad last night if you think this is better.'

'A man is not at his best when he is recovering from a blow on the head,' Kit said. 'Nor when he is bleeding all over the street.'

The major smiled. 'Nevertheless, it's a damned nuisance. The doctor hummed and hawed over me, and said I must be bound up like this for at least a month if ever I wished to regain the use of my right hand. I just wish I could get hold of the men who did it.'

'Has the one I wounded not told you about his fellows?'

'He died without speaking,' said Bowland.

Kit couldn't conceal a shudder, which Lancaster noticed. 'First time you've killed a man?' he asked sympathetically.

Kit nodded. 'I don't regret it, sir, but . . . '

'But it's a shock, nevertheless,' Lancaster finished.

'Yes, sir.'

'You will become used to it in time,' Bowland said.

'No, he won't,' said the major. 'At least I

hope not. I know men who have become used to killing.' He turned to Kit again. The welcoming smile had vanished, as if the shadow of a black cloud had fallen on a sunlit rock. 'I wouldn't wish familiarity with death on anyone.'

Lord Bowland shrugged his well-formed shoulders indifferently. 'Since we are deprived of one source of information about last night's attack, I should be obliged if you would tell us everything you saw.'

'I've only just arrived in London, and I wanted to look around,' she began, conscious of how implausible it sounded: something of a lame excuse. 'I stopped to rest for a while.' At least that sounded likely enough. 'I noticed a dog go into the alley by this house. It came out in a hurry; it looked as though it had been kicked by someone who wanted to stay concealed. I thought that ominous, so I stayed to watch.' From that point she could tell the complete truth.

'So you think that someone was lying in wait for me?' asked Lancaster when she finished.

'It looked that way. Either you or Lord Bowland. I was under the impression that you were the owner of this house when you came out, and it's possible your attackers were equally mistaken.' There, she thought with satisfaction. I've managed to put Lord Bowland on his guard.

'We've been mistaken for each other before in poor light,' his lordship said. 'There may be something in what Mr Jackson says.'

'So I have this arm without even the dignity of being the man they wanted,' said Lancaster in mock disgust. 'Next time I must proclaim my identity more loudly.'

'You think there will be a next time?' said Lord Bowland.

'They did look very purposeful,' Kit said. 'I didn't gain the impression that they were mere footpads, out to rob the first person who came along.'

'It seems, Mr Jackson, that I may be in your debt for this warning. I dislike being in debt,' said Lord Bowland. 'Will you take some financial reward?'

That expresses more clearly than anything his opinion of me, thought Kit in disgust, as she looked at his handsome, contemptuous face. She stood up. 'No, my lord, I shall not.' She stalked out of the room as proudly as her limp would permit, pausing only to say to Lancaster, 'I wish you a quick recovery, sir.'

She was angry as she left, and silently cursed the lost opportunity to get to know

53

Bowland and the major. She was so absorbed that she didn't pay attention as she went out of the door. She collided with a young lady whom, had she really been Kit Jackson, she would have discovered to be staggeringly beautiful. 'My apologies, ma'am,' Kit said and limped away preoccupied.

★　★　★

'Who is that young man who bumped into me?' asked Lady Julia as she greeted her brother and her cousin unceremoniously.

'It's that trick you have of standing in doorways, Julia,' said Lancaster. 'I know they make a frame for your loveliness, but most people have other uses for them.'

Julia sometimes wished her cousin wasn't quite so perceptive. She ignored his remark. 'Why is your arm in a sling, Richard?' she asked instead.

Lancaster and Bowland exchanged glances. Julia knew that look: they were about to conceal something from her. How she hated to be protected!

'Couple of footpads,' said her cousin. 'Did a little damage before that young man's timely arrival. Nothing serious: the doctor says I'll be fit in a month.'

Julia knew he was minimizing it, which made her only the more alarmed. 'How many of them were there? It was more than a couple. You are a match for two footpads, Richard, since fifty thousand Frenchmen failed to kill you.'

'Ah, but remember that English footpads were on my side in the Peninsula; they made up half the army.'

Julia pouted. 'I see that you will not tell me the full story, which will leave me picturing the worst. You and that young man fighting off a company, and both of you wounded.'

'It wasn't a company, and the only wound was mine. Mr Jackson's limp was caused long ago.'

'Mr Jackson,' said Julia, contemplating the name. 'Do you know anything about him?'

'Nothing,' said Bowland. 'Sprang out of the night like a mushroom.'

'If you mean what I think you mean, Edward, then you are being unconscionably rude,' Julia reproved her brother. 'One can see at a glance that he is of good family.'

'Then you, my dear sister, must have remarkably good eyesight. I saw a cripple in ill-fitting clothes.'

Julia protested loudly, and Lancaster joined her. 'I saw nothing but a friend in need, and a brave one at that,' he said lightly.

'Very well,' said Bowland, smiling. 'I am outnumbered. Mr Jackson will be a paragon of all the virtues.'

★ ★ ★

Mr Jackson didn't feel like a paragon of all the virtues later on at her lodgings. She felt extremely irritated. A wonderful chance which she'd had to throw away, at least for the moment. And Harry still hadn't written.

She was distressed at the realization that *he* — the man at the funeral — had turned out to be Major Lancaster. It's going to be hard to work against him, she thought. Hard because he could be such a powerful enemy, and hard, if it comes to the point, for me to put his head in the noose.

But I shall do it, if I have to make the choice between him and Harry. For my brother, I've a lifetime's shared experience and love. For that man I've only a moment of — what? She didn't even have a word for it, her perception that he stood out from his surroundings like a lighthouse in a dark sea. I'm just being silly, she told herself. He's no different from anyone else.

A visitor was announced; too suddenly

for Kit's comfort, as she wasn't wearing her boots. She just had time to throw a blanket over her legs to conceal the fact that there was nothing wrong with them before he appeared. 'Major Lancaster,' she said in surprise. 'Pray forgive me for not rising.'

'If you will forgive me for not shaking hands,' he replied with a smile. His right hand was still bandaged and his arm was in a sling, but he was now dressed more formally.

How does one gentleman entertain another in his lodgings? Kit wondered. She was conscious of a teeming mixture of emotions: relief that her quarry had come to her, fear that he might turn from quarry to hunter, shame at the need to deceive him, and strong curiosity. But most of all, she was acutely aware of a large and powerful masculine presence in the intimacy of her small room.

Lancaster hesitated before sitting down. 'I've come to see if I can make amends for the insult you received lately,' he said.

'Please sit down,' Kit replied hospitably. 'It wasn't you who insulted me, sir, and you shouldn't feel the need to make amends.'

'An explanation, then, if you will accept that?'

Kit nodded. 'You have no need to offer an

explanation, sir, but I shall listen if you feel that you have.'

'My cousin told you that he hates to be in debt,' he began. 'Unfortunately, it seems to be a permanent condition, and one he is doing his utmost to remedy. He has inherited a title but not the means to support it in the dignity which he feels is its due. Consequently he is very careful of his own pride, without perhaps taking enough account of other people's.'

'I see,' she said, non-committally.

'I think perhaps you do, Mr Jackson.'

'Why do you say that?'

'Because I think you also are a man who is careful of his pride.'

'Me? I cannot afford to be,' said Kit with some bitterness.

'That statement is itself a witness to it, is it not?'

Kit smiled, acknowledging a hit. 'I shall try not to be so stiff-necked.'

'Good, Mr Jackson, as I should like to ask you something which may stiffen your neck rather more than it is already.'

'What is it, sir?' she asked, full of curiosity.

'You may consider this a piece of impertinence; I apologize. But am I right in thinking that you would welcome an offer of employment?'

What's coming? Kit wondered. I'd better

leave my choices open. 'I am not rich, but I am not so poor that I must take the first position offered to me.'

'I am in need of a secretary,' Lancaster continued. 'I left my affairs in the hands of an agent while I was in the Peninsula, and I found on my return that he was neither honest nor competent. If you would accept the position . . . '

This is either going to be the best opportunity I have or an unmitigated disaster, thought Kit. If only he were a fool I'd jump at the chance. But he is not a fool, far from it. 'Why me? You know nothing about me.'

'On the contrary, I know a lot about you. You are honourable and intelligent — and you saved my life at no small risk to your own. I should like to know you better, I admit, and that is one reason why I am offering you the post.'

Harry, what should I do? she cried silently.

Lancaster smiled with considerable charm for such a plain man. 'Please say you'll accept. My affairs are in a mess; I can't write; and on top of everything I find myself executor for my brother who has recently died.'

That settled it. To be able to make enquiries — and to do so with full authority — about the late George Lancaster was an opportunity too good to miss. 'I accept with pleasure,' said Kit, smiling and hoping he couldn't hear the loud beating of her heart.

★ ★ ★

'Katherine! You can't!' Lady Fenton was horrified. 'You cannot go and live with him! You will be ruined!'

Kit had gone to tell her aunt about the latest turn of affairs, and to seek her advice — which she now realized she was going to ignore. 'I've done enough to be ruined twenty times over if I were discovered. But the ruin of my reputation is nothing compared to the ruin of Harry's neck.'

'But — Richard Lancaster — an unmarried man! What would he do if he found out? My dear, consider what you are doing!'

'Richard Lancaster will not find out. And if he does, what then? If he did murder his brother, he will be as eager to kill Katherine Faulkner as Kit Jackson to conceal his guilt. If he is innocent I've nothing to fear.'

'No man is innocent if he has a woman in his power.'

'I defended myself against his brother; I can defend myself against him. I have this, now; a lot better than a three-inch needle.' She brandished her swordstick. 'I'll get him in the other arm; that'll fix him.'

'That is a very unladylike way of expressing yourself.'

'Good. I can't afford to be ladylike.'

'Katherine, I think you should wait.'

'For what?'

'For more information than this letter contains.'

Dear Lady Fenton,

If you should happen to see your niece, please let her know that the red colt arrived, but it was hurt on the journey.

Your obedient servant,

Rebecca Coomber

Kit's face paled. 'Harry,' she cried. 'He's injured!'

'I deduced that myself. Who is Rebecca Coomber? Can she be trusted?'

'It's Becky, don't you remember? Our old nurse; she retired into a cottage just outside Eastham. I'd trust her with my life or Harry's.' She looked at the letter again. It contained no more information, no matter how often she tried to read between the lines. 'Harry must be with her. Is he all right, do you think?' She looked at her aunt. Her aunt looked back at her. 'If he was all right, Becky would say so, wouldn't she?' said Kit heavily.

'Or he'd have written himself.'

'I cannot tell. But, Katherine,' her aunt added urgently. 'Don't you see that you should wait? Your sacrifice may be in vain if . . . ' Her voice trailed off awkwardly before her niece's expression.

'If Harry dies? Yes, Aunt Helen. That would be the solution to all our problems.'

4

Despite her assertions to Lady Fenton, Kit was far from confident about the move into Major Lancaster's house. Though it meant that she could keep better watch on him and his noble cousin, she didn't need Lady Fenton's warning that her reputation wouldn't survive the discovery of her sex.

Yet what worried her most when she first arrived was the same problem that would have faced her had she really been Kit Jackson: the etiquette of her position. Was she to be Lancaster's friend or paid servant?

She got no help from McTavish, Lancaster's house steward, a craggy Scot in his fifties with magnificent side whiskers, for he seemed equally uncertain. 'Do ye want me to unpack your valise?' he asked when he had shown her to her room. With a friend of his master, McTavish would have unpacked without asking, while a servant would have been left to his own devices.

She declined his offer. 'I'd rather do it myself. Some of my possessions . . . ' She let her voice tail off and looked significantly at her crippled leg.

'Och, I understand,' said McTavish with ponderous tact.

She took her opportunity: 'McTavish, I wonder — there are times when it needs attention, and I hate anyone doing it for me.'

'A young man like yourself, ye'll be wanting a wee bit of privacy. I'll see to it that you're not bothered.'

She hoped fervently that she wouldn't be there long enough for him to realize that those times recurred once a month.

Yes, she thought with satisfaction when she was alone. I'm all right so far. On good terms with McTavish, and that's important, since he'll know more about Major Lancaster than anyone. Monthly problem solved. Only my position here to sort out, and that I'll leave to my employer.

Major Lancaster settled it with both delicacy and firmness when McTavish ushered Kit into the library. 'Mr Jackson and I will be working for some hours before we dine, McTavish,' he said, not rising from his chair.

So now I know, she thought, and so will everyone else. I eat with him, and am therefore his friend. A much better chance for me to find out about him, but also a much better chance for him to find out about me.

They set to work, and she realized that, in

helping him with his papers, she would have found out a deal about him in any case.

'What are these bills?' she asked after a while.

He glanced at them. 'My cousin Julia's,' he replied. 'They're all sent to me. Oh, that reminds me: make sure that you arrange to pay her chaperon, Miss Maitland. Julia's my ward and it's an understanding we have. In all probability we shall marry when she comes of age,' he added casually, 'but I'd like her to have all the pleasures of freedom before then.'

Kit was shocked. How could a man speak so indifferently of his future marriage? Did he love his cousin Julia? He showed not the slightest sign of it. Was this what marriage meant to the *haut ton*? If that was so, she was glad she wasn't part of it. She could never marry a man who would approach her with such an attitude.

Though it was unlikely that she'd have the opportunity, she reflected. If things had been otherwise, she would at least have had a chance of making a good match. As Lady Fenton's niece she would have gone to the balls and parties, and perhaps she could have found a husband to love and be loved by. She was hardly in a position to find one now.

Lancaster had returned to work. She stifled

a sigh and joined him.

'Damn you, George!' came his exclamation abruptly.

She looked up in surprise.

'Excuse me, Mr Jackson. I was cursing my brother, who got himself murdered and left me his executor. This is the report of the inquest.'

'I am sorry to hear of your brother's misfortune,' she said formally to disguise her acute interest.

'Misfortune, ha!' he said. 'If ever there was a murder that could have been predicted it was George's.'

'Why?'

'My brother thought it was his right to have any woman he chose. It was just a matter of time before one of them produced a husband, a brother or a father who would take it upon himself to rid the world of George.'

'Is that what happened?'

'Yes. He forced his attentions on a young lady,' he looked at the paper in front of him, 'one Katherine Faulkner. Her brother Henry shot my brother, and then made his escape.'

'Your brother's death must have caused you some distress,' Kit managed to say, hoping he wouldn't notice the croak in her voice.

'Not a jot, apart from the damned

inconvenience of having to tidy up his affairs. We never liked each other even when we were boys. Our grandfather, the old earl, made much of him and was always angry that my cousin Edward would inherit the title, not him. And George copied his grandfather, a man whom I would not hold up as a model to the young. George did his best to gamble his fortune away; I doubt it would have lasted another two years. Now I inherit what's left of it.'

'He left his money to you?' she couldn't stop herself saying, but if he noticed her impertinence he didn't comment on it.

'I was his heir, as he was mine,' he replied. 'Though not from brotherly love. By the terms of our parents' wills, his fortune was entailed on me, as mine was on him. Naturally the entails would have gone by the board when either of us married, but we did not. He was a confirmed rake, and I had no desire to marry while I was in the army and my wife might become a widow at any time.'

Kit hoped he would keep on talking, but instead he handed over a sheaf of papers. 'Here are just a few of the bills which must be paid out of my brother's estate. See if you can get some sort of order into them.' With that he stood up and left her alone.

Kit sneaked a look at the inquest report,

which told her little that she didn't already know, aside from confirming that a verdict of murder had been brought in against Henry Faulkner, Esq. The only cause for puzzlement was the fact that her own assault on the constable and her part in Harry's escape were unreported. At least they're not after me, she thought with some relief.

The major has a powerful motive, she reflected as she turned to the bills. Did he kill his brother to inherit a fortune before it disappeared? And does he plan to kill his cousin to inherit the title, which he will have no difficulty in keeping up, with his own fortune and his brother's behind it?

It all fitted. Why didn't she believe it?

★　★　★

They dined together on a small but well-cooked meal of chicken dressed in a way the major said was Spanish. He disregarded opinion and employed a female cook: his confidence in her abilities appeared fully justified.

Kit drank as little as she could, but the major did the opposite; his glass was filled and refilled. Kit had seen her father and his friends down two or three bottles each over a meal, and wasn't shocked by the quantity that

Major Lancaster consumed. But it did seem a lot, especially for a quiet dinner on their own.

'Port or brandy?' he asked when McTavish and the footmen had taken away the remnants.

'I remember the words of Doctor Johnson,' she answered. She had drunk a bottle of the best wine she'd ever tasted and was fighting to keep a clear head; indeed, it was already beginning to cloud. *'Claret is the liquor for boys; port is for men; but he who aspires to be a hero must drink brandy.* I am neither man nor hero, so I shall stay with the claret,' she said, made rash by the wine.

'Nonsense,' snorted Lancaster. He was now imbibing brandy as if it were water, yet his speech wasn't impaired, and his grey eyes were still sharp in the candle light. Only his reserve seemed to have been affected. 'I've seen you act heroically enough, and you're surely old enough to be a man. How old are you?'

'One-and-twenty,' she answered truthfully, on the grounds that truth was always easier to remember than lies.

'See? Why do you not account yourself a man?'

Wouldn't you be surprised if I told you? she thought, but said, 'A man must stand on his own two feet.'

'I hadn't realized the wound went so deep. And yet it need not,' he said, pouring himself another glass. 'We haven't known each other long, Kit — I may call you Kit, mayn't I? — and already I've discovered that you are a better man than three-quarters of my acquaintance. Why do you smile?'

'I apologize.'

'You will not explain?'

'It would be a poor sort of secretary that couldn't keep a secret.'

'True!' he laughed. 'Very well. You can keep your own secrets — can you keep mine?'

'I hope so.' What a dirty game she was playing! She was spying on him, getting his trust, and hoping he would tell her enough so she could send him to the gallows.

'Try this one,' he said, watching her reaction. 'I've killed a man.'

She couldn't conceal her amazement. Surely it wasn't going to be that easy? 'You mean — off the field of battle?'

'Off the field of battle, though God knows I've killed men enough there.'

'Mm?' she asked; it was all she could manage to utter as she tried not to hold her breath in anticipation.

'We'll win this war, Kit, and do you know why?' he asked.

She felt an odd mixture of disappointment

70

and relief; this was nothing to do with her. She shook her head.

'Because our commanders have been slightly less incompetent than theirs. Napoleon wasted the lives of nearly half a million men on the retreat from Moscow: we wasted only a few thousand on the retreat from Salamanca.'

'What happened?'

'When we took Salamanca last year there were still two French armies against us in Spain. We had to retire for the winter, give up most of what we'd won, that had cost us so much, and fall back on our base near Portugal. Four days' march. But those four days were a hell none of us will ever forget. The officer in charge of the supply train decided that he would keep it safe and not risk his precious stores near the soldiers. So we had no rations, and the winter had set in. In four days we lost three thousand men who couldn't keep up with us: three thousand, Kit, men who'd fought and won at Salamanca. We had to leave them to the French. And thousands more died later from typhus; they were so weakened they couldn't fight it off.' He stopped.

Kit could see the horror behind his eyes. 'What happened to the man in charge of the supply train?'

'He had an official reprimand,' said the major, his bitterness plain. 'And then Wellington rebuked us officers for not being able to keep our men in order; no doubt they were dying too rowdily for him. By coincidence, it was then that we heard what had happened to the *Grande Armée*. War didn't seem . . . ' He shrugged. 'Oh, well, I stray from my tale. I decided to seek out the officer in charge of the supply train and force a duel on him, in the full knowledge that I was a far better shot than he. I murdered him as surely as if I'd stabbed him in the back. Wellington ensured that it was all kept quiet, but I was out of his army.'

'Do you regret it?' she asked softly.

'Not for a second, Kit. Not for a second.' His mouth curled in an unpleasant grin, and he poured himself another glass of brandy.

★   ★   ★

Kit soon settled in to the routine of the house. Major Lancaster, having spent years in the harshness of army life, was determined to have a comfortable home. He was fortunate to buy one of the few good houses built since the start of the war with France, and he equipped it with everything that could make life easier.

For a start, there was water that came out of pipes in the upper storeys of the house. No longer did footmen and housemaids have to stagger up the stairs with buckets of hot water for a bath. As a result, Richard Lancaster was one of the cleanest men in London. There was also a privy with one of the new water closets. Kit hadn't seen one before and wasn't certain how it worked, but she learned quickly and approved. It stank somewhat, and she didn't envy the maid whose job it was to clean it.

However, Kit learned that even this most lowly of servants thought herself lucky to be in Major Lancaster's employment. He was a generous master, paying more than he had to. But there was more. Many masters and mistresses didn't trouble to learn their servants' names, calling them all John or Mary, but the major not only knew their names and histories, but would take a real interest in their concerns. In return he expected loyalty and competence: he received both. Any new footman disposed to do less than his best was taken aside by McTavish and given a choice: to mend his ways or to take his leave. All chose the former.

Aside from McTavish there were four upper servants: Gregory, the major's valet, who had been his batman in the army; John, the groom and coachman, an amiable chatty sort of man, passionately devoted to the major's horses; and Mrs Booth and Mrs Rogers, unmarried but entitled to the dignity of a *Mrs* because of their positions as the major's housekeeper and cook.

In addition there were two footmen, two housemaids, a kitchen maid, a laundry maid, and a stable lad. Twelve all told; thirteen if Kit included herself. Rather a lot to look after one man, she thought, considering that her home at Eastham had never had more than eight servants, even while her mother was alive and she and Harry were mess-making children. But, she reflected, Richard Lancaster could afford a regiment of servants if he wanted.

His income was twenty thousand pounds a year: a huge sum. Yet his fortune sat easily on him: he gave no displays of wealth. He insisted on, and received, the best, but he did not show it off. His clothes were the finest his tailor could make, but any attention they attracted was caused by the quality of the cut rather than by their bright colour. His curricle was pulled by a perfect pair of chestnuts, and he rode a splendid horse, Newcastle, but all three were chosen for strength rather than show. He would make an occasional wager at Brookes's, but he had risked his life often enough for the hazards of gambling to seem tame.

He didn't leave his wealth idle, for he was a considerable philanthropist. Kit spent many hours in correspondence with trustees for several charities: schools, returned soldiers, foundlings and hospitals all received his help.

He had, she learned, disconcerted his Tory relations by adopting some distinctly Whiggish — even radical — views since he left the army. He would mutter that the war against the Americans was even stupider than the war against the French, and that the Emperor Napoleon and President Madison were far less of a threat to the welfare of England than the Prince Regent.

Since she'd adopted her father's Tory views, she had to grit her teeth and obey when he told her to send a hundred pounds to the families of some agitators who'd been hanged. Just because a man is a radical, she reminded herself, that does not necessarily mean that he's a murderer — though she wryly acknowledged that her father might have jumped to exactly that conclusion.

He was under considerable pressure to take a place in Parliament. The Whigs, in opposition, were in great need of someone of Major Lancaster's talent, and there was no other man in England who both sympathized with their views and had such a military reputation.

'If it's not impertinent to ask, Major, why don't you stand?' she asked one day, when a letter arrived offering him a borough that was in the pocket of one of the greatest of the Whig aristocrats. 'If I may say so, you would be an outstanding Member of Parliament.'

'There's one overwhelming disqualification: I don't want to. Write to Fitzwilliam and politely tell him no.'

Among her other tasks was settling his brother's estate. She worked at this with enthusiasm, for it meant that she had to visit all of George's circle to see whether there were any outstanding debts.

When she came to think hard, she found to her relief that she still had some traces left of her work of memorizing features at the funeral, despite the overpowering effect of the appearance of the man she now knew to be Richard Lancaster, and she would recognize them if she saw them again.

Of the six men fitting Harry's description at the funeral, she had so far discovered two: the major himself and Lord Bowland. With authority to ask questions as the secretary of George's executor, she now had a magnificent opportunity to find the other four.

At the major's direction, she started with

the tradesmen. She brought immense relief to at least three of them, who between them had outstanding bills worth five thousand pounds. They had faced ruin, since George had shown no inclination to pay them and a remarkable ability to avoid the duns. Their gratitude to her and her employer brought unexpected satisfaction to her work.

For a fleeting second she entertained a completely new idea about George's murder. Could it have been done by a desperate tradesman, seeking the only way to have his debts paid? But no, a tradesman wouldn't have called him George.

One man who certainly would have was Mr Alexander Carstairs, Tory MP and one of the pall-bearers. She made an appointment, saying she was acting for the executor.

When she was shown into his rooms, she could see that Carstairs was a man of the same type as the late George Lancaster: big, handsome in a brutal way, and immaculately dressed. His eyes were a faded blue that could have been described as grey at a pinch. He was not wearing a red rose ring.

'So, you're working for George's upright brother, are you? Want to grab a few more shekels for your master?'

'On the contrary, Mr Carstairs. My instructions are to pay any of the late Mr

George's debts, not to call in any owing to him.'

'Well, then.' He became friendlier. 'He owed me five thousand pounds.'

'You'll understand, sir, that I'd like to see some evidence for that claim.'

'I've got his vowels somewhere. I'll get 'em in a minute.' Carstairs smiled and offered Kit a drink, which she refused. 'You seem mighty young, Mr Jackson, for such a responsibility.'

'It's a fault which I hope to overcome with time.'

'Did you ever meet my friend George?'

'No,' she lied without hesitation. 'I came into Major Lancaster's employment after the death of his brother.'

'Ah, let me tell you about him. Are you sure you won't have a drink? Oh well. George was a great go — always up to every rig. Would never let a friend down — always paid his debts of honour, of course.'

'Of course.'

'It's a sad thing that he's gone. Wish I could get my hands on that bitch who did for him.'

'I understand he was shot by a man,' said Kit as coolly as she could.

'It was this finical cow who screamed when George wanted her. Set her brother on to shoot my poor friend. What call had she to refuse him? Ah, he was a buck of the first head, George. Always had any woman he wanted. Never take no for an answer. Would keep on at 'em until he had 'em.'

'Quite so, sir. Now, if I may see those vowels you mentioned . . . '

'Wait here, I'll get 'em.'

Please let him not have an alibi, she prayed as he went into the next room. I could willingly see this man take Harry's place on the gallows.

Carstairs returned, and gave her a sheet of paper on which was scrawled:

Alexander Carstairs
IOU £5,000.
George Lancaster.

She looked at the writing, then looked at Carstairs. 'This would certainly be adequate evidence for your claim, Mr Carstairs,' she said levelly, 'if only you'd been able to forge the signature a little more accurately.'

Carstairs' face changed in an instant. 'You whoreson cripple!' he shouted. 'How dare you challenge my word!'

'I've become very familiar with Mr George Lancaster's signature, Mr Carstairs, and this isn't it.'

'Listen, cub,' said Carstairs, grabbing her

by the collar and lifting her up so that her face was inches away from his and she could smell the wine on his breath. 'My friend George would have wanted me to have that money. Not that Whiggish, priggish brother of his.' He slammed her down on the floor so hard that her foot jarred in pain.

'Very possibly, sir,' she said. 'As a Member of Parliament you have the power to change the law so that unwritten wishes may be taken account of in disposing an estate. Until that is the case, we must abide by the law as it stands.'

'Ach, get out of here,' he snarled. 'You've picked up too many of your master's ways for my stomach to bear.'

She turned to go. It didn't seem the time to ask him where he'd been on the evening of May the tenth.

'By God, I'm glad of one thing!' Carstairs shouted after her. 'George would have been proud of me if he'd known! There was a special debate in Parliament, and I was putting the knife into those damned Whigs that your master favours at the very hour of George's death!'

Now that's what I call an alibi, she thought as she limped away. Damn!

Three down, three to go.

Her quest followed similar lines among the

rest of George's circle. To a man, they all claimed that George had owed them debts of honour. The major had told her to pay'em and be rid of 'em, but she thought that he deserved better than to be cheated by men who seemed as dastardly as his brother. She insisted on evidence, and the claims dwindled to a mere eighteen thousand pounds.

Three of the men she met fitted Harry's description: the rest were all too old or too short. But Mr Oliver Pool, Lord Reginald Mortimer and Sir Sydney Low were all tall and thirtyish: and they were all pall-bearers.

Each time she had dealings with one, she looked at his hands. Not a trace of the ring she was looking for, though there was a great variety of others. After her experience with Carstairs, she was careful to check their alibis before she demanded evidence of their claims for repayment. She gave the same carefully idle opening to each of them: 'Ah, it's a sad thing when a friend dies in such a way, isn't it, sir? Leaves a mark. We can all remember what we were doing at the time, I dare say.' It had proved fruitless: none of the three had indicated anything of where he had been on the evening of May the tenth.

She took careful note of everything she knew of them, and sent the details to Lady Fenton to pass on to Latimer, her man of business, and Hamlet, Desdemona's brother. Perhaps they'd have better success.

So, she summarized: of the six pall-bearers, one was Bowland himself, one was speaking in Parliament, and three were being quietly investigated by others.

And the sixth man? She had no idea what to make of him, though she was getting to know him very well.

★   ★   ★

If Kit had seen Richard Lancaster only by day, she would have unquestioningly regarded him as a happy and honourable man, albeit with some eccentric views, and she would have dismissed any suggestion that he wore the mark of Cain from killing his brother. But in the evening a devil seemed to get hold of him. He wouldn't go out into company: he preferred to dine alone with Kit, and drink.

Kit had very mixed feelings about their evenings together. She welcomed the chance to get to know him, and hated herself for spying on him. She was afraid the wine would go to her head and make her betray herself, yet she enjoyed the companionship that drinking together brought. She wanted him to drink so he might reveal his guilt, but she feared what he became when he did.

Despite the danger, she gained consider-able pleasure from the evenings when they were alone together, and she believed that he did too. That sense of power she had seen in him at first was disappearing with familiarity. To be sure, she was always conscious of his presence, but it was becoming the presence of a man she could like and respect, rather than of an enemy to be feared.

In his company she felt her mind opening up. She had never realized how confined her experience had been at Eastham, with not even a governess to teach her. Richard Lancaster had a first-class education and a wide experience of the world, and he also had a mind to appreciate it and to share it with her.

But as the evening wore on and the level of the brandy in the decanter sank, he would become morose. He didn't become taciturn and sullen, as did some men she knew when they were drunk, but his conversation took an increasingly morbid turn.

One evening started as an amiable discussion of poetry. It was an unequal match, as Kit had read only what was in her father's library, and Squire Faulkner's tastes had been very conservative. But Lancaster knew the latest poets and their poetry: Kit was interested to learn that he'd shared a mistress with Lord Byron at one time — that was not information Katherine Faulkner could have gleaned.

The discussion turned into a poetry reading, each trying to convince the other by putting forward some favourite works. The major's fine voice rapidly convinced her of the virtues of modern poetry.

She tried to defend her own choice, and he listened to Gray's *Elegy Written in a Country Churchyard* with well-bred attention. When she finished he said, 'Kit, you have a good voice, and I could listen to you read the Army List with pleasure. Now I think on it, I should prefer you to read the Army List: it has far more meaning than Gray's *Elegy*.'

'How can you declare it meaningless?' she protested. 'The way he talks about the people who have lived ordinary lives and are now dead: that may not be strikingly original, but it is beautifully written. After all, that is how Alexander Pope described true wit: 'What oft was thought, but ne'er so well expressed'.'

'That, Kit, is precisely why I dislike Pope, and Gray, and all those poets of the last century.' The brandy was starting to work, and the major was getting vehement. 'It is all so well expressed, and not a new thought in one hundred years! What does Pope know of the depths of the human heart? How can

Gray reach us in our guilt and misery?'

Kit was taken aback. 'What guilt?' she asked. It was unwise of her to be so abrupt, for the question seemed to transform him.

'You don't know?' He leaned over and gripped her upper arm. There was no trace now of the cheerful Richard Lancaster of the daylight. She was suddenly frightened: she felt that those grey eyes would see through her and reveal her as his enemy, and she was afraid of the strength that bruised her arm where he held her. 'Don't you have any guilt?' he asked.

Her gaze dropped.

'I see you have,' he continued. 'Are you going to tell me about it?'

'No!' she cried, shaking her head.

'I thought not. And you will forgive me, then, for not telling you of mine.' He still held her arm but his grip relaxed. It was as if his hand was merely holding her in companionship, but she knew he would tighten his grip if she moved. 'We were talking of poetry, were we not?' he continued, almost as if nothing had happened.

She agreed, greatly hoping to get back to something harmless. But it didn't work out like that.

'Do you know of Andrew Marvell?' he asked, still holding her firmly. When she shook her head he continued, 'An old poet: he came before Pope and Gray and their bloodless friends. Listen to this.' He spoke it from memory, looking into her face all the while:

'*But at my back I always hear*
Time's wingèd chariot hurrying near.
And yonder all before us lie
Deserts of vast eternity.'

His grip tightened. 'It is at my back every night,' he said. 'Every night Death rides behind me.'

She shivered, and her shock made him aware of where he was and what he was doing. He stared at his hand on her arm as if it were something separate from him, then loosed his hold. She rubbed the place he had gripped her.

He noticed. 'Did I hurt you?'

'If that's the strength of your left hand,' she said ruefully, 'I hope to be out of your way when the right is healed.'

He drank no more that night, but he had already consumed enough not to shake away McTavish and Gregory when they came to help him to bed. Kit was surprised by their lack of surprise; they seemed to be expecting the major to drink himself into a stupor.

In the morning she was surprised by the major himself. He showed not the slightest sign of any ill effects of the enormous quantity he had drunk the night before, nor of any consciousness that he had said anything which a man ought not to say to someone whom he'd known for such a short time.

It was Sunday, and the whole household went to church: any church or chapel they wished, for Richard Lancaster had no interest in religious conformity. He and Kit went to St George's where his brother had been fashionably buried.

Kit remembered her previous visit. Then, she had been an outsider, and hadn't even known who he was. Now she was living in his house. In some ways, she had probably come to know more about him in these past few days than any other person did, for she doubted if he talked to many people about his feelings of guilt, or told anyone else that Death rode behind him every night. But she still didn't know what he was guilty of. Was it fratricide? Had he killed his brother, and was he now acting the hypocrite in church?

She knelt and prayed: for help in her quest and for her brother's safety. But most of all she prayed for forgiveness of her own hypocrisy and deceit.

5

'So your cousin Lancaster has taken this young man under his wing,' said Miss Maitland to Lady Julia Lancaster at their fashionably late breakfast.

'It's a wounded wing at the moment. Richard needs someone to write for him.' Julia answered her chaperon far more casually than she felt. Mr Jackson, with his handsome face and his limp, had been in her thoughts frequently since he bumped into her. The news that Richard had employed him interested her exceedingly. Of course he was quite ineligible as a suitor, but she acknowledged a desire to find out more about the stranger who had come out of the night so opportunely. Her doubts about marrying her cousin were increasing. Could she endure marriage with a man who was always right? One who treated her with the same affection that he would a small puppy?

'Nevertheless,' continued Miss Maitland, 'it seems rash of him to choose someone that he picks up off the streets.'

'It was the other way round. I gather that

Mr Jackson picked up Richard.'

'Ah, well, it's another of your cousin's odd ways, I suppose.'

'What odd ways? Richard is one of the most respectable men I know.'

'Of course. Very respectable,' Miss Maitland hastened to say, remembering where her money came from.

'Quite *boringly* respectable,' added Julia provocatively.

'Boring? Major Lancaster? How can a man with twenty thousand pounds a year be boring?'

'Not so much boring as — well, *safe*. He never does anything interesting.'

'I cannot understand you, Julia. Wellington himself said that Major Lancaster was one of the bravest of his officers. How can you say he is safe and uninteresting?'

Julia often wondered that herself. Half her female acquaintance envied her from the depths of their souls. He was strong, brave, and rich. What more could anyone want in a husband? He wasn't handsome, but she'd grown up looking at his face, and she liked it, especially when it was smiling at her. And though she'd heard some comments about his peculiar views, politics was a matter of supreme indifference to her. 'Perhaps it all stems from the same thing,' she said slowly.

'I suspect that if it were not understood that I should marry him when I come of age, I should be passionately in love with him.'

'You have been spoiled by these novels. You should know that you are very lucky. Any other young lady would give her right eye to change places with you.'

'I don't suppose Richard wants to marry someone with only one eye.'

'Julia, what is the matter?' asked Miss Maitland. She was not normally sensitive to other people's feelings, but she knew that something about Julia had changed.

'Oh, nothing. I suppose I must think myself fortunate. But it's dull! All the young men run away when they see Richard coming. He's quite awe-inspiring at times.'

'How can he be both safe and awe-inspiring, Julia?'

'I don't know, but he manages. He manages everything. That's what would be so dreadful if I married him.'

'*If*? Don't you mean *when*?'

'Oh, perhaps. I don't know what I want.' This wasn't quite the truth. Julia knew exactly what she wanted: a chance to charm the mysterious Mr Jackson. She wouldn't fall in love with him, of course not; but it would certainly be pleasant to have him in love with her. And so piquant; it would be under

Richard's nose, which she felt a strong desire to put out of joint.

Miss Maitland was alarmed. Her present very comfortable living depended on Major Lancaster's good will, which would be instantly lost if Julia took it into her head to reject him. What freak had got into the girl? A terrible thought occurred to her. 'Julia,' she asked tentatively. 'It's not — you haven't . . . '

'What do you mean?' asked Julia.

'You haven't fallen in love with somebody else, have you?' she asked desperately.

Julia laughed. 'Oh, no!' she said confidently. 'No, I certainly haven't. Not at all.' She smiled at her chaperon's relief. 'I feel a little dull, that's all.'

'You don't have enough to do,' said Miss Maitland sternly. 'You may help me with the preparations for tonight's dinner.'

Etiquette seemed to demand the absence of any enjoyment tonight, as the family was still in mourning for their grandfather, the old Earl of Bowland; the guests had been chosen mainly for their respectability. Cousin Richard could get away with ignoring etiquette, but she could not. He had at least won for her the concession that she needn't wear black all the time, so long as she avoided colours. She valued this, for she knew that the silver grey of half-mourning became her very well. It matched her eyes, the grey that she shared with all her family.

She was pleased to hear a visitor arriving. Perhaps this would bring some variety on the scene.

'Lady Fenton,' intoned the butler.

'At this hour?' said Miss Maitland in surprise. 'What can she want? Oh, of course. It's . . . '

She broke off as her old friend came in. Helen was a permanent reproach to her; how did she manage to hide so many of the years that sat uncomfortably on Miss Maitland?

However, this morning Helen wasn't looking her best. Her face was slightly haggard and her dress was definitely dowdy. Miss Maitland felt positively amiable when she saw the years at last taking effect on her friend.

After the usual meaningless greetings and exchange of compliments, Lady Fenton accepted a dish of coffee and began. 'I've come, my dear Maria, to ask a favour of you. It's a situation of some delicacy, and only you can help me.'

Julia started to leave, but Lady Fenton beckoned her to stay, saying, 'This concerns you too, Lady Julia.'

'Tell me what it is, Helen,' asked Miss Maitland, hiding her gratification. How pleasant it would be to listen to Helen's story, and then turn her down.

'It is this terrible business about your cousin, Lady Julia.'

'Richard?' Julia said in surprise. 'What terrible business?'

'No, not Major Lancaster. It is his brother George of whom I speak.'

'Oh, yes, poor George,' said Miss Maitland. 'A terrible tragedy. Much loved by all who knew him.'

Julia didn't see why death should have made the family black sheep any more lovable than he had been in life.

'Quite,' said Lady Fenton. 'You have heard the gossip, no doubt.'

Miss Maitland had. 'You mean that your nephew — er . . . '

'My nephew has certainly been accused. He's innocent, of course.'

'It must have been dreadful, Helen,' said her friend, oozing compassion.

'Indeed it was.' She put an elegant hand to her forehead, on which at least one wrinkle appeared.

'How can I help you, Helen?' asked Miss Maitland, having realized that, however pleasant it would be to reject her friend's appeal, it would be even more gratifying to bestow her assistance graciously.

'It is so kind of you to offer, Maria,' said Lady Fenton. 'I knew I could rely on you. I've found myself in an awkward position. There is one person who could help, and that is Richard Lancaster. If it were known that George Lancaster's brother held no grudge against me, who else could?'

'I'm sure my cousin bears you no ill will,' said Julia stoutly.

'I do most sincerely hope you are right,' said Lady Helen. 'If it could only be seen to be the case . . . '

Julia had an idea. 'Miss Maitland, can we not invite Lady Fenton to dinner tonight? She can meet my cousin on friendly terms, and everyone will soon know about it.'

Miss Maitland had never liked to appear together with her friend; she knew that too many comparisons could be made. And Lady Fenton, though fashionable, had too many admirers to be of unquestioned respectability. But she was far from her dazzling self this morning, and looked at Maria with an expression of appeal. 'Of course, Helen. I should be delighted if you could come,' she said in her most patronizing manner. She smiled as a thought struck her. What a blow it would be to Helen if Major Lancaster publicly spurned her!

Lady Fenton's gratitude was profuse as she took her leave. But not as heartfelt as her relief that, with her mission successfully completed, she could go home and get out of these dreadful clothes that she and Desdemona had chosen for the occasion.

'How pleasant it is to help old friends,' sighed Miss Maitland. 'Poor dear, her troubles must be afflicting her greatly. Did you notice how she looked?'

'She was certainly not at her best,' said Julia. 'It was kind of you to invite her. I know how you hate being an odd number at dinner.'

'I forgot! One of the ladies will be without a partner. We cannot possibly invite anyone to come at such short notice, for who would accept?'

'There is someone,' said Julia as casually as she could manage. 'That young man of Richard's.'

Torn between the impropriety of having an unescorted lady, and her unwillingness to show favour to an unknown young man, Miss Maitland couldn't make up her mind. 'Do we know anything about him?'

'Richard obviously thinks well of him,' said

Julia, playing her trump card.

Miss Maitland sighed. 'I suppose he cannot be too unacceptable,' she said as she wrote out the invitation.

*   *   *

Kit was surprised by the invitation, but she accepted with gratitude. She didn't think her stomach could take another night alone with Major Lancaster and the brandy.

It was an excellent chance to continue her hunt. Lord Bowland would certainly be there as host; she had been diligently finding out about both George and Richard Lancaster, but of their cousin she had learned little more than she already knew. And perhaps some of the other men on her list would attend.

As she sat beside the major in the carriage, she smiled. I'm going to my first fashionable dinner, she thought. How often I dreamed of this occasion! I always hoped to have a big strong gentleman by me, and indeed I have, but it isn't quite the way I imagined it would be.

Kit felt an urge to meet Bowland's sister, Lady Julia. After the major's casual revelation that they would probably marry, he had said no more about her, and there had so far been no opportunity to meet. A pretty girl, Lady

Fenton had described her: but exactly how pretty?

Richard Lancaster paid more attention to well-mannered punctuality than fashionable disdain for the hour, so they were among the first to arrive. Miss Maitland and Lord Bowland greeted the major with expressions of concern for his health and no regard for his friend beyond a perfunctory acceptance of Kit's thanks for the invitation. Lancaster was forced to bring Kit forward and introduce her to his cousin, Lady Julia.

Kit saw a golden-haired beauty who bestowed a smile of such charm that, had Kit been what she pretended to be, she would have been instantly smitten. 'I am pleased to meet you,' said Kit politely, wondering why the loveliness of the woman in front of her should depress her.

'And I am more than pleased to meet you, Mr Jackson,' said Lady Julia musically, destroying Kit's hope that she would prove to have a voice like a corncrake. 'I must thank you a thousand times for saving my cousin's life.'

'Once is enough, Lady Julia,' said Kit curtly.

Lady Julia's pretty eyebrows lifted in surprise: she was obviously not used to being snubbed. 'So you think Richard is worth only one word of thanks?' She turned to her cousin. 'I value your life more highly.'

He took her hand in his uninjured one and lifted it to his lips. 'I am gratified by your esteem, Julia. I think I'm worth at least three.'

The major and his cousin obviously liked each other, but Kit could see not the slightest spark from either of them of anything more.

Neither could she see any sign of a ruby ring as she studied hand after hand. Nor were there any of the men on her list, apart from Bowland and the major.

The nearest possibility was Mr Charles Maxwell, who arrived with Miss Lucy Maxwell. They were obviously brother and sister: they shared the same well-formed features and thick dark hair, which in Charles's case had been bleached by the tropical sun that had browned his face. He was tall, but his eyes, unfortunately, were bright blue.

Kit could see that they were old friends of the Lancasters; Julia took Lucy off for a serious discussion of the latest fashions while the major introduced Charles and Kit. 'Charles is one of Sir Joseph Banks's exploring young men,' he said. 'He's recently back from New South Wales where he has been collecting botanical specimens.'

Maxwell started to talk of his adventures,

which meant that Kit didn't pay much attention to the arrival of the other guests, until a hush fell over the room and she looked round. In the doorway was Lady Fenton.

Kit knew that her own mouth was as wide open as her aunt's as they stared at each other. Fortunately no one was looking at Kit. Those who weren't looking at Lady Fenton were looking at Richard Lancaster, to see his reaction to the relative of the man accused of murdering his brother.

Lancaster knew his duty when he saw it. He strode over with his left hand outstretched. 'I am honoured to meet you, Lady Fenton,' he said.

Her eyes snapped away from Kit and she smiled enchantingly. 'And I am honoured to meet you, Major Lancaster. It would indeed be a pity if this wretched business should come between us.'

Kit couldn't understand the fleeting expression of annoyance that crossed Miss Maitland's face. There was nothing wrong with Lady Fenton, was there? Her aunt appeared to be the most ravishingly sophisticated woman in the room.

Kit couldn't spend as much attention on Charles Maxwell's stories as politeness demanded. She wasn't there to find out about the natural history of New South Wales but to discover a murderer.

Maxwell abruptly broke off his description of a kangaroo hunt and his face clouded over as Lord Bowland, released from his duties as host in welcoming the guests, went over to Lucy Maxwell. She was suddenly as blooming as her brother was gloomy. Bowland was speaking to her, too quietly for anyone else to hear, but whatever it was sent a flush to her face. Ah-ha! thought Kit. That's where Bowland's interest lies. But why should Charles Maxwell be worried about it? Surely it would be a fine thing if his sister became a countess?

Maxwell murmured a word of excuse and strode over to where Miss Maxwell was still talking to Bowland. Kit would have liked to follow, but her presence would be unwelcome. She joined Major Lancaster. 'Ah, Mr Jackson,' he said. 'I'd like to present you to Lady Fenton.'

Lady Fenton smiled and uttered inanities; Kit smiled and uttered inanities. The major, who had been thoroughly enjoying talking with one of the most sophisticated women in London, wondered why such a blight had come over the conversation, and disengaged as soon as he politely could.

Lady Fenton kept her smile fixed, and her voice dropped skilfully to one which couldn't be overheard but didn't look like whispering. 'Mr Latimer and Hamlet have been busy investigating.'

'Any news?' said Kit softly.

'Mr Oliver Pool was in a spunging house for debt on the evening of May the tenth.'

That leaves two, thought Kit.

'Mr Latimer has seen the records,' Lady Fenton continued, then added abruptly, 'What pleasant weather this is.'

Kit turned to see who was behind her. It was a man whom she'd noticed arrive; she could hardly miss him, since he immediately drew attention by the glory of his clothes. He was all in harmonious shades of blue: a dark blue superfine coat, a pale blue waistcoat, and sky blue pantaloons. A large ring (sapphire, with no flower) adorned his little finger, and his buttonhole was made of bluebells. Even his cravat, elegantly tied and starched into folds, was a delicate blue. Inside the clothes was a slim man in his late twenties, about Kit's own height. He had long wavy hair, and his features were well formed. His eyes, naturally, were blue.

'Oh, Mr Smythe,' gushed Lady Fenton, holding out her hand. 'I am delighted to see you here, for I can think of no better person to ask about my plans for redecoration.'

'I am always at your service.' The man bowed. 'Will you not introduce me to your young friend?'

'Mr Kit Jackson, Mr Hector Smythe,' Lady Fenton obliged. 'Mr Smythe is our mentor in all matters of taste. Even Brummell acknowledges his superiority in questions of furniture.'

'You are too kind, Lady Fenton,' Smythe murmured. 'You will make me blush, and red is such an unfashionable colour.'

He turned to Kit and smiled. There was something in the way he looked at her that unsettled her considerably. What was it? She didn't know.

She was rescued by the announcement of dinner. With the tact and ruthlessness of a career diplomat Miss Maitland arranged the order of precedence. Kit was definitely last on the list of the gentlemen, but she wasn't displeased as it meant that her partner was Miss Maxwell. Lucy would be as eager to talk about Lord Bowland as Kit was to listen.

If a meal of such immensity can be called elegant, then that dinner was. Dish upon dish, in course upon course, all washed down with quantities of red and white wine of excellent quality. Kit sipped very small glasses of white wine. She knew that nobody was expected to eat everything, and she helped

Miss Maxwell and herself to the dishes in front of them.

The conversation wasn't as fine as the dinner. Kit knew enough about the polite world not to attempt conversation with anyone except those either side of her, and the formidable dowager on her left snubbed her all evening. Lucy would have been willing to talk to her about Lord Bowland, but both realized that the subject of their interest was within ear-shot, so they chatted comfortably about nothing in particular. Of the others around the table, Kit could hear Charles Maxwell's antipodean anecdotes, and Hector Smythe relating as much gossip about the Royal Dukes as befitted the company of ladies. But too many people had too much on their minds for conversation to flow freely.

Lady Fenton had recovered from the shock of seeing Katherine. Of course the girl would move into company; after all, that was the reason for the whole enterprise. Lady Fenton knew it was important to investigate Lord Bowland and Major Lancaster. The major was Katherine's responsibility: Lady Fenton would take Bowland, who was conveniently sitting beside her. She found the task not the slightest bit onerous, and she was aware that he was equally willing to investigate her. A thorough mutual investigation seemed a distinct possibility in the near future.

The thoughts of another lady were different. Miss Maitland felt that she had been imposed on. She didn't mind Mr Jackson, a polite young man who knew his place. But Lady Fenton! That morning she was haggard and dowdy, and had called for compassion. Now look at her! Not the least ashamed of herself, dressed in a gown that cost a fortune, on the easiest of terms with Major Lancaster, and flirting, positively flirting, with Lord Bowland! At her age it was indecent!

Lady Julia Lancaster was also irritated, as precedence had placed her next to the Hon. Waldo Griffin, who was one of the dullest young men in London. She wasn't averse to being adored, but being adored by a man with a face like a turnip was not flattering. Now, Mr Jackson's face was not a bit turnip-like. Mr Jackson's face was as finely featured and smooth as a Greek statue. And Mr Jackson was sitting far away talking to Lucy Maxwell.

To add to Julia's annoyance, Lucy was responding to Mr Jackson's attention. Julia made allowances for her friend's behaviour. Lucy was jealous of the way Bowland was conversing with Lady Fenton, and was trying to provoke his jealousy in turn. Julia was angry with her brother. Why was Edward behaving so badly towards Lucy? Why didn't he marry her? Lucy wouldn't be a good match as far as fortune was concerned, but she loved him dearly. As it was, Edward was practically forcing the girl to flirt with Mr Jackson, and Julia didn't like it at all.

When dinner was over, Miss Maitland made a sign to the ladies to withdraw. Kit almost joined them out of habit, but she converted her move into a salute as the women departed.

Kit had never fully realized how different men were without women. She had guessed that the conversation would become coarser, but she hadn't known how much. Bawdy jokes went round with the port, and Hector Smythe capped them all by relating a story of astonishing obscenity about the Duke of Cumberland. ' . . . and it was absolutely dripping!' he finished among guffaws.

Kit couldn't help blushing; she hung her head, hoping no one would notice.

The conversation turned. 'How absolutely frightful it must be for Lady Fenton,' said Hector Smythe. 'It's bad enough for a woman to be an aunt, but to be an aunt of a murderer!'

'It was well-mannered of you to acknowledge her, Richard,' said Bowland.

'Why not?' remarked Smythe. 'The gallant major doubtless feels that her relationship with someone with a claim to have rid the world of brother George is a matter for congratulation rather than condemnation.'

As the major had felt precisely those sentiments, he couldn't bring himself to reply.

★ ★ ★

Julia always found it dull in the drawing-room with the ladies, and she was relieved when the gentlemen finished their brandy and joined them. The turnip-faced Waldo Griffin took his normal adoring position beside her, but she used her considerable powers of persuasion to direct him to a game of whist. Now she could put her plan into action; to charm that strange young man who seemed to take no notice of her.

But Mr Jackson, troubled by a limp, sat down, and was immediately joined by Hector Smythe on one side and Lucy Maxwell on the other. Lucy took one glance at Lord Bowland, who was deep in conversation with Lady Fenton, and then proceeded to demonstrate great interest in Mr Jackson.

Hector Smythe was not to be left out. 'I am a lucky man,' he said with a smile. 'I am sitting with the most good-looking woman and man in the world.'

Both Kit and Lucy protested at this. 'Very well, then,' he continued. 'Let us confine ourselves to the room, rather than the world. Who are the best-looking man and woman here tonight? What do you say, Miss Maxwell?'

Lucy's eyes went straight to Lord Bowland. 'Of course,' Smythe agreed. 'He is very handsome in his aristocratic way. And whom do you consider the most lovely lady, aside from your delightful self?'

'I protest,' said Lucy, managing a laugh. 'I am no judge of feminine good looks.'

'What is your judgement, Mr Jackson?' Smythe asked.

'I am half of your opinion,' Kit said smoothly. 'I agree that Miss Maxwell on my left is the fairest lady in the world, let alone the room, but the handsomest man must be Mr Smythe on my right.'

'A diplomatic answer,' Smythe said, pleased. 'Now tell us the true one.'

'I also am no judge of good looks.'

'Neither of feminine — nor of masculine?'

Kit stared at Mr Smythe in surprise. There was an odd tone in his voice as he'd asked the question. Kit could understand Lucy Maxwell's motives, but Hector Smythe was a mystery.

'Will you not tell us, Mr Jackson?' he pressed.

Kit surveyed the room, considering. Mr Smythe would think her grievously wanting in taste if she confessed to preferring Major Lancaster's rough-hewn features to those of any other man, as he stood conversing cheerfully with his unnecessarily beautiful cousin Julia. What were they talking about to make them laugh so together?

In fact, they were talking about her.

Julia, when she was foiled in her plan to talk to the mysterious young man, had seen her cousin leaning against the mantelpiece, an amused expression on his face. She joined him, recognizing that he was always entertaining, for all that she wasn't enthusiastic about marrying him.

'An interesting party, Julia,' he said.

'It seems decidedly flat to me, Richard.'

'What, no devoted admirers save my humble self? You shouldn't have disposed of Waldo Griffin so rashly.'

'I can live without Waldo's devotion. I wish you'd have a word with him.'

'When you've reproached me before for scaring off young men? I wouldn't dream of spoiling your pleasure. Besides, it would take more than a word to conquer his passion. A dictionary, at least.'

'Preferably administered over the head.' Now was Julia's chance. 'Richard, I fancy Mr Jackson is in need of assistance. He looks decidedly uncomfortable sitting between Lucy and Hector Smythe.'

'An odd trio, certainly; they are doing a good job of appearing happy together. For whose benefit is it?'

'You are a monster of cynicism, Richard,' protested Julia. 'Lucy is being very brave, and I can sympathize with her desire to show Edward that she doesn't care that he flirts with a woman old enough to be a grandmother.'

'Jackson and Smythe seem to be amusing her.'

'I don't think Edward would consider Mr Smythe much of a rival.'

'If you mean what I think you mean,' he said repressively, 'then you shouldn't. A well brought up young lady ought to know nothing about such things.'

'Don't be so stuffy. I know perfectly well where Hector Smythe's tastes lie. My concern is that Mr Jackson may not.'

'You may be right. There's something very innocent about that young man.'

'I shall rescue him before he finds out,' she said, and she sailed across the room with a dazzling smile and a clear conscience.

'I've wanted to talk to you all evening, Mr Jackson,' she said, spiriting her quarry away from Smythe and Lucy with a request to fetch her a drink.

Kit obliged, and returned with a glass of champagne. 'I wonder why the most beautiful woman in the world should wish to talk to me?'

'Flatterer,' laughed Julia. 'I wager you say that to all the women.'

'Quite right, Lady Julia. I told Miss Maxwell she was the most beautiful woman in the world not ten minutes ago.'

'Do you always do that?'

'Of course. I have a happy disposition that makes me think that any woman I am with is bewitchingly lovely.'

'I wish you'd be serious, Mr Jackson.'

Kit put on a serious expression. 'How can I help you, Lady Julia? Do you wish me to talk, sing, juggle three plates in the air, fly to the moon? I'd ask you to dance, but my foot prevents me.'

'You are a very rude young man.'

'I? Rude? How can you say that? I've told you that you are lovely, I've offered to fly to the moon for you. What more can you want of me?'

As the main thing that Julia wanted was that Mr Jackson should fall in love with her, she found it difficult to answer. 'I wish you'd treat me seriously, Mr Jackson.'

'Treat you seriously? If you really wish me to, I shall: if in exchange you will tell me why a lady of rank and beauty sets out to charm a penniless cripple, of whom she can want nothing except another heart to add to her collection.'

Julia recoiled. 'Mr Jackson, you have obviously mistaken good manners for something more,' she said haughtily.

'Have I made a mistake? Good. I am glad that a woman of your honour and sense wouldn't stoop to such meanness. I offer my apologies.'

Kit started to go, but Julia put out a hand. 'Stay, Mr Jackson. I am not offended by what you say. But I am unused to such treatment.'

'You asked me to take you seriously, and now you find you don't like it?'

Julia looked up into the brown eyes which studied her. 'I think I do like it. I've been told that I am beautiful until I am sick of it, but nobody has credited me with honour and sense. You are a most unusual young man.'

'Lady Julia,' said the unusual young man. 'Do you really wish me to take you seriously, as a human being, not just as a pretty woman?'

'Oh, yes,' she breathed, entranced at the prospect.

Kit glanced around the room to make sure they wouldn't be overheard. Julia waited in anticipation. Then, taking Julia by the hand, Kit asked in a low voice, 'Tell me, Lady Julia: has your brother any enemies?'

That was not at all what Julia expected.

6

Kit was pleased when she looked back on the dinner. She had found an ally, when she explained to Lady Julia that Lord Bowland might be in danger. She didn't mention the real reason for her concern, but repeated her tale that the cut-throats who had attacked the major might have been after his cousin. Julia, after a surprise which Kit thought excessive, promised to keep watch on her brother.

Kit felt that she could have been friends with Julia if things were different. She was an intelligent woman, and although she obviously set out to charm anything in trousers, that was only natural in someone of her beauty. She was clearly very concerned with her brother's welfare, and such sisterly affection was pleasant to see. Kit thought it was also pleasant to see how she treated Richard Lancaster with an affection equally sisterly.

Kit found another source of satisfaction in her aunt's behaviour. It was most kind of Lady Fenton to take so much trouble to get to know Lord Bowland. A pity that it made that nice Miss Maxwell jealous, though.

Kit was also pleased to discover that, when Major Lancaster went into company, he drank no more than the next man. At the end of the dinner he bade farewell in a gentleman-like fashion, he drove home with Kit chatting pleasantly of nothing very important, and he required no assistance to climb the stairs to his room — though she had a suspicion he might have a bottle beside his bed.

One thing puzzled her: the odd behaviour of Mr Smythe. But since everyone regarded him as an authority on taste, she had to assume that he was acting correctly and that she was ignorant of the ways of London life.

She worked hard and efficiently, trying to assuage the guilt she felt about her deception of the major with the thought that she was, after all, serving him well in his affairs. She was conscious that she was good at it: she had been in charge of the accounts at home in Eastham for many years. She felt she might earn the generous wages of eighty pounds a year that he was to pay her. When all this is over, she thought, I might even get him to give me a reference.

If I don't get him hanged first, she added. Too often it slipped from her mind that her main aim in working for him was to take the rope from Harry's neck and put it on his. Oh, damn it! she thought. I wish I hadn't come to — to like him.

But there were still two other men whom it might be: two others who could have been free to murder George.

Only one, she discovered half an hour later, when a letter from Lady Fenton was delivered which said:

Don't worry about Bowland: I'll get to know him and keep watch over him.

On the evening in question Lord Reginald Mortimer was playing whist with the Prince Regent.

The major had gone to a meeting of the board of trustees of a hospital for injured soldiers with which he was connected. He would sometimes protest about the time it took: he would have been pleased to donate twice the sum he had given if only they would leave him alone.

She finished her work for the day, and in the absence of the major until the evening felt she could return to her novel. She had chosen *Caleb Williams* merely to broaden her reading; the author, a notorious radical, was not represented in her father's library. Then she discovered that it was about a good rich man whose character changed after he committed murder and who persecuted his secretary for discovering his guilty secret. She was reading it with far more terrified fascination than any Gothic horror story.

McTavish announced a visitor, 'Mr Hector Smythe.' His face was unmoved at the sight of that remarkable person, today clad in varying shades of green.

She set her book aside and Mr Smythe sat down, crossing his elegant legs in their sea-green pantaloons. He surveyed the furnishings of the room with a critical eye. 'He has style, the major,' he approved. 'Very modern, very masculine. Not my taste at all, of course, but stylish nonetheless.'

'Major Lancaster is out at the moment,' said Kit.

'Oh, dear, what a pity,' said Smythe. 'I shall have to content myself with paying my respects to you, Mr Jackson.'

'I hate to be inhospitable,' she said. 'But I'm not sure Major Lancaster likes me to receive visitors in his house.'

'Oh, dear, is he really such an ogre?' Smythe said. 'In that case I shall invite you out. My coachman is waiting with my carriage outside: would you care to come for a drive round town?' She accepted. *Caleb Williams* could wait, and it was a fine day.

But it was a pity Mr Smythe had a closed carriage, she thought as she joined him: an open one would have been more pleasant.

As they rattled over the cobbles, the bouncing of the carriage kept jogging Mr Smythe close to her. She edged away, but soon came to the end of the seat and could move no further. It was a pity, for otherwise she would have enjoyed the drive. He was an amusing companion, and she knew it was a great honour for such as Kit Jackson to be noticed by this leader of fashion. He soon discovered her newly-acquired taste for modern poets. 'You know Byron, of course,' he said.

'Only his works: I've never met him.'

'You're not unlike him, you realize,' Smythe continued. 'You both have a limp, and there's this air of mystery that you both carry about you. And then there's something else,' he said. He turned to face her and put a hand on her knee. 'You are both desperately hand-some.'

Kit couldn't understand him. If she'd been wearing woman's clothes she would have known exactly what he was doing, but she didn't believe that he'd seen through her disguise. She had to assume that an arbiter of taste had the right to pass comment on anything from furniture to faces. But she was quite uncomfortable, and she would prefer to talk of other matters.

'What do you think of Gray's *Elegy in a Country Churchyard*, Mr Smythe?' she asked, the first question she could think of. He smiled, gave her knee a friendly squeeze, and accepted the change of subject.

He set her down outside the major's house, and he gave a little wave from the carriage as he drove away. 'Bye-ee!' he cooed.

What a strange man, she thought. But very friendly.

After dinner that evening she learned the reason.

The meal had been cleared away and McTavish was putting out the brandy when one of the footmen brought in a parcel. 'For Mr Jackson. A messenger has just delivered it,' he said, then left the room.

It was a book: *The Giaour*, Lord Byron's latest work. She opened it and read the inscription: 'Kit Jackson, with the warmest and most affectionate regards.'

'Oh, how kind!' she exclaimed. 'See, Major: it's from Mr Smythe. I went for a drive with him this afternoon, and I mentioned that I'd like to read it. Wasn't that generous of him to buy it for me so quickly?'

But then she looked at the major. He had fallen back in his chair with an expression of stunned amazement. 'You went for a drive with Hector Smythe?'

There was a suppressed snort from McTavish, but a thunderous look from the major sent him out of the room.

'Mr Jackson,' Lancaster said in a strangled voice. 'What are your — er — sentiments towards Mr Smythe?'

'I like him, and I am honoured by his regard. Though I confess I am at a loss to explain why such a man as he should extend his friendship towards me.'

'Ah,' he said, obviously relieved. 'You're not.'

'Not what?'

'You don't know?'

'No, I don't know. I've displeased you in some way, but I don't understand how.' She was upset. 'Please explain to me.'

'Oh,' he said, embarrassed. 'How can I put this?' He looked at the ceiling as if for inspiration. 'You wouldn't happen to know the word *molly*?'

'No. What does it mean?'

'It means — well — someone like Smythe.' He was hardly explaining matters. 'Someone who is not altogether — er — the same as other men.'

'I've noticed that,' Kit said, trying to be helpful. 'One or two of the things Mr Smythe has said are a little queer.'

'Ah. Yes. Quite.' He tried again. 'Mr Smythe — doesn't like women.'

'Really? He was getting on famously with Miss Maxwell last night.'

'It's not so much that he doesn't like women; it's more that he does like men.' He paused, but she still hadn't grasped his meaning. 'Rather too much.'

Kit's eyes opened wide with astonishment. 'You mean — he commits the sin of Sodom?' she gasped.

'That's rather a biblical way of putting it, but yes, Hector Smythe commits the sin of Sodom,' said the major, relieved at her comprehension, long though it had been in arriving. 'You have never met someone like that before?'

'No, never. I've read about it in the Bible, of course, but to meet a genuine Sodomite — I'd as soon expect Noah's Ark to come sailing up the Thames.'

'I deduce that you didn't attend an English public school.'

'Is it so common there?'

'It is common anywhere that large numbers of men are kept together out of the company of women. Prisons, the navy. Certainly the army. Unnatural circumstances breed unnatural acts.'

'So those heroic sailors at Trafalgar I've been taught to admire were all Sodomites?' she said, taken aback.

'Not all of them. But some, yes.'

Kit said nothing, distressed. She knew now what Hector Smythe had tried to do, and she rubbed her knee where he had squeezed it as if it were dirty.

There was also the realiztion that she'd nearly betrayed herself. If sodomy was as common as the major said, any man would have understood Smythe's behaviour, even a country bumpkin like the supposed Kit Jackson. Fortunately the major seemed to accept that she was merely naïve, but she dared not make another mistake like that.

She could do one thing. 'With your permission,' she said, and rang the bell. When McTavish answered, she handed *The Giaour* to him. 'Can you have that returned to Mr Smythe? And if he calls again, tell him I'm not at home.'

'Aye, Mr Jackson. I'll do that.' He left.

Lancaster nodded. 'Yes, I think that's the right course of action.'

'I hope so,' she said quietly.

'You are a little dejected, I see.'

'A little, yes. And ashamed of myself.'

'Do you have anything to be ashamed of?'

he asked very gently. 'Did he — did he do anything?'

She looked down in embarrassment. 'He got rather close, and he put his hand on my knee,' she said, rubbing it again.

'That's nothing for *you* to be ashamed of.'

'It isn't that. It's — well, I was so stupid!'

'Innocence is not stupidity, Kit. Don't mix them up.'

'Thank you,' she said, smiling gratefully at him. 'All the same, if it wouldn't embarrass you, I should be grateful if you could tell me more about *mollies*. I don't want to make the same mistake again.'

'I don't know if I can, for I don't understand that sort of man myself. What goes on in the army, when there are no women — well, I've seen enough of that, and I know why it happens even if I cannot approve. But Smythe? He's a man of high standing, admired by some of the finest women in the land, a gifted talker — no, I cannot comprehend what drives him.'

'There is something else that concerns me. He may have thought I was like him. For though I didn't encourage him, I didn't discourage him either. I thought it was simply friendship.'

'He may well have done. He probably thought that you'd understand his behaviour.

You haven't been approached in that fashion before?'

'No, never.'

'That surprises me. I'd have thought the Hector Smythes of the world would have been attracted by your sort of looks long before now.'

'But why?'

'Well,' he said, embarrassed. 'You are — something of the beardless youth.'

'You think my appearance is effeminate?' she dared to ask.

'I shouldn't put it that way,' he said. 'But Smythe isn't the only man who might be interested in you. I suggest you be on your guard in future. You make me wonder. Where were you brought up? It must be a very virtuous place.'

'So virtuous that my boyhood was quite out of this world.'

'Ah, we're back to your mystery again. I shan't dig any deeper, not tonight. Let me fill your glass,' he said, and they conversed on other matters until he called for Gregory to help him to bed.

★   ★   ★

I have been putting it off too long, Kit thought next morning as the major went out.

123

She had been many days in the house of the man most likely to have committed the murder, and she still hadn't searched it for a red rose ring.

She had excused herself in the first days with the notion that she dared not risk being discovered while rummaging around the house; but an excuse had occurred to her a few nights ago, and she knew what she would say if she had to.

She took the seal that she used to stamp the wax when closing the letters that she wrote for him, and stuffed it down the side of an old sofa, so that she could pretend that she was looking for it.

Not that I need an excuse to search here, she thought as she explored possible hiding places in the library. I'm his secretary: of course I may look through his desk. But she found nothing; and with dread she knew that she could not avoid searching his bedroom.

Gregory, his valet, was in the kitchen occupied with some leathers, and the housemaid was not yet due to tidy the major's bedroom: Kit had watched her and knew that she did it early in the afternoon. The search was best done before the room was tidied, so that any trace of disorder would be whisked away by the maid. There would never be a better time than right now.

She climbed the stairs as if to go to her own room, next to his. When she saw that she was not observed, she opened his door and slipped quietly in. She didn't lock it behind her; that would be even more suspicious if anyone tried it.

She leaned heavily against the door, her eyes closed, trying to calm her breath and her racing pulse. I have an excuse, she told herself. I know what I'll say if Gregory comes in. With her eyes closed and her deep breaths she could smell the room, and the masculine traces that the major had left in it: the brandy, the leather of his boots, the shaving soap, and the smell of him from his bed.

She opened her eyes: the sheets were still crumpled, the imprint of his body still on the mattress and the pillow. His bed was against the wall that divided his room from hers, and she realized that he slept less than a yard away from her every night. Next to the bed was a small table, and on it was a half-full decanter and an empty glass. In the corner of the room was a basin cabinet, the water from his wash and shave still in the bowl, and a towel hanging beside it. It made her realize that she had been neglectful of her disguise: she must buy a razor and brush to leave wet by her own wash-basin.

Where would I keep a ring? she wondered.

In a jewel case. And where would I keep a jewel case? In that chest of drawers.

She went over to it. At first she tip-toed, but she corrected herself: I must behave as though I have every right to be here. She bent down and pulled out the bottom drawer as quietly as she could; there was no sense in drawing attention to her presence, even if she did have an excuse.

She was surprised at first to see how tidy it was; Harry kept everything from dog-chewed cricket balls to his gold signet ring in such a drawer. But Harry had no valet. Gregory kept the linen clean, pressed and folded: so well folded that it would be instantly apparent if she searched through it. The best she could do was feel down the sides and back: nothing there.

The next drawer held something more promising: a leather case. She opened it, and saw a pair of obviously well-used and well-cared-for duelling pistols. These have killed at least one man, she thought. Have they killed two?

In the top drawer she found it: his jewel case. Almost empty; he was not a man to wear much. Only a small cravat pin, a gold watch that had stopped for ever, and a few unobtrusive studs. No rose ring.

She was closing it when the heart-lurching

sound of the opening door came from behind her. She dared not turn round — nothing would conceal such obvious guilt on her face — but she could bless the foresight that allowed her to say casually, 'Oh, Gregory, have you by any chance picked up the major's seal? I can't find it anywhere, and he'll murder me if I've lost it.'

'You think I'm a murderer, do you?'

She couldn't hold back a squawk of terror. There was no help for it but to stand up straight, turn round, and face him.

'Well, Kit Jackson,' he continued as she did so. 'If I were a suspicious man, I might have my doubts about you at this moment.'

'I've lost your seal, sir,' she said, allowing herself to hang her head in shame. 'I was trying to find it.'

'So instead of telling me, you come and search my room for it?'

'Yes, sir,' she mumbled.

'You're a bloody fool, man! I could well have thought you a thief or a spy, catching you like this.'

She knew what she had to do. She forced herself to look him straight in the eye and say, with some indignation, 'I'm not, sir.' Only half true: but she had been living with half-truths for long enough to enable her to say it convincingly.

'I'll believe you, Kit, if you'll believe that I'm no murderer.'

If only she had the composure to study his face as he said it! But her confusion and relief were too great. 'Thank you, Major. I'm glad you trust me.'

'I do, but fortunately I have evidence as well.' He reached in his pocket and produced the seal. 'Here. It must have slipped down the side of the sofa in the library; one of the housemaids found it and gave it to me as I came in.'

She took it from him, carefully avoiding touching his hand as she did so. I've got away with it, she thought.

'And take this too,' he added, smiling at her and reaching for a packet that was tucked under his arm. 'It's what I went out for.' It was *The Giaour*, with an austere inscription: 'To Kit Jackson, from Richard Lancaster.' He'd written no word of his warm or affectionate regards; he didn't need to.

In the privacy of her room, her face splashed with water to cool down, she looked at herself in the mirror, loathing what she saw, and thought, I haven't got away with it at all.

★ ★ ★

128

Hector Smythe called the next day when the major was out, and Kit felt guiltily relieved as she heard McTavish telling him that Mr Jackson was not at home. She mentioned the visit that evening.

'I doubt you'll be troubled again,' said the major. 'Smythe will not need telling more than once: he's an intelligent man.'

'He seems to be nobody's fool,' Kit agreed.

'Not in that direction, certainly. But in other ways, he's a damned idiot. He knows that he risks his neck, yet he persists in his behaviour.'

'Risks his neck? What for?'

'He is a much liked man, but it would take only one enemy to denounce him to the authorities. Sodomy is a capital crime.'

'Hanging? What, even when both men agree to it?' she said, too astounded to be embarrassed at her question.

'Oh, yes. Sodomy is one of over two hundred capital crimes, along with murder, treason, stealing goods worth more than ten shillings, and impersonating a Chelsea pensioner.'

'Why so many?'

'God knows. Our revered Lords and Members of Parliament appear convinced that only the hangman stands between us and anarchy.'

'I suppose hanging is all right for serious crimes, if someone was really guilty . . . ' she said uncertainly, repeating her father's opinions but knowing all too well that an innocent man could face the noose.

'Have you ever seen a hanging?'

'No, I haven't.'

'Then you must, before you say again that it is ever right. Tomorrow they are hanging a man for theft. We shall go.'

She would much rather not have, but there was no way out. She found herself the next day limping behind the major's broad shoulders as he forced a way through the press of shouting men and women round the scaffold at Newgate. The language around her was indescribable: filthy language and foul jokes, and curses at the work of pickpockets who were plying their craft at the place where they might finish their career. The noise of the crowd became even louder when the main attraction arrived. He was white and shaking, and the crowd started to jeer at him for putting on a poor performance as he stumbled to his place on the scaffold. There was no cessation of the jeers and curses, not even while the chaplain spoke to him, or while the hangman put the noose over his head. When the trap opened and the rope jerked tight as he fell, the jeers were replaced by applause, which turned to abuse of the hangman when it became apparent by the struggles of the body that the execution had been botched. It was half an hour before the man was pronounced dead and his body was cut down.

'Now, Kit, will you tell me that it is ever right to send someone to his death in such a way?' said the major as the crowd began to disperse.

Kit could not answer: she was concentrating on trying not to vomit.

The major seemed unaffected that evening; he was more silent than usual, but that could have been because his companion was unusually silent also. The vision of the man struggling on the end of the rope wouldn't leave her while she was awake, and when she went to sleep she dreamed of Harry and the major engaged in a ghastly dance with nooses round their necks.

Could she bear a part in hanging a man? Could she go through with it, when it came to the point? Could she put a rope round someone's neck? Even on the neck of her one last candidate for murderer, Sir Sydney Low, who appeared to be as dastardly as his friend George had been?

To take it off Harry's, yes.

The dark shadows from her sleepless night

must have been apparent to her employer. 'Perhaps I shouldn't have forced you to the hanging,' said the major. 'It wasn't the most edifying of sights, was it?'

'It was the crowd more than anything else,' she said. 'To behave so when a man dies; it makes me ashamed to have been part of it.'

'No crowds are so vile as the one around the gallows. What say we go to something that might restore your faith in humanity?'

So on the next possible occasion he took her to see a cricket match. There was a cheerful crowd, and though the language wasn't such as to be fit for ladies' ears, neither was it so vile as that of the mob round the gallows. Yet Kit was sure that many had been to both, and if they enjoyed the cricket match more than the hanging, it was only because the Gentlemen of Kent put up a good showing while the hangman had not.

Major Lancaster was greeted by many, from one-eyed soldiers to elegant dandies, all of whom appeared pleased and honoured by his regard. One hero-worshipping young subaltern on leave told Kit that she was the luckiest of fellows, and warned her that she had better serve the major faithfully, or the regiment would hear of it.

Over dinner that evening they discussed the match in the kind of detail that would be interesting only to someone else who had been there: or rather, the major did, while Kit, no connoisseur of the sport, confined herself to asking what she hoped were intelligent questions.

'I was accounted something of a bowler myself,' said the major, after the dishes had been removed and the brandy set out. 'We had some fine games in the Peninsula. He refilled his glass. 'And you? Before that — ' pointing to her supposedly wounded leg — 'were you a batsman or a bowler?'

'Neither,' she replied. 'I never played the game.'

'So, neither sodomy nor cricket; a boyhood singularly lacking in incident.'

'Fencing, though,' she asserted, piqued. 'I was taught to fence.'

'Of course. Had you not been I would be in my grave, so I am in no small debt to — your fencing master.'

'And to me, too!' she exclaimed indignantly.

He laughed. 'I was waiting for you to fall into that trap.' He rang the bell for a footman. 'D'you know, I've a mind to see you in action. After all, I was then in no position to judge your style, though of its effectiveness I have no doubt.' The footman arrived. 'Jeremiah, bring Mr Jackson's stick; it's by the front door.'

'You can't mean to fence in here!' Kit exclaimed.

'I can. We're well matched; we each have only three good limbs apiece.'

The footman arrived with the swordstick, handed it to Kit, and departed.

'Hold it out,' said the major, coming towards her armed with the poker that he'd picked up from the unlit fire. He stood shoulder to shoulder with her, measuring the reach of her right arm with the sword-stick, and his longer left arm with the poker. 'There, that's about equal. You will oblige me, and keep the blade in its sheath, I trust. *En garde*!'

'If I stabbed you through the heart it would serve you right for your ingratitude in laying that trap for me,' she retorted, taking her position. 'Be warned, I'm used to fighting with unusual weapons. I defended myself with a three-inch needle once.'

Damn, I shouldn't have said that, she thought, remembering that it was his brother against whom she had defended herself. To distract his attention she made a hurried and inadequate lunge at him.

The first few minutes would have been the despair of their fencing masters. Kit's lame foot stopped her attacking well, but the major's left hand was equally clumsy in defence. And both were far from sober.

He lunged, she parried successfully. The wooden sheath of the sword-stick began to suffer from the assaults of the poker, and Kit began to suffer from loss of dignity, for he soon came to grips with his unwieldy weapon, and he showed an ungentlemanly ability to kick furniture out of his way. More than once she parried unnecessarily, drawn by his feinting attack: there wasn't a question of who was the better fencer. But Kit defended stoutly and wouldn't admit defeat. She was being manoeuvred round the room, and she could do nothing about it. Time for action, she thought. Handling her stick like a sabre, she took a swipe at his head.

He ducked, and kept on with the movement downwards. With astonishing speed for such a big man, he knelt, dropped the poker, grabbed the rug onto which he'd forced her, and pulled. She flailed about wildly, but succeeded only in pulling over with her a table laden with bottles as she hit the ground.

'You cheated, you scoundrel!' she cried, indignation making her forget the respect due to her employer.

'No such thing. Good tactics I learned from Napoleon: get the enemy onto bad ground, then surprise him.'

'You — you — ' Words failed her, and she picked up one of the fallen bottles and hurled it at him.

It missed by a long way. 'As you said, Kit. Not a bad fencer, but no bowler.'

She threw another: this time she got a bowl of flowers, which splattered all over him.

So when the servants rushed in to investigate the crashes, they were treated to the sight of Mr Jackson on the floor in a mess of broken bottles, and Major Lancaster on his knees drenched in water and covered in tulips.

It was too much. On the face of each was an expression of dismay and guilt so ludicrous that the other took one glance and howled with laughter.

★   ★   ★

When Edward, Lord Bowland, drove his sister, Lady Julia Lancaster, out in his phaeton, all turned to look. The judgement as to whether the brother or the sister was the better looking depended entirely on the sex of the judge: the men swore that Lady Julia was a diamond of the first water, while the ladies thought that Bowland was without question the handsomest man in the peerage.

Even the few who looked neither at

handsome man nor pretty woman still turned to admire, for the phaeton with its immense wheels and immaculate yellow varnished wings was pulled by the finest greys in London: high spirited creatures whom only the touch of a master could control.

The park was at its most beautiful, and Julia enjoyed herself as her brother drove her out. She knew the effect she was making, in her grey velvet coat, cut in a military style with gold trimmings and epaulets, and her cap set at a rakish angle that belied its mourning hue. Though Kit Jackson was not in the park there were plenty of others to admire her. She had just smiled at Captain Porter of the Fifty-first (and stolen that young man's heart in a way that has nothing to do with this story), when her brother spoke. 'Julia, I've something to ask you.'

'Yes, Edward?'

'You may think this impertinent, but I need to know. What are your feelings towards Richard?'

Julia was taken aback. 'I — I like him,' she managed.

'Do you wish to marry him?'

'Why do you ask, Edward?'

'Can you trust me when I say I have reasons of my own?'

Julia was in a dilemma. Was Edward

thinking of ending the arrangement between her and Richard? If he did, would she be pleased or disappointed? She would tell her brother the truth, or at least some of it. 'Edward, I don't know. I like Richard; who could not? But I don't love him; or if I do it is in precisely the same way that I love you.'

'Do you wish to marry him?' he asked again.

'I wish I had a choice,' she acknowledged ruefully.

'Thank you, Julia, for speaking frankly. I know what I must do now.'

'Will you tell me?'

'No, Julia. There are some things it is better that you don't know.'

When Julia heard that tone from either her brother or her cousin, she knew from experience that argument was useless. It was infuriating. But she was determined to have a piece of the truth out of him in return. 'Edward, I think you must tell me something, since I've been honest with you. What are your feelings towards Lucy Maxwell?'

'Why do you ask?'

'She is my friend; we have known each other since we were girls. She loves you, and at one time I thought you loved her.'

'I still do, Julia,' Bowland acknowledged.

'Then why do you torment the poor girl?

Why do you pay so much attention to Lady Fenton?'

Her brother sighed, and repeated her own words. 'I wish I had a choice,' he said despairingly.

★ ★ ★

The night after their impromptu fencing match, Major Lancaster drank so much that he passed out and had to be carried to his room. Gregory stayed with him to put him to bed, but McTavish came downstairs with his face grim.

Kit was waiting for him, and grabbed his arm. 'Why does he do it, McTavish?' she asked urgently. 'I could understand it if it had been the other day after the hanging, but there was nothing to have upset him today.'

'I dinna ken,' McTavish sighed. 'I thought that you might. He talks to you, Mr Jackson, like he talks to no other. You've been doing him a power of good since you arrived here. Och, it did my heart good to see him yesterday. I've not seen him laugh that way since he came back from the Peninsula. It was worth the mess the pair of you made — though the housekeeper was not of that opinion.'

'But why does he drink so? What's it all for?'

'Did he say aught tonight?'

'It wasn't what he said, McTavish. It was what he did. We were just talking; nothing much, just about military strategy; and then he seemed to — well — his mind wasn't in the room any more. He was somewhere else, somewhere hellish, I could see it in his face. Have you seen him do that before?'

'Aye, I have often enough, but not since you came. He's not drunk so much while you've been here.'

'You mean he was drinking even more then?' Kit was amazed. 'His liver must be made of leather.'

'Och, even if it was, no man can keep drinking like that.'

'But why is he doing it?' she cried again. 'He has everything a man could want. Fortune, strength, a fine mind . . . '

McTavish shook his head sadly. 'A fine mind, ye say? I tell ye this, Mr Jackson. The things the major has on his mind — I dinna ken what they are, but I'd not wish them on my worst enemy.'

★   ★   ★

Lady Fenton drummed her elegant fingers on the dressing-table while her hair was brushed

140

into gleaming chestnut waves.

'You've got the fidgets this morning,' Desdemona scolded. 'Stop worrying. You'll get wrinkles.'

'I cannot help worrying,' Lady Fenton confessed. 'Katherine and Harry: what will become of them?'

'Your niece is doing very well, milady. I told you: my brother is courting Major Lancaster's cook and keeps his ears open in the kitchen — his mouth open too, I think, seeing as how she's a good cook. Everyone in the house thinks your niece is a fine young man; a bit of a boy, but one that they all like.'

'But what of Harry? All we have heard is that one letter from this Coomber woman, with a message about the red colt being injured. She doesn't have to write in code: nobody would dare to open my letters. But I wish I knew: I cannot help feeling that no news is bad news.'

'There you are, milady,' said Desdemona, finishing her mistress's hair. 'All nice for Lord Bowland.'

'Oh, blast Lord Bowland,' said milady inelegantly.

'I thought you liked him.'

'I accept his company purely in the interests of my niece and nephew,' said Lady Fenton in her grandest manner. Desdemona sniffed disbelievingly. The sound that came from her ladyship's throat would have been described as a giggle in a girl from the schoolroom. 'But I must admit,' she said, 'a handsome young earl is remarkably pleasant company.'

Her toilette finished, she went downstairs to sort out the day's business: she kept her household in very good order, and traders who thought that such a pretty head must contain a foolish brain were soon disillusioned.

The mail was brought in. Her wish was to be granted. There was a letter on top of the pile, in the sprawling handwriting of Rebecca Coomber.

★   ★   ★

Half an hour later, in a different street, Kit and the major finished reading the day's post, and Kit started writing at the major's direction. They heard the sound of a messenger arriving with another letter. Kit put down her pen and waited for the footman to bring it in.

She opened it as befitted a secretary, and glanced at its contents. What she read seemed to knock all the breath out of her, and she heard the major's voice as if from a great distance. 'Good God, what's the matter?'

'Nothing.' Somehow she managed to keep both the joy and the dismay out of her voice, for the letter read:

Rebecca Coomber wishes you to know that the red colt is recovering.

Sir Sydney Low was at the theatre and afterwards went with a whore.

7

'I know you fence, Kit, but do you drive as well?' the major asked one evening after dinner.

'A little.'

'Good. I'd be obliged if you'd take the ribbons on Monday. I've a journey to make, and this hand of mine stops me driving far. I don't want to take John; he's damned good with horses, but he talks too much. I've a suspicion that I may need someone who can keep a secret.'

Kit poured herself a glass of claret and asked, 'Where are we going?'

'You've done a fine job in sorting out my brother's affairs, but it's time I took a hand myself,' he said. 'I'm going to look at the place he was murdered; it's an inn called the Rose and Crown. Are you all right?'

Kit appeared to have choked on the claret, and was coughing violently.

* * *

'When I said I could drive a little, I was telling the truth,' said Kit as she found herself

144

in charge of Lancaster's curricle and pair. 'I wonder you trust me with these excellent horses.'

He settled himself beside her. 'I trust them with you, rather: they are good-tempered creatures.'

'If their tempers are as good as their looks, I've no need to worry,' she said, and then spoke no more. She needed all her concentration to get through the busy streets of London. Only when they left the suburbs could she relax. 'You were right,' she said. 'They are good-tempered beasts. I pointed them in the right direction and they did the rest. A lot different from my father's old cart-horse.'

'So you have a father?'

Her guard had slipped with the relief of reaching the open road. 'I do, Major Lancaster. But as you may have guessed, I am not his legitimate son,' she added truthfully. 'Please may we talk about your horses?'

Without a pause, Lancaster said, 'There are more high-spirited teams than my chestnuts about town, but none, I think, with such sense. One of the advantages of having been a soldier is that you don't need to prove yourself a hero every time you drive round the park.'

Kit laughed, and the miles passed easily in

good-humoured conversation. She put away from her mind the risk of discovery she would face at the Rose and Crown and let herself enjoy the moment.

But she couldn't forget that it was four weeks ago that day that she had been driving towards the inn from the opposite direction, coming from Eastham. The day that George Lancaster had come into her life, and gone out of his own.

She took a glance at George's brother beside her. Had he too driven this road four weeks ago? If he had, it was at least not in this carriage, nor riding his own horse: that information had been easy to glean from his talkative groom.

But horses and carriages could be hired. Had he arrived at the inn and shot his brother? From her knowledge of his character she would have said not, but who else could it have been? He carried an immense burden of guilt for something, and fratricide was a crime to weigh on anybody's conscience.

However, the charm of the day had its effects, and she found herself ignoring her worries and whistling cheerfully.

'You're very happy,' the major observed.

'Why should I not be? Here I am, bowling along a well-made road, with these prime cattle in my hands, and the sun is shining.'

146

'You don't mention one thing which may make for your happiness; it certainly makes for mine.'

'Yes, Major?'

'You have a friend beside you.'

She felt a lurch of her heart: did she really want to be his friend?

★　★　★

The nearer they got to the Rose and Crown, the more happiness was replaced by worry, and the more she wished the journey would take for ever. But it wasn't even long enough to require a change of horses, and they reached the inn by the middle of the afternoon.

The yard was crowded as they drove in; even such a splendid rig as theirs had to wait before being attended to. 'I'm glad I engaged a couple of rooms for us,' said Kit, hoping they would not be the ones she'd shared with Harry four weeks ago; she would rather not see Richard Lancaster in the place where she'd fought off George. 'I doubt if there'd be any for us otherwise.'

'If necessary, we could have gone to the Vicarage; it's a place my cousin Edward keeps for the duck shooting.'

'A vicarage for duck shooting?'

He laughed. 'Yes, it really is a vicarage; it's an old parish that's lost all its inhabitants about three miles from here. My grandfather bought it years ago for next to nothing. It's on the marshes, you see, which means that the air is very unhealthy, but the shooting is first-rate. It's kept up by a scoundrelly old vicar, who's not fit to look after his own soul, let alone anyone else's. All the same, it's best to stay here, where we can talk to people who know what happened.'

Despite the crowd, the landlord himself found time to bustle up to them. Kit recognized him; she hoped fervently he wouldn't recognize her with her hat pulled down so her face was in full shade.

She heard the landlord apologizing: 'I'm sorry, sir, there was no time to reply to your letter. We only have the one room free tonight, so I've put you both in that. I hope it's all right: it's the best room in the house.'

No, it's not all right, thought Kit in unutterable dismay, but the major thought quite the reverse. 'Excellent!' he said. 'That's if I'm right in thinking that you put a certain George Lancaster in there a month ago?'

The landlord nodded. 'I wondered about that, Major Lancaster, when I saw your name. May I offer my condolences?'

'I'd rather you offered me half an hour of

your time. I'm his brother and his executor, and I'm here to try to find out more about how he died.'

'Very well, sir, I'll make sure the room is ready for you, and I'll be with you shortly afterwards.' He bustled off, yelling for servants.

'Ah, well,' the major said as the horses were led away. 'Looks as though we'll have to bed down together.'

'We couldn't go to your cousin's place?' she said faintly.

'What, sleep in the marsh-land when we have the luck to be offered the very room where my brother died?' he asked incredulously. Then his voice softened. 'It's that leg, isn't it? You don't want anyone to see it.' She didn't deny it. 'You mustn't be so touchy. I've seen the terrible things that can happen to the human body. Whatever it is, I won't be shocked.'

You shouldn't put a wager on that, she thought as she followed him in.

Their room was made ready, and they entered. Lancaster could show his interest in the place his brother had died, but Kit had to keep secret the reason for her curiosity. The landlord soon joined them; Kit took a place in a shady corner, pulled her hat over her face and prepared to take notes.

'Tell me in your own words what you know of the death of my brother George. Don't mince matters; I've read the report of the inquest, and I know there was some sordid business with a woman, so don't feel you must conceal anything out of respect for the dead. My brother wasn't the best of men living, and I don't see why dying should make him appear any more virtuous.'

'Well, seeing that you've been so frank, sir, I didn't take to him much myself. Though in my trade I can't afford likes and dislikes. He was supposed to be in this room here, see, but somehow he walked into some other rooms taken by a brother and sister. Country folk they were, respectable enough. Henry and Katherine Faulkner, their names were. The brother was out and the sister was parading around in her petticoat, thinking she was private. Mr Lancaster comes in, sees the young lady in her undress, and takes his opportunity.'

'That sounds like George. The lady, I take it, was unwilling.'

'Yes, sir. Put up a fight, yelled for help, and stabbed him with a needle.'

I wish he hadn't said that, thought Kit, remembering her slip, but the major appeared not to notice the connection.

'She darn near scratched his eyes out,' the

150

landlord continued.

'A resourceful young lady, it seems.'

'Indeed so, sir. Well, her brother comes back and takes amiss at what he sees. Wallops the gentleman. When I come in, your brother is saying that the lady was willing all the time, and it was as well I was there, because Mr Faulkner would have killed him, else. Though as it turns out, it made no difference, as he killed him anyway.'

'Tell us more about that, landlord.'

'It was about two hours later. I heard a shot coming from this room, and I rushed in to see what was the matter. There was the lock bust open, your brother dead on the floor, and Mr Faulkner standing over him with the gun.'

'Did he say he'd done it?'

'No, sir: he said he'd seen someone else climbing out of the window as he'd come in.'

'And you didn't believe him?'

'Well, no, sir. Not really. Mind you, I don't blame him much for it, not after what happened to his sister.'

'So then what happened?'

'I had Mr Faulkner taken to the constable, and your brother taken to the coroner. They brought in a verdict of murder, but if you've read the report of the inquest you know that already, sir.'

'This Mr Faulkner escaped, it seems.'

'Right, sir. Not hair nor hide of him or his sister have we seen since. Constable Webb can tell you more about that. He's in the taproom now, if you'd like to see him.'

'Yes, I would. One or two more questions, though. I am concerned about these Faulkners. The young man had provocation; I'd hate to see him hang.'

'I agree with you, sir. Nice young fellow he was.'

'Perhaps he's in touch with people round here. Could you spread the word that I can have the sentence commuted to transportation? He may come forward if he knows that he has to face Botany Bay rather than the noose. What is it, Kit?'

'Nothing,' said Kit gruffly as she picked up her pen from the floor where she'd dropped it.

'As I was saying,' he continued, 'I am also concerned about the sister. Miss Faulkner is innocent, and it seems hard that she should share her brother's flight. I am acquainted with her aunt in town, and I shall tell Lady Fenton the same as I am telling you, so that the news may perhaps reach her. I'll do my utmost to help her, and I shall ensure that she isn't forced to reveal her brother's whereabouts.'

'I'll spread the word. She was a brave young lady.' The landlord stood up to go. 'Oh, here are your brother's bags, sir. I kept them, not knowing what to do with them.'

'Ah, thank you. And thank you for your valuable time.'

The landlord departed with a gold coin and a promise to fetch the constable.

'What do you think of that?' said the major when they were alone. 'Do you think the message will get to young Faulkner and his sister?'

'I think it might.'

'Miss Faulkner seems a resolute young woman, doesn't she? I'd like to meet her.'

'Perhaps you will, one day,' she said, resolutely answering him calmly.

'But she needs more than resolution in her present danger. I must help her. Oh, damn you, George!' he cried to the room as if he could be heard. 'One more bloody problem of yours that I'll have to sort out!' He turned to Kit. 'Or you will, rather, as you've sorted out so many of George's problems for me.'

'I'll do my best for Miss Faulkner and her brother, Major.'

'I know you will, Kit. What do you think of the landlord?'

'I think he's telling the truth as he sees it.'

'Why do you say that?'

'I wonder about Mr Faulkner's story of another man.'

'You think it's possible?'

Careful, Kit reminded herself. Don't appear too eager in Harry's defence. 'If Mr Faulkner is a nice young fellow, as the landlord says, would he not challenge your brother to a duel, rather than shoot him down like a coward?'

'To challenge someone to a duel requires more confidence in your aim with a pistol than in the justice of your cause.'

'Perhaps,' said Kit, unwilling to press the matter.

'Now let's look at George's effects,' said the major, struggling with the gold clasp of the bags. 'Oh, damn. It needs two hands. Open them for me, will you?'

She unclasped the lock and they rummaged through the dead man's belongings. Half a dozen cravats, shirts, and other necessaries of a night's stay to a man who was careful of his appearance. Nothing very interesting. Except . . . '

'What's this?' Kit held up a ball of dark cord.

'Why would George have this in his possession?' he asked in surprise. It was very strong, black, and about eight yards long when they stretched it out. The ends were slightly frayed, as if they had been tied round something, and there was another patch of fraying in the middle. 'What could you use this for?'

'Flying a very small kite, sewing a very large button, wrapping a parcel, stretching across a river, strangling someone — too many things to be much help,' she said.

There was a knock as Constable Webb arrived. Kit retreated hastily to her shady corner and began writing. She was glad he showed no ill effects from the weighted stocking with which she'd hit him, but she would have been very happy if in the past four weeks he had been promoted and sent to a distant part of the country.

The major settled the constable down and led him quickly through that part of the story which corresponded to the landlord's. 'Now, Constable, can you tell me what happened once Mr Faulkner was locked up with you? I understand it must be a matter of some embarrassment, having a prisoner escape, but I'm sure you've been forced by your superiors to tell the story. Please tell me too.'

'Well, sir, it was like this. He kept telling me that he didn't do it. Kept saying that while he was locked up the real murderer was getting away.' Kit saw a fleeting expression of embarrassment cross his face.

155

'Then his sister come in, the young lady that the fuss was all about. Crying her eyes out, she was. I couldn't help feeling sorry for the poor young lady; it wasn't her fault, none of it. So I let them talk it over, making sure she wasn't close enough to pass him anything, and I listened to what he said.'

'Now, what did he say?'

'As far as I remember, he said he'd been planning to challenge Mr Lancaster to a duel. He was outside this very room, and he heard voices. He didn't want to break into them, duelling being a delicate matter. Then he heard something.'

'What was it?'

'Now, sir, this is what we call hearsay evidence. This is me remembering what Mr Faulkner is remembering your brother saying. It wouldn't stand up in a court of law.'

'I take your point. But say what you remember.'

'I think it was like this. Mr Faulkner said your brother said something like, 'It's a hanging matter.' Then he says, 'It's not too late.' Then he says, 'You want to kill Bowland.' Something like that.'

'Bowland!' cried Lancaster in astonishment.

'The name mean something to you, sir?'

'He's my cousin. And my late brother's cousin also.'

'I find that very interesting, sir,' said the constable levelly.

'So do I,' said the major. He turned to Kit, attracting the constable's attention to her in a way that she could have done without. 'If this story is true, it may be as you suspected. The men who attacked me may have been after Bowland, and mistaken me for him.' He turned to the constable and briefly explained what had happened.

'And the young man was fortunately at hand to save you?'

'That's right.'

'Very interesting. You wouldn't mind both telling me where you were on the night Mr George Lancaster was murdered?'

Lancaster guffawed. 'I come down here to investigate a murder, and I find myself a suspect!'

'Not at all, sir,' said the constable, unmoved but persistent. 'In case you've forgotten, it was Monday the tenth of May.' Kit listened eagerly; that was the question she had wanted to put for weeks, but hadn't yet found a way.

'I'm afraid I can't tell you,' the major said casually. 'After all this time, I can't remember.'

'Not remember the day your brother died?' said the constable, an edge of polite incredulity in his voice.

'George and I were not on such terms as to make it important to me. But what about you, Kit? Tell the constable that you were here at the Rose and Crown and make him a happy man.'

The constable was not in a position to press a man like Major Lancaster, but an unimportant nobody like Kit Jackson couldn't afford such a bad memory. 'I hadn't arrived in London. I must have been in Aberdeen,' she said, nonchalantly naming a town as far off as she could think.

'Have you ever been in these parts before, young sir?' the constable asked.

'No,' she lied flatly.

'Because there's something mighty familiar about you, and I just can't bring it to mind.' Kit shrugged indifferently; she couldn't say a word. 'I'll perhaps remember it some day.'

'Constable,' said Lancaster firmly. 'We came here to listen to your story, not the other way round.'

'Very well, sir. Now, where was I?'

Kit's heart started beating again. She looked down at her notes. 'You were telling us what young Mr Faulkner was saying to his sister.'

'Now there it gets difficult to tell you, sir. I was listening to Mr Faulkner's story, and

158

— well, sir, you know how it is when you have a blow on the head? You sometimes can't recall the few minutes before it happened?'

Kit scrutinized the constable intently. Was he telling the truth? Or was he simply reluctant to admit that he'd been overpowered by a woman acting alone? Either way, it accounted for the fact that there'd been no search for her.

'You can't recall anything about the men who attacked you?'

'Well, sir, you know how it is. When I came round, Mr Faulkner and his sister were gone.' As one who had great experience in the past weeks in the art of uttering misleading truths, Kit recognized the ability in another. He hadn't said a word of a downright lie, but he remembered what had happened perfectly well.

'Hmm. Can you say anything more about these two? Give a description?'

'Young man, aged about twenty, red hair, medium height, square build, blue eyes. Speaks in a gentlemanly manner,' he reeled off with practised ease.

'And the young lady?'

'Well, now, let me think. Nobody's asked about her. She was a long lass, taller than me. Nowhere near as tall as you. Thin — regular beanpole Black hair. Brown eyes. Not what you'd call pretty, but not ugly, neither.'

Huh, Kit said to herself at this candid portrait.

'And you've searched everywhere for them?'

'Well, not me personal like. But the word's been sent out, and all the likely places have been checked. Bill Lawson, the constable over at Eastham, that's the young man's place, he's keeping an eye open, for what that's worth.' The constable's face showed clearly the contempt in which he held Bill Lawson, a view with which Kit entirely concurred. 'And the Runners have talked to their aunt. Some fine lady in London, I understand. Didn't get much out of her.'

'Constable, what do you think of Faulkner's story?'

'I don't believe it, and I don't disbelieve it.'

'Have you investigated it?'

'Some, sir. There was nobody here saw anything of this mysterious gentleman that Mr Faulkner claimed did the deed.' Kit's heart sank. 'But,' the constable continued impressively as he got out of his chair and went to the window, 'I did find something. You see that spinney yonder, sir? There was a horse tethered there that night.'

'How do you know?' Kit cried, unable to control herself.

'Because I got eyes, young sir, and I use 'em,' said the constable stiffly. 'I thought to meself, if I was this mysterious gentleman, I'd probably come on horseback. And where would I leave me horse if I was going to murder somebody? Over there. You want to come and see?'

Lancaster went off with Constable Webb while Kit pleaded her leg. The less time she spent with that sharp-eyed man the better.

She walked to the door of the room and looked around. This was where Harry must have stood when he burst in. He'd seen the body on the floor: where? A rug out of place caught her eye. She lifted it. Yes. Vigorous scrubbing hadn't removed all traces of blood that had soaked into the floorboards. She shivered. She walked over to the window. This was where he — whoever he was — had climbed out, his hand resting on the sill, the ruby ring on his finger.

Who was he? Was it Richard Lancaster?

It's time you thought coldly and clearly about him, she told herself. Forget the fact that he stands out like a lighthouse in whatever company he is. Forget the fact that you've come to like him — to like him far too much for comfort. There is a good chance that he's a murderer.

He could have done it. He had something

161

horrible on his conscience. He couldn't — or wouldn't — say where he'd been on the tenth of May. The offer of commuting Harry's sentence and helping his sister could have been a trick to bring the witness into the open.

But the major, in the weeks that she had lived with him, worked for him, drunk with him, watched him and listened to him, had done not one thing that revealed more knowledge than he should have had of the death of his brother. In fact, she reflected, I've made more slips than he has. He is either a first-class actor, or an innocent man.

She looked out of the window. Lancaster had taken leave of the constable and was returning. He caught sight of her, smiled and waved. Innocent, or very clever? she wondered as she waved back.

★   ★   ★

To Kit's immense relief a second bed arrived. It was only a truckle bed, small and uncomfortable-looking, but in her eyes it was more blessed than the many mattresses of the princess who slept on a pea. Sharing a bedroom she thought she could manage — but sharing a bed! Wild schemes of pretending to have smallpox or the plague had been racing through her mind.

She planned how she would retire for the night. She'd slip out discreetly, giving him time to get undressed. Then she'd come back, turn off the lamp, and get to bed in the dark. If he drank as much as he usually did he'd be in no condition to notice much. In the morning she'd keep her eyes shut and the blanket around her chin until he left the room.

The major ordered dinner in their room, and as they ate her mind went back to the last time she'd stopped at the Rose and Crown. If only George Lancaster had stayed in this room, instead of wandering into hers! She would have been safe in her aunt's house, with no more to worry her than the colour of a new ball gown.

Instead, here she was sharing a room and a bottle of brandy with a man who was immensely powerful, certainly shrewd and possibly a murderer. She'd have to keep her mind clear if she was to keep her secret under these conditions.

'I didn't know you come from Aberdeen,' said the major, smiling.

'Neither did I,' she smiled back cheekily.

'You'll have to ask McTavish about it. That's where he comes from. Strange view of morals, apparently: they have the highest number of bastards in the country. Must have something to do with the long nights and the cold weather.'

'You don't enquire where I really was?'

'No, because I know that you won't tell me.' He emptied his glass. 'So, here we are in this room where my brother died. Not afraid of spirits, are you?'

'No,' she said, reflecting that she'd love the chance to say a few choice words to George Lancaster's ghost.

He did not speak for a moment, then said, very quietly, 'I am.' He swirled a drop of brandy round his empty glass. 'I don't mean ghouls and goblins, but the spirits that eat into the mind. And not these spirits, either,' he said, picking up the bottle and pouring himself some more. 'They help to drown the other sort.' He studied her for a second. 'You don't know what I'm talking about, do you?'

'Do you want to tell me?' she asked gently.

'It's just that I have bad dreams,' he said with hardly a trace of emotion. 'The brandy helps me to sleep more easily.' He could have been talking about the weather.

'Mm?' she said. It was all that was necessary.

'When I was your age, I thought war was glorious. It isn't.' He stared into his glass. 'It isn't just the battle; you can get used to the sight of blood, though it's not pretty. It isn't even the fear of death. You never get used to that, by the bye; you just learn to control it. I can even live with the incompetence that lets thousands of men die of hunger and disease. It's the sheer damned evil of it all that weighs on my conscience.'

'Evil? To fight Napoleon?'

'It's the way we do it. I don't know if you read about it, when we captured Badajoz?'

'Yes. And I read of the courage of our men: how they stormed the walls, through the grapeshot and cannon. Are you going to tell me that it wasn't true?'

'Oh, no. It was perfectly true. The men were brave enough; they went on, though they had to climb over the bodies of the men who'd gone before. It was what happened afterwards. The city was looted.'

'I read that, too.'

'You read it. Everyone read it. Did you think what it meant? It wasn't just food and gold that the soldiers wanted. They wanted women too. There's a picture in my mind that won't go away. Three of our brave soldiers — and they had been brave just an hour before, very brave — with one poor woman, her husband lying dead beside her. They killed her baby, too: it was crying so they smashed its brains out.'

'But that wasn't you,' she whispered.

'No, but I watched it happen and I didn't stop it. Orders, you see. Wellington gave the town over to our men for three days. It's the cheapest way of paying them.' His lip curled. 'It encourages their bravery, if they can do what they want with the town once they get into it.'

'But surely all the soldiers aren't like that?'

'What d'you expect? Perhaps some of them had ideals of glory like me, once, but they don't last long. Our soldiers are badly paid when they're paid at all; if they are wounded they're left to beg in the streets; they are trained for nothing but killing. You expect well-behaved gentlemen to come from this?' he sneered. 'In any case, the finest gentleman in the army is made of the same stuff as the meanest soldier — blood, bones, bowels.' He finished his glass. 'So now when they call me a hero, you can understand why I get a touch cynical about it.'

'But you are a hero,' she urged.

'Oh, yes, that,' he said indifferently. 'I didn't run away when someone was shooting at me. That's all there is to being a hero. Not much, is it?' He refilled his glass again.

'I understand why you get nightmares,' she said softly.

'No, you don't,' he snapped. 'You understand damn all about why I get nightmares.'

'Will you tell me?'

'I don't know why it should be that which gave me nightmares — in God's truth I saw things far, far more nightmarish than that. But somehow — No, I'll not burden you with it.'

'You will not share your burden with a friend?'

He sighed deeply, put his head in his hands, and spoke without looking at her. 'It was that hellish retreat from Salamanca. There was a man, an ordinary soldier — I never knew his name. I could see he was wounded and couldn't keep up with us, so I let him ride behind me: it must have been the first day or so, because we had to eat the horse before we reached journey's end. I told the man to hold on tight, and we rode all day, his arms wrapped around me.' His voice became choked. 'When we came to a halt for the night, he was dead.'

She reached out to touch his shoulder, and she could feel him trembling.

'He must have been dead for some hours, and his arms had stiffened. They had to break the bones to get him off me.'

'No!' she breathed, appalled.

'In all my dreams he's there, clutching me, stifling me. Every night he comes to me: I can only keep him away if I drink myself unconscious.'

She could say nothing; she kept her hand on his shoulder, as if the compassion she felt would flow into him. They stayed unmoving for perhaps a minute. 'You must think I'm a weakling to be overcome by such as that.'

'No, I don't think you're a weakling.'

He lifted his head and looked at her; he was no longer shaking. She made to take her hand away from his shoulder, but he stopped her, gripping her wrist with his good hand. 'What is it about you? Why can I tell you all this?'

'I must be a good listener,' she managed to say.

'I owe you a great debt. Not that you saved my life: it may seem ungrateful, but a soldier gets used to that. But you've done something for me which no one else could. You've sat by me and comforted me. You reached out your hand to me when I needed it.' His eyes held hers as strongly as his hand gripped her wrist. Neither spoke. Then he smiled and let her go. 'I think you may have rid me of my nightmares,' he said, standing up.

Kit sat immobile. She tried to control the conflicting emotions that rose in her: anger at what a soldier had to endure, pity at his pain, tenderness that he found it possible to share that pain with her, and horror at the story he'd told her; she knew now what he meant when he'd said that death rode behind him.

For a second there was also joy: she had learned the name of his devil, and it wasn't fratricide. He wasn't carrying the weight of a brother's murder.

But a nasty little voice within told her that the fact that he wasn't feeling guilty at his brother's death didn't mean that he was innocent of it. He'd told her himself how he killed a man in a duel without the slightest remorse.

She felt remorse, though: bitter remorse at what she was doing. He trusted her, so much that he could tell her the horror he had kept enclosed for so long, and reveal to her what he thought was his own weakness. But she was nothing but a spy; if he told her anything she could use, she would betray him.

There was another feeling, one she dared not put a name to. It was as if he still held her wrist; the skin felt warm where he'd touched her.

He stood beside her. 'You're troubled. Perhaps I shouldn't have told you.'

She shook her head. 'I'm glad you did.'

'So am I.' He smiled at her, then ruffled her hair in a brotherly fashion. 'Come, Kit, time for bed. And for once I'm tolerably sober.'

This was the moment when she had

planned to slip out discreetly. She stood up and headed for the door.

'Oh, Kit,' he said, stopping her in her tracks. 'Lend me a hand to get my clothes off.'

She stared hopelessly at the door. 'But — '

'Well, I can't do it on my own, not with only one hand, and Gregory isn't here to help me,' he said reasonably, pulling his neckcloth off one-handed.

She was trapped. Wordlessly she went over to him, and helped him out of his coat, so finely cut that it fitted his muscular body too well to be taken off without assistance. She took it and hung it up.

Then the waistcoat. Then the shirt.

She couldn't stop staring at his chest. She had never seen a man like this before. The curls of black hair and the firm muscles under the skin almost made her reach out and touch him.

'Help me with my boots, will you?' he said, unaware of her fascination, as he sat down and put his feet out.

She knelt in front of him, not daring to look up. She could feel the muscles of his legs; the masculine smell of his body mixed with the leather of his boots as she pulled them off. She stood up, hiding her blushing face as much as she could, and put the boots outside the door for the bootboy.

'Now, the trousers — ' he said.

Oh, no!

'- I can manage by myself,' he continued.

She sank down on a chair in relief. But he misunderstood her reason for sitting down. 'Your boots, now,' he said affably, coming over to help her while he was half undressed.

She shot up again. 'No!'

'What is it?' he asked gently. She backed away; he moved closer. Soon she could move no further; she was against the wall.

'It's that damned mystery of yours, isn't it?' She said nothing. He reached out to her. 'Tell me.'

He was almost touching her. Her eyes dropped and she looked down at his body, virile and strong.

'Kit, don't you think it's time to give up this absurd secrecy?' he said, both command and affection in his voice. 'What's so horrible that you can't tell me?'

She couldn't speak. He gripped her shoulder, and with his other hand, the injured one, he touched her chin and made her look up. 'I bared my soul to you this evening because I trust you,' he said. 'Don't you trust me?'

Their eyes were locked together; his mouth was inches away from hers. Feelings she'd tried desperately to conceal from herself at last escaped and overwhelmed her. She wanted his arms around her, his body against hers, his mouth on her lips.

She was a woman, and she loved this man.

She understood what it would mean. He would know what she was, and he would kiss her, and then he would take her to his bed and make love to her. She wanted him to strip her clothes off, and with them the deceit she'd been living.

Her lips parted; her hands began to reach up to his head to pull him to her. But from somewhere came a last flutter of resolution. 'No!' came a voice she knew as her own.

It was as if she'd struck him. For a second she could see disgust and contempt written on his face, and then he almost threw her away from him.

What had she done? He'd asked her if she trusted him and she'd said no. 'Major Lancaster,' she pleaded. 'I didn't mean . . . '

He turned his back on her and he would not look at her. He was as stiff as a rod, and his voice was hard as he said, 'Have no fear, Mr Jackson. I shall leave you in peace.'

He stripped off no further, but climbed into his bed, where he lay rigidly with his back to her, facing the wall. She put out the lamp, then took off only her boots and outer clothes before she too got into her own bed.

All night she lay, barely moving, fully awake, fully aware of him, with the blankets around her ears so she couldn't hear him, and her face in the pillow so he couldn't hear her, whimpering in misery at her success in keeping her secret.

8

The return journey was hellish. Kit drove; Lancaster sat beside her. They exchanged hardly a word beyond the barest directions. The major's silence seemed to echo around the country, louder than anything he could have said to her. She felt his reproach: he had bared his soul to her, he had taken her into his confidence in a way that he had shared with no other — and she had held back. She gave nothing, he gave everything, his silence seemed to say.

She too said nothing. Not from any desire to hurt or reproach: that was the last thing she wanted to do. Her silence stemmed merely from the lack of anything safe to say. Even a simple comment about the weather carried an unspoken comparison with the pleasant companionship of yesterday's journey in the opposite direction.

He had offered her his friendship, and she had rejected him. She would never forget that look of revulsion in his eyes as he had turned away from her last night. The irony ate into her heart: she had repelled him at the moment that she realized that she loved him.

She didn't know whether he was as relieved as she when they finally reached London and drew up outside his house. But before the servants came to attend to their master and his horses, she knew she had to say something to him. 'Do you wish me to resign my position, Major Lancaster?' she croaked, not able to look him in the face.

'Do you wish to resign it, Mr Jackson?' she heard him say, in a tone of voice she couldn't understand.

She forced herself to look at him. She couldn't read his face: there was nothing but a mask looking back at her. It would be dreadful to stay with him, but it would be dreadful to leave him too. And for Harry's sake she had to remain where she was. 'No. I do not wish to resign.'

'Then stay, Mr Jackson,' he said, jumping down from the curricle. 'There is, after all, something to be said for the ability to keep a secret — in a secretary.'

★ ★ ★

'So you see, Edward, you may be in danger. Somebody wants to kill you.'

'On the contrary, Richard, you exaggerate. You've heard from a village constable what an accused man told his sister that he heard.'

The three of them, Kit, Lancaster and Bowland, were seated beside the earl's hearth the day after the return from the Rose and Crown. Kit was carrying the notes she'd made of the conversations with the landlord and the constable.

'Someone may have tried already,' Lancaster urged. 'Mr Jackson always did think the attack on me might have been meant for you.'

'So what do we have, Richard? A story that has come by a roundabout journey, and a possible assault by footpads. What is it that disappearing young man is supposed to have heard? Nothing more than your brother getting alarmed — and that was hardly unusual for George.'

'I don't know, Edward.' Lancaster turned to Kit. 'Read out what George was heard to say, Mr Jackson.'

She looked at her notes. She knew the precise words that Harry had overheard, but the constable hadn't got them exactly, right. She had to relay the constable's incorrect version. ''It's a hanging matter', then, 'It's not too late', and finally, 'You want to kill Bowland',' she recited dutifully.

'Who wants to kill you?' Lancaster asked.

'I can think of half a dozen,' said Bowland airily.

'I take objection to you being killed even if you don't. I'll inherit your title if someone does away with you before you produce a son, and I can think of nothing I'd like less than to sit in the House of Lords. Who are these half-dozen potential murderers?'

'My creditors, hoping to be paid out of my estate. On second thoughts, make that two dozen. Charles Maxwell would like to see my blood, too.'

'Charlie? Why? I thought to see him your brother-in-law.'

'Do you really wish to discuss my private affairs?' said Bowland, looking very pointedly at Kit.

She was annoyed. The conversation was getting most interesting. But recognizing the inevitable she mumbled a transparent excuse and left the room.

She was standing outside the door vainly struggling to catch a word when Lady Julia appeared, having left her unsuspecting chaperon upstairs. 'Mr Jackson!' she cried prettily. 'What brings you here?'

'Business with your cousin and your brother, which has turned private.'

'And they've thrown you out. How discourteous! Come with me and let me entertain you.' Since Kit was wasting her time eavesdropping behind a thick oak door, she accepted Julia's invitation with good grace.

Her hostess was in fine form: had Kit been any sort of a man she would have been captivated. Lady Julia listened to the story from the Rose and Crown with attention, she expressed her heartfelt gratitude for the warning, and she promised faithfully to be attentive to danger.

She was naturally affectionate in referring to her brother, and equally — but no more — affectionate in her attitude to her cousin Richard. Kit also seemed to be coming in for a share of concern. 'It was good of you to let me into the secret. Most men think that women are liable to be overcome with a fit of the vapours at the mention of danger.'

'A woman's heart can be just as strong as a man's.'

She leaned forward. 'Do you mean that, Mr Jackson?'

'I am sure of it. And they usually have more common sense. I think your brother's life would be safer in your hands than his own.'

'You talk of women's common sense, Mr Jackson. I'm not convinced of it.'

'Why not?'

'Women are too often guided by the heart rather than the head. I see it time and time again. A woman, blessed by fortune, marries not the highly eligible gentleman that wisdom would have chosen for her, but some unsuitable man, perhaps poor, unconnected. Is that common sense?'

'It is certainly not common sense to marry someone whom you do not love,' said Kit stoutly. 'That is sheer folly, no matter how eligible he is.'

'You think that love is more important than anything else?'

Kit thought the conversation was getting too close to home. 'In marriage, certainly,' she said lightly. 'In cricket I don't think it matters overmuch.'

Julia wasn't to be diverted. 'Please be serious, Mr Jackson. I am talking of something that concerns me deeply.'

'I know, Lady Julia.'

Julia looked closely at her. 'You do know, don't you?'

'What do you mean?'

'I mean that something has changed in you since we last talked. You seemed so cool and dispassionate then: but now there is some emotion, some fire in your eyes that wasn't there before.'

Kit looked at her feet. 'I beg you, please don't say any more.'

'You have found what love is.'

Kit couldn't take it. Not those searching eyes, not that heart-wrenching talk. She jumped up hastily, limped to the window and stared out into the street. Behind her Julia said, 'And you think there is no hope.'

'None.'

'Are you sure of that?'

'Yes.' Kit was conscious that Julia had risen and was standing close behind.

'Perhaps you think that the one you love is too high above you?'

'That is true — but if that were the only thing I shouldn't care.' Kit turned round. Julia's face was very close, and Julia's grey eyes searched Kit's face. 'There is something else, something that I cannot overcome.'

Julia stepped back dismayed. 'You are too young to be married already!'

'I am not married, nor is my honour engaged.'

'Then tell me what it is!' cried Julia.

The door opened. Richard Lancaster stood and surveyed the scene with great interest. 'Ah, Julia,' he said suavely. 'I gather that you too have been bitten by the desire to know Mr Jackson's secret. Mysterious young man, isn't he?'

Julia rallied. 'I wager that I shall find out before you do, Richard.'

'Done. The pick of my stables against your mare Bess.'

'Do I have no say in this?' asked Kit.

'Not the slightest,' replied Julia lightly. 'Unless you care to tell us both now and spoil a good wager. My cousin has excellent taste in horseflesh, and my choice from his stables is a prize worth winning.'

'That reminds me,' he said. 'Mr Jackson, will you drive my carriage home? I'll drive Bowland's phaeton and greys, which I find myself owning now.'

'What! Edward's greys! He can't mean to sell them!' exclaimed Julia.

'I am sorry to contradict you, cousin Julia; he not only means to sell them, but he actually has sold them.'

Julia looked up at him. 'You mean you have given him a lot of money, and have accepted the greys to salve Edward's dislike of being in debt.'

'On the contrary,' he said in a voice that deceived nobody, 'I've been guilty of covetousness for some time, and Edward has agreed to give me the supreme pleasure of driving the fastest team in the country.'

'Oh, but you can't, Richard, not with one hand.'

'I shall certainly attempt to.'

'But you mustn't. I don't want any harm to come to you.' She glanced at Kit, then deliberately turned away and smiled coquettishly at her cousin. 'You know how much I care for you,' she said in a voice full of affection.

The major was taken aback only for a moment. 'And I care for you, Julia,' he said tenderly.

Kit coughed. 'I'll take your carriage back now, Major. I've work to do.'

'No, stay,' Julia entreated.

'You hear Lady Julia, Mr Jackson?' Lancaster commanded. 'You will not displease her. You will stay.' He smiled at his cousin. 'I'd not have anything displease you, Julia.'

I can't bear it, Kit wanted to cry out. But she couldn't say anything of the sort. She took her place by the window. She was forced to listen to them, but at least she didn't have to watch as Julia and Lancaster exchanged their tender words. For this wasn't the cousinly banter she had heard before. This was getting close to a declaration of love on both sides.

She stared out of the window. Over the road was the alley in which she had waited and watched this house, what seemed like years ago, but was in fact less than a month. What if I hadn't been there? she thought. I wouldn't be here now having my heart torn out, unable to utter a word. Because Richard Lancaster wouldn't have been here either, she reflected. He would have been dead.

Why are they doing this to me? she wondered in anguish. Why are they forcing me to be an audience to their love-making? What are they trying to prove to me? To each other? To themselves?

'The phaeton is ready, Major Lancaster.' It was Slater, Bowland's butler, never before seen as an angel of mercy.

'Thank you, Slater,' said Lancaster, releasing Julia's hand with reluctance.

They all went round to the stables and saw Bowland giving a last carrot to his greys. 'I've been saying farewell to them. I hate to part with them, Richard,' he said. 'But needs must when the devil drives.'

'I'll look after them, don't worry, Edward. And of course if you ever want to borrow them . . . '

'You are the soul of generosity, cousin,' said Bowland formally.

'Now, let's have a look.' Lancaster started to walk round the phaeton. It was in fine condition, sparkling clean, its immense springs gleaming.

'What the devil are you doing?' asked Bowland as Lancaster squatted down.

'Looking, Edward, looking.'

'You won't find anything wrong with it,' Bowland exclaimed irritably.

'I'm sure I won't. But — ' he said, kicking a wheel ' — I once knew many fine young men in the Peninsula who were so sure there was nothing wrong with their equipment that they didn't check it.' He grabbed one of the springs, trying to bend it. 'I don't know 'em now, because they're all dead.'

'You take caution too far!'

The major ignored him, as he bent down and looked carefully at one of the axles. He took a previously spotless handkerchief and rubbed at a patch of grease. He stood up, frowning. 'Edward, come and have a look at this,' he said quietly.

'What is it?' Bowland peered where his cousin pointed.

'See that axle? It's about to break.'

'No!'

'Oh, yes. And it's about to break because it has been sawn through.'

Bowland poked at it. 'Yes! You're right! And smeared with grease to disguise the cut!'

'Now do you accuse me of over-caution, Edward? The first time you'd taken a fast turn, that phaeton would have crashed down around you. Now will you believe that someone is trying to kill you?'

'Or you, Major,' said Kit, shuddering.

'And with your hand, you'd have even less chance of escape!' cried Julia.

'No, not me,' Lancaster said. 'It's been less than an hour since I said I'd buy it. Nobody's had a chance to get to work on this since then, have they, Edward?'

'No,' said Bowland. 'I or the groom have been here the whole time. I suppose you'll take back your offer to buy?' he added almost hopefully.

'Do you want me to?' asked Lancaster.

'Damn it, take them!' he snapped. 'And the other things you've been so generous as to give me twice the value of.'

'Edward!' protested Julia. 'If Richard has helped you, don't be ungracious.'

Bowland smiled and put out a hand. 'I'm sorry. It's just that I hate this retrenching, and I hate being in anyone's debt.'

Lancaster unwisely put his injured hand out, and grimaced as his cousin shook it over-heartily.

'And to show there are no hard feelings, let us share the honour at the play on Friday,' said Bowland. 'Julia, my box at the theatre has had to go. You will have to cajole Richard if you want anyone to take you.'

'Julia knows that I am hers to command; she has no need to cajole,' said Lancaster gallantly, as he escorted her indoors.

Bowland, left alone with Kit, looked down at her with an unreadable expression on his handsome face. 'Ah, yes, the major's minion.'

She tried to remember what a minion was: she didn't think it was meant as a compliment.

'This time, Mr Jackson, your care was unnecessary,' he continued. 'My cousin saved his own life.'

'And I am thankful for it, as we all must be.'

'Quite so. Would you care to join our party at the theatre?'

'What's on?' she asked, taken aback that Lord Bowland should invite her.

'Now there, Mr Jackson, you betray your country origins. In town, one does not go to see a play, but to be seen.'

★ ★ ★

There was a letter waiting for her when she arrived at the major's house, one which had been redirected to her from Lady Fenton's. In an instant she recognized the handwriting: Harry's!

Dear Kitty

How's the investigation? Sorry I didn't write before. I was shot in the back, and it took a while to recover. I'm staying at Becky's. I wouldn't be alive if it weren't for her. But I am alive, and getting better. Write to me and tell me what's happened. It's frustrating to be here and not know what's going on.

I don't like you doing this, Kitty. Are you in any danger yourself? Promise that you will tell me. If there is anything I can do, just write — I've blackened my hair and I'll come straight away.

I've been lying here not able to do anything much except think, and I've been thinking about you. I feel a poor sort of man, relying on my sister to get me out of trouble. But if ever there was a sister a man could rely on, it's you. I don't often say anything sentimental — perhaps it's easier to write it. God bless you, Kitty.

Your very loving brother,
Harry

Harry's letter came when Kit most needed it. The news that he was well was the only thing that could have brought her any happiness that day. The knowledge that her brother loved her came at a time when she most needed affection; his praise of her and trust in her helped overcome the feelings of doubt and worthlessness that beset her.

She sat in her own room, writing a long letter back to him. She would send it through

Lady Fenton, who would undoubtedly read it, so she tried to keep the tone cheerful. Kit would have told Harry of her love for the chief suspect, but she wouldn't tell her aunt.

Writing the letter helped her sort out her own thoughts. She was getting close to the murderer: it must be someone who had access to Bowland's stables. It could be Richard Lancaster: who else but the man who did it could have found the damage to the phaeton so easily?

Harry would come if she asked him, but she thought it a needless risk, blackened hair or no. She was totally accepted as Kit Jackson, an unimportant nobody, the major's minion.

Word of a Faulkner, I do not see myself in any greater danger now than I have been since I started this masquerade.

She hoped that would satisfy him. She sealed the letter and addressed it to Lady Fenton. She went downstairs to the library, slipping her letter into the pile that she'd written on the major's behalf.

There was a solution readily available to one of her problems at least. She took Dr Johnson's Dictionary from the shelf, and read:

Minion. A favourite; a darling; a low dependant; one who pleases rather than benefits. A word of contempt, or of slight and familiar kindness.

When Major Lancaster came into the library, Kit appeared to be busy writing. He didn't say anything beyond a stiff greeting as he entered; he walked to one of the shelves, took a book and sat down to read it.

It was impossible for her to ignore his presence, but sorting her thoughts out to write to Harry enabled her to maintain a tolerable composure. She continued to work through his business, the large figures on the bills for Julia's clothes and jewels dancing madly round the smaller ones for the major's own. Writing wasn't easy, but she wanted a task that would keep her eyes occupied, for otherwise they would go over to him.

But when she had finished, she couldn't help it. She glanced at him, only to find that he was studying her.

'Yes, Major?' she asked, thankful that she could appear so calm. 'Is there anything you want?'

'I want many things, Mr Jackson,' he replied. 'But it's not possible to have them all, is it?'

She took a knife and began to mend her

quill pen. 'I meant: is there anything you wish me to do for you?'

'Yes, but it would probably be as well if you didn't.'

'I'm sorry, I don't understand you.'

'Don't you?' He was observing her intently.

'Not at all.'

'If that's true, Kit, you're a lucky man.'

He stood up, and for a moment it seemed as if he was reaching out to her, but it was nothing. 'I'm going out,' he said. 'I'll be dining with my cousins tonight, and then I'll escort Julia to Almack's.'

She found the strength to force her lips into a smile. 'I hope you have a pleasant evening.'

'Well done, Mr Jackson. That sounded almost as if you meant it.' As he went out of the door he added, 'I think that pen is sharp enough, now.'

Without noticing what she was doing, she had whittled the quill into nothing but shavings.

★   ★   ★

Kit had never been to a proper theatre. The height of her theatrical experience had been the troupe that performed the Christmas play in the village hall. But she'd read a lot;

190

Shakespeare, Gay, all of them. Not having anyone to disapprove her choice she had devoured them all, including the ones that ought to have brought a blush to a maiden's cheek. She knew whole passages of Shakespeare off by heart; she'd agonized with Hamlet, hated Iago and laughed at Falstaff.

So that Friday she hoped to bear the evening at the theatre with reasonable fortitude. She wouldn't have to watch Julia and Lancaster; she could watch the play instead.

The major was his usual polite self, and ordered the carriage for the sake of Kit's foot, though he said it was for himself. She couldn't reproach him as an employer. He was unfailingly civil to her, and she hated it. He wasn't avoiding her — he could have done that by terminating her employment — but he certainly was far from seeking her company as he had before. Apart from that odd episode in the library, his conversation was stiff when they were alone together, as if it were an effort to talk. Ah well, Kit thought as she sat beside him in chilly silence; at least he's not drinking himself to sleep any more. He prefers Julia to the brandy, which is no doubt good for his liver.

At the theatre she followed him into their box, where they found that Bowland had already brought Julia and Lucy Maxwell. He left as soon as there was male company for the ladies, saying he would bring the final member of the party, but not disclosing who this was.

Julia was as lovely as ever, but Lucy was radiant. Hope, springing from Bowland's invitation, had made joy shine out of her. Kit preferred her conversation to listening to Julia's exchanges with the major, and they chatted throughout the entertainment that preceded the evening's main offering.

Kit was well aware that Lucy's thoughts weren't with her but with Lord Bowland. Every time someone came to their box Kit, whose back was to the door, could see Lucy's eyes opening in expectation, only to fade as the newcomer proved to be just another visitor exchanging civilities.

But Lucy could be polite, and appeared to forgive everyone for not being Bowland. Indeed, she seemed quite pleased when one rap on the door of their box was followed by the entrance of Hector Smythe.

Kit rapidly moved as far away from the newcomer as she could, which wasn't very far; she ended up almost on the major's lap. 'You're safe here.' Lancaster was so close to her that he had no need to lean forward to whisper quietly in her ear. She looked up at him gratefully.

As it happened her alarm was unnecessary. Other than glancing at her occasionally, Smythe paid Kit little attention, concentrating instead on the ladies and conversing with considerable wit and charm.

Lucy and Julia joined in with his banter. Kit studied them in wonder. They appeared to like him. Did they know what sort of man he was? She exchanged glances with the major, who gave a slight shrug as if to say that he didn't understand women either.

'No, Lady Julia,' Smythe reproved. 'Topazes, with silver-grey satin?'

'I like them,' said Julia, not offended by his criticism. 'They are a gift from my cousin Richard.'

'His taste is far too good to approve of your wearing his gift with that dress,' Smythe retorted.

'Not at all. Whatever Julia wears is always delightful,' Lancaster replied promptly.

Kit gritted her teeth and said nothing.

Shortly after, Smythe took his leave, distinguishing Kit with no more than a smile and a gaze that lingered a fraction too long. But the others must have noticed it, for Julia said, 'You have an admirer, Mr Jackson.'

'Julia!' thundered the major in awesome tones.

'Sorry, Richard. Sorry, Mr Jackson,' said Julia in seeming penitence, spoiled when she exchanged glances with Lucy and the two girls started to giggle.

'Julia,' Lancaster said icily, white-faced with anger. 'Do you consider bad manners amusing?'

Abashed, Julia said, 'It was very rude of me, Mr Jackson. I offer my most sincere apologies.'

'They are unnecessary, Lady Julia. I wasn't offended,' Kit replied. With what she felt to be considerable heroism, she said to Lancaster, 'Indeed, I hate to be the cause of a quarrel between you and your cousin.'

'Mr Jackson pleads your cause well, cousin,' he said. 'But he doesn't need to.' His voice became gallant. 'Your lovely face is your own best advocate, Julia.'

I believe I'm going to be sick, Kit thought. She was aware that she was a poor companion to Lucy as Julia and Lancaster talked to each other, but it didn't matter, since Lucy was preoccupied waiting for Bowland's return.

At length Lucy's wait was over; her face lit up, and Kit, with her back to the door, could deduce that Bowland had entered. She was just about to swivel round when she saw Lucy's face change: the light went out like a snuffed candle, and the smile changed to a gasp of dismay.

I know who's walked in, thought Kit, and turned to greet the person that Bowland was ushering into their box.

'It's Mr Jackson, isn't it?' said the lady vaguely.

'Yes, Lady Fenton,' said Kit with a sigh. It was kind of her aunt to help in her investigations, but did she have to be so energetic about it?

As Lord Bowland had said, it did seem more important to be seen than to see. Below, a raucous crowd cheered and flirted, drank and ate: the smells of oranges and beer mixed with those of unwashed bodies and prostitutes' perfume. On their own level, in other boxes, ladies and gentlemen waved to each other across the theatre.

Kit was talking to Lucy, since nobody else paid much attention to either of them. Her heart bled for the girl. Bowland was by no means rude to Lucy, but he was making it plain that Lady Fenton was his partner for the evening. Lucy's beauty wilted in the frost.

Both Julia and Lancaster tried, awkwardly, to be kind to her. The major ensured her chair was comfortable; Julia regaled her with the latest gossip. 'You've heard about Lady Gascoyne's remarkable baby,' she was saying. 'Born ten months after her husband left for Spain.'

Lucy didn't even smile.

Kit joined in the attempt. 'I think Miss Maxwell has too good a heart to think badly of anyone,' she said.

Lucy's lips twitched. Relieved by Kit's small success, Julia and Lancaster thankfully returned to their determined flirtation. Bowland and Lady Fenton ignored all of them.

The music struck up; the play was about to begin. There was a slight lessening of noise, enough to hear the opening line: *If music be the food of love, play on.*

Kit recognized the words with horror, and felt a strong urge to run out of the door. The play was *Twelfth Night*. Oh, why had she not persisted in her questioning and found out what was being performed tonight? She knew the story well, and of all plays, this was the last in the world that she wanted to see or be seen at. She looked at her aunt in despair, but found that there was no help from that quarter.

Lady Fenton had never been a bluestocking and so she was unaware of the story of the play. She didn't take much notice at first, paying more attention to the people in the box with her.

She was pleased that Bowland was so assiduous in his attentions. She understood his motives perfectly: he wanted her fortune. But it was certainly no discomfort to be courted by a good-looking earl. She felt a mixture of remorse and pride at cutting out such a lovely young lady as Lucy Maxwell.

Lady Fenton paid little attention to Major Lancaster and Lady Julia, beyond noting that their compliments to each other were about as sincere as the words uttered on stage. But what was wrong with Katherine? Lady Fenton wondered. The girl — the young man, she corrected herself — was staring at the stage as if it were covered with poisonous snakes. Lady Fenton followed her niece's gaze, just in time to hear the actress on stage declare that, since her brother was lost, she must protect herself by dressing up as a boy.

Oh, no! Lady Fenton thought in dismay. What a dreadful choice of play! And for the first time in her life she watched a Shakespeare performance with undivided attention.

★　★　★

'Preposterous stuff,' said Julia when the play was finished and they left, not staying for the farce which was to be staged at the end. 'They must have all been blind not to see that Viola was a girl in boy's clothes.'

'I quite agree,' Lady Fenton echoed her. 'No woman could possibly dress up as a man and hope to get away with it, could she, Mr Jackson?'

Kit gave her a look of pure loathing. 'Of course not, Lady Fenton.'

'And then such a ridiculous story,' Julia continued. 'Viola's in love with her master, he's in love with another lady, and the lady falls in love with Viola dressed as a boy. How absurd!' She turned to Kit. 'What did you think, Mr Jackson? You were interested in the play to the extent of being rude. I spoke to you once or twice and you ignored me.'

'I apologize, Lady Julia,' said Kit, who had indeed been absorbed by the fate of Viola on the stage — so like her in some ways, but so unlike in others. For Viola's story had a happy ending: she was rescued by the timely arrival of her long-lost brother. But Kit could see no way in which Harry could come to her aid.

Bowland had taken little part in the conversation. 'Mr Jackson, I should be obliged if you would escort Miss Maxwell home,' he said abruptly. Kit was startled into

198

agreeing. 'I shall take Lady Fenton,' Bowland continued. 'You won't mind taking Julia, will you, Richard?'

Kit watched them go in dismay. There seemed to be little to stop Lancaster proposing to his cousin tonight. Would Julia accept him?

Bowland and Lady Fenton went off together, and Kit was left in a carriage driving through the dark London streets facing a woman who was even more miserable than herself. Lucy, who had sat 'like Patience on a monument, smiling at grief' for several hours, could no longer contain her tears. She put her head in her hands and wept.

'My dear Miss Maxwell,' said Kit, cut to the heart. She sat beside the weeping woman and put an arm round her. 'What you are going through; believe me, I sympathize deeply with your trouble.'

Lucy buried her head on Kit's shoulder and sobbed desperately. Kit stroked her hair and made what consoling noises she could. Damn Lord Bowland, she thought. What a poltroon! He hasn't even the courage to face this woman himself but leaves it to me. 'There, there, Miss Maxwell, Lucy,' she said. 'Have my handkerchief.'

Lucy blew her nose and sat up straight, realizing the impropriety of weeping on the shoulder of a man she barely knew. 'I'm sorry, Mr Jackson,' she sobbed. 'What you must think of me!'

'I think you are a brave woman who's kept grief unexpressed for too long.'

'I believed, tonight, when he invited me out to the play I believed he would — he would — ' she sobbed again. 'He's forgotten me. He wants to be rid of me, and I still love him. It was sheer cruelty, what he did tonight.'

'Can you not take that to console yourself? A man who behaves as dishonourably as that is not worth a single tear.'

'Oh, if that were all, Mr Jackson. If only that were all. But — no, I can't say it.'

Kit knew the agony of unwelcome questions and didn't press Lucy further. 'If there is anything I can do — '

'No, there is nothing, except don't tell anyone about the way I've behaved. I have enough to bear without the mockery of the world.'

'Miss Maxwell, anyone who knows your situation and knows you will not mock but will sincerely pity you.'

The carriage drew up outside a modest house in an unfashionable area. Kit helped Lucy out and escorted her inside where her brother was waiting. 'Lucy,' said Charles.

'Did he — ?' Then he saw her distress. He exchanged glances with Kit, who shook her head sadly. 'Come and tell me all about it.'

Kit started to back out. 'If you will excuse me . . . '

'Thanks, Jackson, for bringing my sister home. I needn't ask you to remain silent about this, I'm sure.'

'Of course. If I can do anything for your sister, you or she need only ask.'

'If only another were so gentlemanly,' he said, gently guiding Lucy away.

That's a remarkable compliment, thought Kit as the coach took her back. Someone thinks I'm more of a gentleman than the Earl of Bowland.

* * *

The following Sunday Kit recalled the words of St Matthew: *Come unto me, all ye that labour and are heavy laden, and I will give you rest.* She was very heavily laden and she felt great need for rest. The major appeared disinclined to attend, so she limped alone to the nearest church.

At the end of the service she limped back, preoccupied. There was a carriage waiting close to the major's house when she approached it, but she took no notice until the instantly recognizable figure of Hector Smythe alighted from it.

She went to dash up the front steps to the safety of the house when Smythe called to her in a voice of entreaty. 'Don't run away from me, please, Kit.'

She stopped and looked at him. The day being Sunday, he was clad more sombrely than usual, in shades of black and grey. There seemed to be nothing offensive or importuning about him, other than the look of appeal in his eyes. 'I've been waiting for you. It seems the only way I can see you. I guessed you might be going to church: I think your mind is unquiet.'

'I don't believe that the state of my mind is a concern of yours, Mr Smythe,' she said stiffly, going to the steps.

'Don't go. I just want to talk. What harm is there in talking? What can I do here, in a public street?'

Again the note of entreaty in his voice stopped her. There was nobody near, but the street was not deserted: she was in no danger. 'Very well, Mr Smythe. Say what you have to say.'

'Will you tell me why you returned my gift, and why you are not at home when I call?' he asked. 'Why are you so cold to me? It wasn't like that at first.'

'At first I thought you were offering me friendship. I didn't realize what sort of a man you are.'

'Wasn't it something else? Perhaps you didn't realize what sort of a man *you* are,' he said quietly. 'You didn't realize that you are — like me.'

'I know exactly what sort of a man I am, Mr Smythe. And I assure you, I am not like you,' she said whole-heartedly.

But Smythe didn't believe her. 'I'm sorry, Kit, it's no use denying it,' he said. 'I saw you at the theatre: I saw the way you looked at Richard Lancaster.'

Oh, damn! she thought, turning away to hide her face. Is it so obvious?

She said nothing, and he continued, 'You realize it's futile, don't you? He'll never return your affections.' He put out a hand to her. 'But I could. I'd be good to you, Kit, very good.' His voice was soft. 'I love you.'

This is very awkward, she thought. What do I do now? 'I am sorry, Mr Smythe. You are making a great mistake,' she said firmly.

He didn't take any notice. 'What's your future here? What will you do when he marries his cousin Julia? Will you watch him every day, loving him and knowing that you can say nothing, that he'd be disgusted if he even knew of your love for him?'

This was so close to her own picture of the future that she couldn't speak for a second. Smythe saw her distress. 'You must accept it,' he said sympathetically. 'Major Lancaster is not one of us.'

The front door opened: Major Lancaster himself stood there, glowering. She was so relieved to see him that she ran up the steps and stood beside him, comforted by his massive presence.

'Is he pestering you, Kit?' Lancaster asked protectively.

'Just talking,' Smythe cooed innocently. 'Just talking, weren't we, Mr Jackson?'

'I think you've talked enough, Smythe,' Lancaster said grimly. 'If you value a whole skin, you had better go.'

Then followed an exchange which Kit didn't understand. Hector Smythe's eyes opened wide. 'Oh, that's it!' His voice was full of surprise. 'I'm terribly sorry,' he added in exaggerated tones. 'But how could I have guessed?'

Lancaster's face went white. 'What do you mean, Smythe?' he snarled.

Smythe stepped back in alarm. 'I don't mean anything that could offend a man of your reputation with a pistol, I assure you,' he said hastily. He smiled ruefully at Kit. 'You were right, Mr Jackson. I was making a great mistake.' He returned to his carriage. 'I shan't trouble you again,' he said as he drove off. 'I understand now.'

'Well, I don't,' said Kit. 'Major, what was — ?'

But her question remained unfinished, for he turned and strode furiously back into the house.

9

'Ye'll pardon me I'm sure, Mr Jackson,' said McTavish one evening when the major had again escorted Julia to Almack's, leaving Kit to dine in gloomy solitude, 'but would ye care to take a wee dram with me?'

'McTavish, I should indeed care to take a wee dram with you. And I thank you most sincerely for your offer.'

She limped after him. They went down the stone-flagged back stairs into his room, which seemed to be lined with bottles. McTavish beckoned her to a chair, then ceremoniously got two glasses and poured out the golden liquid from one of the bottles. She sniffed her glass uncertainly.

'Have ye not tasted whisky before?'

'No, I never have,' she confessed.

'Well, for your first glass, most Scotsmen will tell ye to drink it' — he up-ended his glass straight down his throat — 'like that.'

Dubiously she lifted her glass to her lips. The smell was strange; but since her host was still alive she thought it could do her no harm. 'Like this?' she said, throwing the contents down as she'd seen him do. The whisky hit the back of her throat and fought all the way down before it exploded.

'Like that,' he agreed amiably. 'And now ye ken why most Scotsmen will tell you to drink it like that the first time; they love to laugh at the Sassenach.'

He poured her a glass of water, which followed the whisky down extremely quickly. The fire died down to a smoulder.

'Now I'll teach ye to drink it properly,' he said, pouring out another glass.

Two hours later they were like long-lost brothers. 'Ye ken, Kit, we're not so badly off.' They had stopped being Mr Jackson and McTavish after the first half bottle, and they'd solved the problems of slums, enclosures, smallpox and quack doctors after the second half.

'No, Hamish, we're not.'

'We've a guid master, a guid cook, and some verra guid whisky.'

'Very good, all three.'

'Ye ken that a guid master is the most important?'

'And we've got a very good master.'

'Och, 'tis a shame that he drinks too much, but he's a fine man for all that.' He refilled their glasses.

'He's not been drinking so much in the past week or so.'

'Aye, ye're not wrong. D'ye ken the reason for it?'

'Well . . . ' she said reluctantly.

'Dinna tell me: I'll not ask ye to go blabbing the master's secrets.'

'Thank you, Hamish, I appreciate that.'

'Let's drink to him.'

They lifted their glasses to the major, celebrating his newfound sobriety.

'To the best master in the world,' said Kit.

'Aye, that he is. And me, I ken some bad ones. Och, I do indeed.' While Kit listened avidly, he launched into horror stories of the dreadful things that some gentlemen did to their servants. 'And the worst of the lot was the ol' man.'

'Which ol' man?'

'Lord Bowland, of course.'

'Hamish,' said Kit. 'I may be very drunk; indeed, I shertainly am very drunk. But Lord Bowland was not an old man last time I saw him.'

'Och, not Master Edward. The old one, may he rot in Hell.'

'What was wrong with him?'

'What was right with him, ye'd better ask. He was a stone-hearted, small-minded, evil-living profligate: cruel, unhallowed, miserly, and a lecher till the day the devil took him. There was not a maid in the house that was safe with him; not a man that he'd not beaten with a horsewhip; not a tenant that he'd not ground into the dirt; not one of his sons or grandsons that he'd not humiliated.'

'Doesn't sound like a nice man.'

'Tcha, that he was not. The only one of God's creations he had time for was his horses; and when one of them threw him to the ground and broke his neck and ended eighty years of evil living it was a judgement to us all.'

'God moves in mysterious ways,' she said, keeping enough discretion not to add that God — or the Devil — had taken an unconscionably long time about it.

'And now there's poor Master Edward with the title and not a penny to go with it. He ruined the estate, the old man. Rack and ruined it. Should an earl be forced to be selling all his property? He hates to be in debt, Master Edward. Always has. Strange wee lad he was. Would steal from the servants rather than borrow. Och, we knew what he was doing and we felt sorry for the lad. His mother would always make it up to us, for all she had to go short herself. It was comical to see the shifts they all went to to give the poor lad some money. Not Master George — the only way he was better than his grandfather is that he left the world younger — but Master

Richard would leave his breeches pockets full so that Master Edward could take what he needed.'

'Did he?' asked Kit brightly. 'That was just like him.'

'A fine lad, Master Richard, and a fine man noo.'

'The finest man I ever met.'

'Indeed he is.'

'I love him, Hamish. I love Major Lancaster.'

'And dinna we all? There's not a one of us that doesna love Major Lancaster, and we love you too, for saving him that night, Kit. Kit?'

But Kit made no reply, for she had slid gracefully under the table.

★ ★ ★

'Ugh.'

'You ain't feeling well, Mr Jackson?' said Lizzy the housemaid, pulling back the curtains and letting a vicious shaft of morning sun into the room.

'Don't do that!' The effort of shouting made Kit feel even worse.

'Sorry.' Lizzy drew the curtains again. 'Is there anyfink you want?'

'I want to die.'

'I'll leave you in peace, then.' She left, closing the door gently.

Oh, hell, groaned Kit. I shouldn't have done that. Her head felt as if it was the wrong size, her throat burned, and her stomach heaved. She hadn't the slightest recollection of getting into bed. The last thing that she remembered was telling Hamish McTavish that she loved Major Lancaster.

Oh, hell, she groaned again. She was fully dressed apart from her coat and boots. My boots! she thought in alarm. Who took my boots off? Did they find the stones? She sat up. It was a mistake, since a hammer seemed to crack the back of her head open. She crawled out of bed and peered into her boot. No stones rattled in the bottom. She grabbed a drink of water and crawled back into bed again, pulled the blanket over her head, and spent the next quarter hour trying to die.

'Kit,' she heard the major's voice as he lightly touched her shoulder. 'What's the matter?'

She groaned.

'I'll send for the doctor.'

'No!' she yelled, her head throbbing. 'I'll be fine.' She pulled the blanket back down and rolled over in bed to look at him.

He knelt by her bed, concern in his face, and he reached out as if to feel her forehead:

his hand stopped for a moment in mid-air, then continued its journey. His touch on her brow cut through the ache in her head; but then he took it away. 'There's a slight fever,' he said, worried.

She knew it wasn't fever that heated her where his hand had rested.

'You don't look at all well. What's wrong?'

Lizzy came in carrying a tray. 'Mr McTavish sent me up with this,' she said. 'He says porridge and coffee'll set you right; 'e's 'aving the same 'imself.'

'You were drinking with McTavish!' The major let out a bellow of laughter that echoed round the room and burst in Kit's head. 'So that's the matter with you! I thought you were really ill!'

'I am,' she said hollowly.

He stood up and his voice returned to its formality. 'Bearing in mind your youth and inexperience, I shall not insist you perform your duties this morning, Mr Jackson. McTavish, on the other hand, will. He should know better.'

'Thank you,' she said with sincere and heartfelt gratitude. The only thing she wanted him to do at that moment was to leave her alone.

He did, pausing only to say at the door, 'I presume you have learned something. Never drink whisky with a Scotsman.'

And what else did I learn last night? she wondered. There was something. Something very important, I'm sure. But for the life of me I can't bring it to mind. It was no use to hammer her brain; the effects of the whisky were doing that perfectly well. She dozed all morning, thinking and regretting, trying to recall her conversation with McTavish.

But the only thing which kept returning was the awful moment when she'd said, 'I love him, Hamish. I love Major Lancaster.' McTavish, of all people. What a choice of confidant!

As the headache receded and she began to feel she might live after all, she consoled herself. She remembered McTavish's reply to her confession: 'Dinna we all?' He'd taken it as no more than a declaration of loyalty to a good master. At least he had then; what he would think of it now was another matter.

But how had she got into bed? Who had taken off her boots? Had she done it herself? If only she could remember!

At noon she got up and washed herself. The cold water provided blessed relief, and she started to feel more like a human being. She went carefully down the stairs, and saw McTavish in the hall receiving the day's letters. His face was greyer than normal but he seemed otherwise unaffected. She seemed to be living in a household of men with iron livers.

'Good day,' she greeted him formally. She didn't know whether to call him Hamish or McTavish. After last night . . .

He looked at her oddly. 'And good day to you, too.'

She had to ask. 'Last night. Did I — was there — ?'

'Was there anything ye shouldna have said nor done, ye mean?' She nodded. 'I canna remember too well. And if there was, why, it's a poor friend that'll go blabbing things told in drink.'

She shook his hand gratefully.

'Ye ken, I'm not saying that I approve. But well — ye're old enough to make your own choices, he's a fine man, and I come from Aberdeen.'

With that incomprehensible comment he departed below stairs.

★　★　★

I should be grateful if you would visit me this morning, said the curt note signed by Lord Bowland.

'Your cousin wishes to see me,' said Kit, passing the note. She was tired since she'd woken from a nightmare of a man dangling from a rope — not the first time she'd dreamed it. She hadn't been able to go back to sleep.

Lancaster had come down to breakfast with her and was his usual civil self. 'Why does Julia wish to see — Ah, no, it's Edward that wants you. Well,' he said, finishing the devilled kidneys he was eating, 'if you wait until I am properly dressed, we may go together. I wish to see my beautiful cousin.' He looked hard at Kit. 'She is beautiful, is she not?'

'Indeed she is.'

'We have always held each other in great affection, Julia and I.' He stood up. 'I had intended to wait until she came of age, but why should I?'

'Quite so,' said Kit dully. 'She is old enough to know her own mind.'

'I doubt that very much, Mr Jackson,' said Lancaster as he left the room. 'I doubt if any one of us ever reaches that advanced age.'

★ ★ ★

'Ah, Mr Jackson, come in,' said Bowland as Kit was ushered in. Behind her, outside the door, she knew that Lancaster was paying his regards to Julia. Perhaps more, she reflected

215

sadly. Perhaps the next time she saw him he would be an engaged man. She shook the thought away, and sat down in the chair that Bowland indicated.

Bowland stood up and started pacing round the room. 'Mr Jackson,' he began. 'I wish to ask you some questions. I've no wish to pry into your affairs, and I shan't regard it as impertinent if you refuse to answer questions I may ask.'

I may regard it as impertinent of you to ask, she thought, but held her peace.

'I have my reasons for knowing, Mr Jackson,' Bowland continued, still pacing the room with some agitation. 'And, if your answers are satisfactory, I shall reveal them. Is that clear?'

What is he after? Why does he want to find out about me? She felt cold inside as she waited for his questions.

'First, Mr Jackson, who is your father? What is his station in life?'

Kit considered. 'My father was a gentleman, a country squire, recently dead. His name I prefer not to reveal until I know the reason for your desire to know.'

'A fair answer. Are you his heir?'

'So far from being his heir, I am not even his legitimate son.'

'Ah!' That seemed satisfactory. 'I can tell

216

that you've been brought up as a gentleman.'
Kit nodded. 'You have little in the way of
fortune, I presume?'

'You presume correctly.' Where was all this
leading to?

'You are not married?'

'No, nor engaged to be.'

'And you know, no doubt, that your
present position is temporary?'

'I am aware of that.'

'So you will be seeking some way of
improving your financial situation in the near
future?'

'Are you offering me employment, my
lord?'

'Yes — no. I may be about to offer you
financial security, so that you don't need to
seek employment again. But one or two
further questions.' Here he paced around the
room again. 'You like Miss Maxwell, I gather.'

'Yes, very much so. But what — ?'

'Have patience, I've nearly finished. She
appears to like you, is that not so?'

She certainly likes my shoulder to cry on,
Kit thought, nodding assent.

Bowland faced Kit. 'I should like you to
marry her.'

'What!' Kit jumped up in astonishment.

'Pray sit down. I said that I wished you, Mr
Jackson, to marry Miss Lucy Maxwell.'

Kit sat down, mouth gaping. Of all the things she had dreaded in this interview, this was one she'd never expected.

'I can offer something in the way of financial inducement, Mr Jackson. You are no doubt aware that most of what I have is either mortgaged or entailed,' he said, obviously disliking his private affairs being revealed, 'but I still have a small estate out on the Thames marshes. It is yours and Miss Maxwell's on the day you marry each other.'

'But why do you want us to?' she exclaimed.

'I trust your discretion here. Miss Maxwell is in urgent need of a husband. Her condition will become obvious in a matter of months.'

Kit said nothing, but her mind was full. You are a swine, Lord Bowland, she thought. You are an appalling swine. So you want me to marry that poor woman and provide your baby with the father that you refuse to be.

'This has no doubt come as a surprise. But consider the advantages of my offer. You will be comfortably settled in a station somewhat higher than you can expect; in time I expect to improve my affairs, and you will not find me ungrateful, I assure you. You will have an estate and a beautiful wife.'

'And a ready-made family,' Kit said acidly.

'And a child that I shall support to the best of my ability.'

'Why me?'

'Because she appears to like you. I have some regard for Lucy; I wouldn't wish to make her unhappy.'

'The action that would make her happiest would be to marry her yourself.'

'Lucy Maxwell is an admirable young lady, but she is no fit person to be the Countess of Bowland. She has no fortune and no connections. I cannot afford a poor wife. Besides, her honour is manifestly not beyond reproach.'

How like the man, Kit thought disgustedly. He seduces a woman and then despises her for unchastity. 'I don't think, my lord, that Miss Maxwell's honour, nor yours, nor mine, is to be served by this conversation,' she said, rising.

'So you desert Miss Maxwell and leave her child a bastard, Mr Jackson.'

'That is in your hands, not mine,' said Kit, and stalked out of the door.

★   ★   ★

'Ah, Mr Jackson!' It was Julia, who'd obviously been lying in wait for her.

'Major Lancaster has gone, then?' Kit asked.

'Yes,' replied Julia. 'He seemed in no mood to wait on anybody. Come with me.' She led Kit into the drawing-room and closed the door.

She stood looking at Kit for an age; Kit returned her gaze. She's favoured with beauty and nobility, Kit reflected bleakly, and I have nothing. He has loved her since childhood; he doesn't even know I'm a woman.

'Mr Jackson,' Julia began, 'I must ask you something.'

Kit licked her lips apprehensively. First Bowland's disgraceful proposition; now what was coming?

'I should tell you,' Julia said, 'that my cousin Richard has just asked me to marry him.'

Kit felt the blood draining from her face. She swayed, and had to lean for support against the wall. She had thought herself prepared for such an announcement, but the event was so much worse than the fear of it.

'You say nothing, Mr Jackson. I see the news has discomposed you.'

'And have you — did you accept him?'

'I have not rejected him, and neither have I accepted.'

The blood flowed back in a wave of relief. And why, fool that you are? Kit berated herself. Why the relief? It can only be a matter of days. But, fool or no, her heart was singing.

'I wish to ask you — I need your advice, Mr Jackson,' she heard Julia's voice. 'For I don't know what to do.'

'*My* advice? Oh, no. Never ask my advice in this. I am not to be trusted.'

'I will have your advice. I will have you tell me what I should do. For I cannot act until I know.'

'Do you love him?'

'I respect him. I like him. He is rich, brave, kind and clever.'

'Do you love him?' Kit cried again.

'I love him as I have always loved him, my big cousin Richard.'

'That isn't enough for you?'

'It could be. It would be, if I didn't know what real love was. It will be, if the man I really love doesn't ask me instead.'

'And will he?'

Julia looked at the floor, blushing deeply. 'I don't know.' She looked up again, into Kit's eyes. 'Will he?'

Oh, no! thought Kit in utter dismay. The only way I can stop the man I love marrying the woman he loves is by proposing to her myself.

'Julia,' Kit said, gently taking Julia's hand. 'You know that it would tear me to pieces to see you marrying him.'

Julia's eyes filled with hope. 'Do you mean that?'

'From the bottom of my heart.'

'Then . . . '

'But I cannot ask you myself.'

'Why not?' she cried. 'In God's name, why not?'

'I cannot say. I can only beg you not to marry him.'

'It's not fair!' Julia cried. 'It's not fair of you to ask. Why should I not marry him? He is everything a woman could want in a husband.'

'I agree with you completely.' Kit let go Julia's hand. 'You are right. It is not fair of me to ask. But love makes us unfair.'

'I shall marry him,' Julia cried with desperate firmness. 'I shall write and tell him so now!'

'Wait!' Kit pleaded as Julia ran to the desk. 'I beg you, don't accept him now. Only wait.'

'For how long?'

'I don't know.'

'But how can I? I like Richard, and he deserves an answer. How can I expect him to wait while I wait, neither of us knowing what we are waiting for?'

'Wait a few days, Julia, please,' Kit begged. 'Something may happen — I don't know. What harm can it do? A few days are nothing to you in a lifetime of marriage — but it's a long stay of execution when the axe is about to fall.'

Julia studied her toes intently. 'Very well, then. Three days.'

'God bless you, Julia,' said Kit. She couldn't say any more; she couldn't stay any longer. She walked blindly out into the street.

⋆ ⋆ ⋆

All that afternoon, Kit wandered alone through the streets of London. She didn't know where she was going; she took no notice of either the broad fashionable streets or the narrow dirty slums. The pain in her foot made her rest; the pain in her heart made her walk on again.

What was she to do? She had three days. Three days to do what? Even if she found the man who'd murdered George Lancaster, what could she do? She could become a woman again: but it was sheerest folly to believe that she, even in woman's clothes, could compete with Julia. If she told the major the truth she could guess what would happen: he'd be disgusted at her shameful behaviour and grievously offended at the way she'd deceived him.

Perhaps she could ask for his help, as Kit

Jackson, Harry's illegitimate brother. Perhaps together they could find the murderer.

But perhaps he *was* the murderer. There was no one else it could have been. What other tall gentleman was there, aged about thirty with grey eyes, who had any reason to kill both George Lancaster and Lord Bowland?

She knew he could kill without remorse. But could he kill and then let an innocent man take his place on the gallows? She wished she hadn't read *Caleb Williams*, which told her that a good man could do exactly that.

But that's just a novel! Major Lancaster would never be so cruel and ruthless, would he?

He didn't do it, she thought. I'd stake my life on it.

But could she stake Harry's?

Could she test the major out? Ask, innocently, if he'd seen a ring with rubies set into a rose? No. For she was no impartial observer; besides, if he were guilty he was certainly an excellent actor.

With all her doubts and questions there was guilt. When Harry was still facing death, what was she doing worrying about her own problems?

She should face the facts, she told herself

sternly. Major Richard Lancaster was going to marry his cousin Lady Julia. And since she couldn't bear to live in the same house, she would have to move.

Hector Smythe would take her, she thought sardonically. Hector Smythe knew something about the major that she didn't: that was obvious from the incident on Sunday. What was it? And why was Lancaster so wrathful about it? Could she go to Smythe and ask him? If she did, would he tell her? If he told her, what would he expect in return? And what would he do when he found that he could never get what he expected?

I'd do better to marry Lucy Maxwell, she thought. At least that way I'd stay close to Bowland. The irony struck her. She had to protect a man whom she disliked, perhaps from the man she loved. If Bowland treated everyone the way he treated her there'd be no shortage of potential murderers.

An idea struck her. What was Charles Maxwell doing the night of the murder? Now there was a man with a motive: Bowland had seduced his sister. She liked Maxwell, and she would be sorry to see him hang for doing no more than Harry had wanted to do for her, but if it came to a choice between Lucy's brother and her own . . .

But Maxwell seemed an honourable man;

would he not have rather challenged Bowland than tried to murder him by stealth? 'To challenge someone to a duel requires more confidence in your aim with a pistol than in the justice of your cause.' She could hear Lancaster's voice saying that — and her thoughts were back in the same old rut.

The afternoon was over, and the long June evening was coming in. She had made no more progress than a resolution to find out where Maxwell had been on the night of the murder and whether he owned a ruby ring.

There was another thing that nagged her; she wasn't treating Julia in the way that an honourable man should. But I'm not an honourable man! she protested. I'm neither man nor woman; I'm not even the nobody I pretend to be. Kit Jackson would have friends, a history, a future. He would have tastes to go with his clothes. He would think it heaven to have the beautiful Julia Lancaster talk to him the way she had this morning.

She kept on walking and thinking. Sometimes the bizarre side of things surfaced in her mind, and she would sit down on a wall and laugh. Counting Hector Smythe's offer, she thought, I've had three proposals in a week. I wonder if I'd have done so well in woman's clothes.

Then there was the Shakespearian complexity of her relations with Lancaster and Julia. I love him; he loves her; she loves me. Now, if this were *Twelfth Night*, Harry would turn up to the rescue and Julia would marry him, having mistaken him for me. But Harry and I couldn't be mistaken for each other except in a coal cellar on a moonless night.

I am not in a play, she told herself. If I were, would it be a tragedy or a comedy? What's the ending going to be? Will the stage be littered with corpses, or will everyone get married and live happily ever after?

But perhaps Harry could come to her rescue in a different way: Harry had seen the murderer. If he could only be brought safely to London in the next three days . . . There was the rub: *safely*. It would be asking Harry to risk his neck merely to sort out her love life. And she knew perfectly well that Harry would do it, which was why she couldn't ask him.

The day had been dull, and the evening was cold and unseasonable. She found herself on Westminster Bridge, and she looked over the parapet. Beneath her the Thames flowed, slow and stinking.

She thought, briefly, of those who had thrown themselves over the edge. No, she wasn't in that bad a state. She had something to live for. She wouldn't be the first woman in the world who hadn't married the man she loved. Others survived: so would she. Compared with Lucy Maxwell she was lucky.

I've had enough, she thought. I can manage no longer on my own. Tomorrow I shall — I shall leave London, and go to Harry in Eastham, and we can work things out together.

Or I shall tell the major the truth, and work things out with him.

Which?

I know I should go to the man I both love and trust rather than the one I love and don't trust: but it's hard. Oh, God, it's too hard.

She heard a horse stopping behind her, but she didn't look round until a familiar voice said, 'Kit.'

She turned and smiled bleakly up at him, while Newcastle snorted and stamped.

'I was — concerned about you, Kit.'

'I'm sorry, Major. I didn't mean to cause you any alarm. I just needed to be alone for a while, to think.'

'Have you come to any conclusions?'

'No, not really.'

'I don't see why you should think more clearly on a windswept bridge than in a comfortable house.'

'No. Perhaps you're right.'

'Come with me, then. Come home.'

'I shall.'

'Tired?' he asked.

'Yes, a little.'

'Then Newcastle shall carry us both.'

He reached a hand down to help her climb onto Newcastle's back. His right hand: gloved, not bandaged.

'Oh, your wound is better,' she said, feebly stating the obvious.

'Yes. The doctor came this afternoon. But we may have to call him in again if we stand here much longer in this wind. Haul yourself up.'

He gripped her as she clambered up while the well-disciplined horse stood steady. 'Set?' he asked.

'Set,' she affirmed.

She found she wasn't as soon as they started. With no saddle to keep her on she kept slipping uncomfortably. She wanted to grasp hold of him, if for no other reason than to stay on the horse.

But she remembered another passenger who had ridden where she was riding, and whose clasp had haunted him since. Nevertheless, she was in danger of falling off, so she tentatively put her arms round his body. But as she did, she could feel him flinch in her embrace. She let go and resumed her uneasy grip on the back of the saddle.

He pulled Newcastle to a halt. 'Hold on to me if you need to,' he said. 'Why did you let go?'

'I apologize. I should have known that you wouldn't want someone riding behind you to hold you like that.'

'Kit,' he said, rather huskily. 'There's all the difference in the world between the deadly thing that rode behind me once, and the warm and human embrace of a friend.' He coughed. 'Besides, my devil hasn't been back since you routed him that night. So put your arms around me, and welcome, if it means that you don't fall off. But don't die, Kit. That I couldn't bear.'

So she did wrap her arms around him, and she even rested her head on his broad back, and he didn't flinch. As they rode she forgot everything: Harry, Julia, the murderer, Bowland, the ruby ring. There was nothing in the world except him and her, riding together through the streets of London.

★　★　★

But even the longest journeys have an end, and theirs was a short one, much too short.

'We're home,' he said as the stable lad ran out to hold Newcastle. 'It's time to let go.' He gave her his hand to help her get down, then dismounted himself.

McTavish opened the door for them, and she could see the lights in the house, bright against the dark grey evening outside. 'I hope dinner hasna spoiled, sir,' said McTavish gloomily as he took the gloves the major removed.

'I hope not too,' Lancaster replied amiably. 'Investigate, will you?'

Then he took her by the elbow and guided her into a room where a fire was blazing. 'You're cold, as well as tired, aren't you?'

'Yes,' she said as she stood facing the fire warming her hands.

'Hungry?' she heard him say behind her. 'When did you last eat?'

'Breakfast,' she admitted.

'And your foot hurts.'

'It was foolish of me to walk so far.'

'You're distressed in spirit, too.'

She nodded, glad she had her back to him and he couldn't see her face.

'It would be cruel of me to press you now, when your body is at its weakest,' he said, and she welcomed his chivalrous consideration. But he added, 'We'll talk after dinner. And then you'll tell me.'

His voice was gentle, yet there was a command in it that she knew she would obey. She was at the end of her strength: he had only to ask, and she would hide the truth from him no longer.

'There'll be no more secrets between you and me, Kit, because I — ' he continued in a low voice ' — because I have something to tell, too.'

She was too exhausted and miserable even to wonder what it was.

'But while we wait for dinner,' he said, his voice changing to one of cheerful unconcern, 'a glass of Madeira would be welcome to both of us, eh?'

'Yes,' she said, turning from the fire now she didn't need an excuse for hiding her face. 'A glass of Madeira would be extremely welcome.'

His back was turned to her while he poured out two glasses. 'It's a blessing to be rid of those damned bandages,' he said, coming towards her. His newly healed right hand held out a glass. 'I can write for myself, and I can put this thing on at last. It's an heirloom; it's worn by the next in line to the Bowland title. Absurd pretension, of course: our family has no real claim to the red rose of the Royal House of Lancaster.'

There was a roaring in her ears, and blackness closed in around her. The last thing she was conscious of before she passed out was the ring on his finger: blood-red rubies set in the shape of a rose.

10

She opened her eyes. She was lying on the sofa, and she could feel that her neck cloth had been pulled off and her shirt had been torn open. He must have picked her up when she had fallen, and loosened her clothes to let her breathe.

He had his back to her. He was leaning against the mantelshelf, his face buried in his hands. His body was shaking, and she heard his tortured voice. 'The guilt! The bloody guilt!'

She was terrified. Misery would have to wait — at the moment she felt only fear. She knew she was in desperate danger. He had murdered his own brother without showing a qualm until now. He wouldn't hesitate to kill her if he knew she was a danger to him.

What did he know? What knowledge had she betrayed when she fainted? Had he discovered she was a woman when he picked her up and ripped her shirt open? She cursed her feminine weakness. If only she had kept control of herself when she saw the ring on his finger, she could have made an excuse and left safely. Now she was trapped. He held the power now, the power of life and death over her. Her safety depended on his belief that she was no threat to him. She must convince him: but her wits had almost left her. She shut her eyes and feigned unconsciousness to gain time to think.

She heard his footsteps as he came towards her. She sensed that he was kneeling beside her, waiting for her to come round. Then he would question her, and she hadn't the slightest idea what answers to give. It took all her resolution to stay still. She believed she was safe when he thought she was unconscious.

'You're awake now,' she heard him say. Her eyes blinked open. She saw his face close to hers as he knelt beside her. 'Who are you?'

She didn't reply — she dared not, for she didn't know what he knew.

He put his arm round her shoulders and firmly lifted her. He held a glass in his hand: the right one, with the ring. 'Drink this. It'll make you feel better.'

Was it poisoned? But if she refused to drink, he'd be sure that she knew he was a murderer, and then he would kill her. What was she to do? There was no way out. She had to drink, or betray her knowledge of his guilt. His arm was around her, holding her as she'd once dreamed of being held, but now it

235

was not the fulfilment of her dream but a terrible threat.

She looked at the glass. Madeira, or so it seemed. She studied his face, but she couldn't read him. One thing she could tell: whatever he felt, it wasn't mere concern for her welfare. There was some strong emotion, barely held in check. 'Drink it,' he insisted, bringing the glass to her lips.

Knowing that it might be the last thing she ever did, she drank.

It tasted of nothing but the best Madeira. There was no way she could stifle a shudder of relief, and no way he could miss her reaction.

'What is it?' he asked her. 'Why did you shiver so?' She couldn't answer him. He set the glass down, then put his hand up to her face. He held her chin, forcing her head round. Her eyes met his. She couldn't tear her gaze away from his face, so close they could almost kiss.

'Look at me,' he commanded. 'Tell me who you are and why you are here.'

Her lips opened, but no words came out. She couldn't say anything, but dared not say nothing. For a second, or for an eternity, they stayed there, a breath apart, his arm round her shoulder, his hand holding her face.

Then the door opened and McTavish

coughed. 'Dinner is served.'

Lancaster swore violently, and loosened his grip on her.

It's now or never, she thought. The terror that she'd so far kept under control rushed through her and gave her legs speed as she leaped up from the sofa. McTavish wasn't nimble enough to catch the form that darted past him in fear of her life.

'Wait!' she heard Lancaster's cry. 'For God's sake don't go!'

She was in the hall. Safety lay before her. Once she was out in the street he wouldn't dare touch her. She rushed to the front door. It wouldn't open.

Lancaster and McTavish appeared in the hall. She turned to face them. 'The door is locked,' said Lancaster quietly. He stepped towards her, McTavish following.

Out of the corner of her eye, she saw her sword-stick in the stand by the doorway. If she could reach it she'd at least have a way of defending herself.

But McTavish saw it too. He glided forward fast and picked it up. She slumped in despair. She couldn't fight the two of them. And now she'd betrayed her knowledge of his guilt. He would kill her, as surely as he'd killed his brother.

Then, suddenly, she found the sword-stick

in her hand. 'Ye'll be wanting to go out, then,' said McTavish, as he moved to the front door, holding the key.

'McTavish!' roared Major Lancaster in fury.

McTavish turned to face his master. 'If the lassie wants to leave, I canna find it in my conscience to stand in her way,' he said resolutely.

The door stood open to the street, and Kit limped out.

★　★　★

Lady Fenton was angry. Bowland had ruined everything. They had been having a delightful time; what had started out as a mere flirtation on his part, and a dutiful care for her niece and nephew's affairs on hers, had developed into a relationship that might have raised eyebrows, but had given the two of them nothing but pure — or impure — pleasure.

Why had he spoiled it all by proposing? As if she couldn't guess. It was galling that his intentions were strictly honourable, as the saying goes: he wished to rob her of her fortune by way of marriage.

Infuriating man. So handsome, and such an accomplished lover! Was it worth giving up her freedom for him? She had asked for a few days to consider, and she was by no means sure that she would refuse.

Her irritation left her when Mr Jackson was announced, replaced by curiosity. But when Kit staggered into the drawing-room, her face white and drawn, Lady Fenton jumped up in alarm. 'What's the matter?' she cried.

Kit stared at her for a second, her face filled with pain. 'I've found the murderer.'

Lady Fenton's well-managed household burst into activity. A glass of brandy was brought, and a room was prepared for Mr Jackson. Desdemona's brother Hamlet was sent to continue his attentions to Major Lancaster's cook. A meal was summoned from the kitchen, and Kit was cajoled into eating a few mouthfuls, for Lady Fenton knew that misery is made no easier to bear by hunger.

'So it was the gallant major all the time,' said Lady Fenton when Kit had finished her story. 'The most obvious person. He may have killed his revolting brother George to keep his mouth shut, but no doubt the money he inherited will be welcome. So he plans to be Lord Bowland, with fortune enough to maintain the title.'

Kit didn't say anything, but sat gloomily sipping the brandy that Stewart had brought to her.

'It was just bad luck that you didn't find out before,' Lady Fenton continued. 'He didn't wear the ring because his arm was bandaged, and nobody mentioned it, because nobody except the two of us thought it important.'

'I know where it was, now. Rundell and Bridge's, being repaired. I had the bill in my hand and I didn't understand what it meant!' Because he had been in the room with her, and she hadn't been able to think of anything else. 'I was such a fool!'

'No, my dear, you were not a fool. You were pitting your wits against a clever, powerful and ruthless man: and it's no wonder that you never caught him out in anything until today.'

'I knew he had a troubled mind, but I thought it was the war.'

'You had a very lucky escape. If it hadn't been for that man McTavish!'

'He must have known I was a woman for days. I foolishly shared a bottle or two of whisky with him, and I passed out. He must have put me to bed while I was unconscious, and that's when he discovered what I was.'

'I wonder why he didn't say anything to the major.'

'He thought he didn't need to. From something he said, he must have assumed I was the major's mistress, smuggled into the house in disguise. That's why he let me go — and Richard Lancaster couldn't do a thing about it.'

'His one weak spot — he had everything else under control. My dear, that is a very formidable opponent you have defeated.'

Tears sprang into Kit's eyes. She couldn't help it.

Her aunt saw, and understood. 'There was a price to pay, wasn't there?'

Kit nodded.

'It was uncommonly stupid of me not to foresee it. To be living in such intimacy with a man of so many attractions! My poor child!'

Kit's lips trembled.

'You were in love with him?'

Kit could bear it no longer. 'I still am!' she cried, sobbing into her aunt's dress and ruining the lace.

★   ★   ★

Kit went up to her room, closed the door and locked it. She wanted nobody to disturb her in the agony of her dilemma. She stripped her clothes off, the men's clothes that had brought her to this. She put nothing else on, but knelt naked by the bed, praying for help, praying for strength, praying for a way out.

241

She had thought it bad all those weeks ago, when she first heard that Harry was taken for murder and would hang for it. But then she had only one thought in mind, to save her brother's life.

She had thought it bad that morning — God, was it only that morning? — when Julia had told her of the major's proposal. But now she would rejoice if he were to marry Julia and live with her in happiness — if only he would live!

Memories came to her. His laughter after their fencing match, his faith in her when he had told her of his torment, his strength that had laid out two of the men who were attacking him, his gentleness when he asked her to trust him.

No! she cried out silently. I cannot do it! I cannot betray him and send him to the gallows. And for what? For the murder of a man who deserved to die?

No, not for that. To save her brother's life. Because if she did nothing, if she kept quiet about the major's guilt and managed to persuade her aunt to do likewise, Harry would go to the gallows instead. He couldn't keep in hiding for ever — sooner or later he would be found and hanged.

Memories of Harry came to her also, a lifetime of them. The time when she had glued the vicar's teacup to the saucer, and he had taken the blame and the flogging. The tree house they had built and shared in the old oak at Eastham. The way they had cried together when their mother had died. His angry strength that had nearly broken the jaw of George Lancaster, a man six inches taller than he. His trust in her to save him.

I love both of them, she cried in the silence of her room. I would do anything to save them — anything except sacrifice the other. It's like asking me which arm I want chopped off, the left or the right. Worse — if my life would save both of them, I'd willingly give it.

How can I choose which one to save? How can I choose which one to betray to his death? There is no worse than this.

And then she realized that there would be worse, far worse. There would be seeing one of them dangling on a rope, and knowing that she had put him there. There would be living with that knowledge until the day she died.

To let Harry go to the gallows knowing that she could have saved him, but hadn't because she'd fallen in love with the murderer? Impossible.

But just as impossible was sending Richard Lancaster there instead after he'd trusted her as he'd trusted no one else in his life.

The early dawn was fighting its way

through the sooty London air. She had not moved for hours. Her body was stiff with kneeling and the cold was eating into her, for though it was the height of summer, the night was chill. She welcomed the physical discomfort — far better than her mental torture.

There was a shaft of sunlight through a gap in the curtains, and a voice came to her. It didn't bring illumination; there was no sudden light on a way out. Instead it was like a knife blade, stabbing through her, cutting her heart in two — but cutting it cleanly.

You must betray one of them. You cannot save them both, said the voice, cold, hard and merciless.

Save the one who is innocent.

★ ★ ★

Edward, Lord Bowland, spent a long time dressing. On his mantelshelf was a letter, neatly folded.

If Lord Bowland would visit Lady Fenton at noon today, he would learn something to his advantage.

So she'd decided to accept him, had she? She would become a countess, and he would become rich. A fair exchange. They didn't love each other, and she was considerably older than he, but she was still a lovely woman, and she would die well before he did.

Now, if only that fellow Jackson would marry Lucy . . .

Bowland felt some remorse about Lucy. He loved her, in his fashion. He was doing his best by her, wasn't he? And she could still be his mistress if she was safely Mrs Jackson. If only he had enough money he could do what he wanted.

So he spent a long time trying to look his best. And, it should be noted, succeeding. When he arrived a mere quarter hour late, Lady Fenton realized that she would have to work hard to persuade herself to refuse him.

He was taken aback when he saw Lady Fenton's guest: the last person he could have expected. 'Good day to you, Mr Jackson,' he uttered as coolly as he could manage.

'Ah, my lord,' cooed Lady Fenton charmingly. 'This may seem unnecessary, but I should like to introduce to you Mr Kit Jackson — the child of my late brother-in-law.'

Lord Bowland was too well-bred to look startled. 'Tell me, pray: why conceal the connection?'

'I think that will become apparent as Mr

Jackson tells you his story.'

This was the moment Kit had been dreading so much. But it had to be done. 'You have heard, I think, that Lady Fenton's nephew Harry Faulkner is wanted for killing your cousin George?' she began.

'Yes, but what has this to do with either you or me?'

'It has to do with me, my lord, because Harry is my brother. We share the same father, and we have always played together and loved each other. I know Harry didn't kill George Lancaster, and I came to London to find out who did.'

'I still don't comprehend why you are talking to me about this. Surely Major Lancaster is a more suitable person?'

Kit managed to continue without wincing. 'I shall come to that. I know Harry is innocent. He did have a fight when your cousin assaulted his sister, as I'm sure you've heard. He intended to challenge your cousin to a duel, and went to his room to do so. But there he overheard George Lancaster and somebody else talking about killing you.'

Bowland snorted with impatience. 'I've heard this story before. 'Killing Lord Bowland — it's a hanging matter.' You were there when my cousin Richard warned me about this: the constable had told him about it.'

'It is the truth, my lord.'

Bowland shrugged.

'Harry heard a shot,' Kit continued. 'He broke down the door in time to see your cousin dying on the floor, and somebody climbing out of the window.'

'That is your brother's story. He needs a mysterious villain climbing out the window, doesn't he? Are there any traces of this man?'

'Yes,' she said, stung by his indifference. Telling him cost her so much, and he didn't seem to care. 'He tethered his horse in a nearby spinney.'

'Is there anything else you know about him? Would your brother recognize him again?'

'Oh yes. He gave me a good description. A gentleman of about thirty, tall, with grey eyes.'

'That description fits half a dozen people I know.'

'There was one more thing, my lord. The man was wearing a very distinctive ring. An old-fashioned ruby ring, in the shape of a rose.'

The blood suddenly drained from Bowland's face. It was futile for him to protest the story was worthless. He believed what Kit was telling him, and it showed.

'You know the ring, I see,' said Lady Fenton. 'Worn by Major Lancaster.'

'Richard?' said Bowland incredulously.

'I'm afraid so.'

'My God!'

'Yesterday Mr Jackson saw it on his finger: he realized he had found the murderer, and he knew his own life might be in danger. That is why he came to me, and that is why he is telling you the story now.'

'Let me just ensure that I've understood you, Mr Jackson. You think my cousin, Major Richard Lancaster, killed his brother and now wants to kill me?'

'Yes, my lord.'

'You say your brother can identify him.'

'Well, he could. But my brother is wanted for the murder himself. He cannot patrol the streets with a Bow Street Runner beside him.'

Bowland put his head in his hands and thought. 'I find it difficult to believe this story,' he said at length. 'In fact, I don't think I can, not from you. I must hear it from your brother's own lips. Where is he?'

'I am sorry, my lord, but I cannot tell you that.'

'Cannot, or will not?'

'Will not, then, for reasons which I need not explain.'

'I'm sure you have some way to communicate with him.'

'I do.'

'I suggest a meeting outside London. Your brother wishes to remain in hiding, no doubt. I've a lodge about three miles from the Rose and Crown: it is secluded, so your brother can approach and depart in secrecy.'

'It sounds suitable,' Kit acknowledged.

'How long will it take for your brother to be informed, and for him to reach my lodge?'

Kit calculated rapidly. 'About two days, my lord.'

'Next Monday, then, at noon.' His tone did not admit of any argument. He sketched the directions to find his hunting lodge, then took his leave, without any of his former gallantries to Lady Fenton.

When he had gone, Lady Fenton heard a sigh escape from her niece's lips, but no more. What a shame, she thought. Two of the most eligible men in London, but one's mercenary and the other's a murderer.

Kit went and lay down on her bed. She was desperately tired, not having slept the previous night, but she could hardly gain even a doze.

Lady Fenton's servants tiptoed round, knowing that the mysterious Mr Jackson had performed some arduous service for

249

milady. To their annoyance, 'that Desdemona' appeared to know something about it, since she was the only person allowed in Mr Jackson's room. But Desdemona wasn't saying anything.

It was four o'clock when Kit arose, not much refreshed, and went into the drawing-room.

'Here's a letter for you,' said Lady Fenton as she passed it over. 'It's from him,' she added laconically.

Kit ripped it open and read:

I understand your fears last night. You must know that I would not harm you. If I did anything to frighten you, I beg you to forgive me: I was in no more a condition to think rationally than you were. I know you are in a situation of the utmost delicacy, and I have no wish to add to your burdens. However, I think we should see each other and talk together. Explanations are due from both of us, as I am sure your heart will tell you. Until then, believe me to be
   Your friend
   Richard Lancaster

'He wants us to meet,' said Kit.

'Are you going to?' asked Lady Fenton, who was itching to read the letter, having heroically refrained from opening it in the hour since it was delivered.

'No.' Kit stared down at the carpet.

'Very well.' There was a pause. 'Why not? You could meet here, where he wouldn't dare to hurt you.'

Kit lifted her head. 'Do you think I could be in the room with him for a single minute and not tell him everything?'

'Perhaps not,' Lady Fenton concurred. 'Richard Lancaster isn't an easy man to fool. Have you noticed what's on the outside of the letter?'

Puzzled, Kit turned it over and looked at what the major had written. Her mind was still hazy, and the significance of the name he had used escaped her for a few moments. Then she realized what it meant, for he had written: 'To Miss Katherine Faulkner'.

11

Even at noon on Midsummer's Day the marsh mists seemed reluctant to clear, and wisps of them hung like a shroud round Lord Bowland's lodge, the Vicarage. This was the property he would settle on Lucy the day she married.

Once it had been the centre of a small village. The church still stood, though the windows had long been broken. The cottages had crumbled, and the inn was nothing but a fire-blackened shell. The people had left, those who hadn't been brought down by the bad air of the marshes to lie under the weed-covered headstones in the churchyard.

Only the lodge was still in fair condition. It still was a vicarage according to law, which hadn't caught up with desolate reality. This was still a parish, and it still had a vicar, though the only parishioners were in their graves. The old earl had never spent anything on this land, and was hard pressed to find anyone who would pay him anything to be made the incumbent of a parish with no tithes, until Reverend Marcus Fazakerley came to his notice.

Fazakerley nursed ambitions to be a bishop when he was first ordained. But greater than his desire for preferment was his desire for drink: he twice barely escaped disgrace. A parish with no parishioners was the answer.

The pittance the old earl granted him was as much to keep the lodge in good repair as for any religious purpose. It was nowhere near enough to keep him in brandy, and he looked for an additional income. He soon realized that there were advantages in a parish church that was away from neighbours, yet only a few hours from London. There were many who wanted christenings for babies who shouldn't have been born, or funerals for those who shouldn't have died, and would pay handsomely for ceremonies that were both discreet and legal.

The old earl had known of the vicar's activity but ignored it, since it cost him nothing and meant that Fazakerley could maintain the lodge in return for a very small stipend. The lodge was used fairly often, since the marsh provided some of the finest fishing and duck-shooting within easy reach of London.

Leading down to the river was a track used by hunting parties to reach the wildfowl and fish. It was also used by some of the vicar's guests, to get to the ships which sailed down the river to all countries of the world, and which might, for a fee, take on a man who didn't wish his departure from England to be known.

In the other direction a poor road, little more than a track with its ruts and pot-holes, led from the lodge to the highway over which the Rose and Crown presided. Since the vicar knew that some of his guests might not feel very gregarious, there was another path to the lodge, one that conveniently avoided both the inn and the constable's lock-up nearby.

Down this convenient path came a man on horseback. His hair was flaming red, like a signal of freedom. For six weeks he'd been a fugitive in disguise, wanted for a crime he did not commit. Now, thanks to the love and courage of the finest sister in the world, he was within an hour of liberty.

His horse picked its way down the muddy path and turned a corner. Ahead of him he saw his goal. But for some reason he didn't feel as happy as he expected, as he surveyed the unwelcoming old building with few windows, the ruins of a village, and the dilapidated church. It would be easy to set a trap here, he thought, then shook the idea away. There was no trap; his sister had vouched for the place and the man he was to meet.

But he still felt unease, which didn't abate when he rode up to the door of the lodge; the gentleman waiting there wasn't such as to inspire confidence. 'Reverend Marcus Fazakerley,' he introduced himself, extending a trembling hand. It was impossible to say whether he was forty or sixty, but it was clear that many years of drinking had gone into making the red bloom of his nose.

The horse was taken by a man who looked more like a boxer than a groom: two equally burly men stood by, watching with seeming indifference.

'Lord Bowland is waiting for you,' announced Fazakerley, opening the door. There were separate rooms in the upper storeys, but on the ground floor there was just one single enormous room with no dividing walls. There was a large fireplace, but no fire, since it was midday at the height of summer.

By the fireplace a tall man was standing, his back towards the newcomer. 'This is the man you wanted,' said the vicar, then stood back.

'Henry Faulkner, I presume,' said the man by the fireplace. And then he turned round.

★　★　★

It would be too painful to dwell on the torture Kit had suffered over the past two days.

Lady Fenton was seriously worried about her niece's condition. In a rare display of genuine unselfishness she abandoned her entertainments and her admirers, including Lord Bowland, to stay with Kit and try to console her.

Kit had slept hardly at all and eaten almost nothing until yesterday evening, when her body's demands had made themselves felt and she had fallen into a deep sleep, from which she woke this morning ravenous.

Over and over again, she tried to think of a way out that would save both the men she loved. There wasn't one.

But her aunt had kept assuring her that a man so clever, powerful and ruthless as Major Lancaster must surely find a way to escape the gallows; these assurances had had some effect on her mind. Her aunt had also advised her that she should cease to love a man so clever, powerful and ruthless; this advice had made no difference whatsoever.

So Kit's physical health was as good as it had been for days, as she paced back and forth in the drawing-room just after noon on Monday, even though her mental health was little better. Lady Fenton, feeling she deserved a reward for her days of compassionate service to her niece, had gone out to buy a new dress.

'Lady Julia Lancaster,' announced Stewart. 'I've told her that Lady Fenton isn't at home, but she says she wishes to see you.' Stewart was plainly at a loss to see why such a dashing young lady in such smart riding clothes and with a liveried groom in attendance should wish to see Mr Jackson.

With all that had happened, Kit had almost forgotten that Julia had given her three days' grace. Kit felt guilty at the neglect; she knew what it was to love hopelessly, and she must let Julia down gently. Though perhaps it wouldn't be gentle to let Julia become engaged to Richard Lancaster if he might shortly be charged with murder.

Kit greeted Julia formally when she came in, and Julia followed suit. 'I hadn't known you were a connection of Lady Fenton's,' she said. 'Though now I do know, it explains the glances I've seen you exchange.'

Julia was jealous! Kit hastened to put her mind at ease. 'Lady Fenton is my father's sister-in-law,' she said, slipping into the misleading truth with practised ease. 'An aunt, if you like,' she stressed that harmless relationship. 'But we have been forced to conceal our connection.'

'Is this your secret? Has Lady Fenton anything to do with — with — why you cannot marry?'

'I can assure you she has nothing to do with it.'

There was an awkward pause. They both knew why she had come — and neither could say so. Finally Julia took her courage. 'It has been some time since I saw you. Three days.' She blushed.

Kit hunted for words. 'Lady Julia, last time we met I urged you not to marry your cousin. You gave me three days. Something has happened since, something which makes me urge you again: you must not marry him.'

'Will you tell me?'

'No, but your brother will tell you when he returns from his lodge.'

'What is this? What does Edward know? Why don't I?'

'I'm sorry to make such a mystery out of it, but you will find out soon enough. You mustn't marry him; ask your brother if you don't trust me.'

'You want me to make Richard wait again for an answer.' Julia privately thought that her cousin wouldn't mind very much. She had asked him for three days to consider his proposal, expecting a storm of passion. But to her surprise he had said that he had no desire to force her into something she didn't want to do, and that if there was the slightest doubt in her mind she shouldn't accept him. However, she wasn't going to tell Kit that.

She tried another tack. 'I understand why you felt it necessary to leave my cousin's house,' she said. 'The situation must have been difficult.'

'It was. Very difficult.' Kit couldn't resist the next question. 'How is he?'

'Looking well now his arm is out of bandages,' Julia replied, not averse to changing the subject. 'I'm glad he can wear the Lancaster rose ring now. Did you see it before you left?'

Kit's mouth was dry. 'Yes, I saw it.'

'It's a family heirloom, worn by the person who's next in line to the Bowland title. With his arm bandaged up like that, it's the first time Richard's been able to wear it.'

Kit felt as if the floor had lurched beneath her feet. 'What did you say?'

'Eh?' asked Julia, bemused. 'I said it was a family heirloom.'

Kit, feeling that she would scream, stepped over to Julia and gripped her by the shoulders. 'After that, Julia. You said something after that. It was the first time Richard had worn it, you said.'

'You're hurting me,' Julia protested, frightened by the eyes that seemed to drill into hers.

Kit didn't slacken. 'Julia, tell me this. When was the first time the major put that ring on?'

'A few days ago.'

'Who was wearing it six weeks ago?'

'It was Edward.'

'Edward? Lord Bowland?' Kit said incredulously.

Julia nodded.

Kit let go of Julia's shoulders, stood up straight, took a deep breath and said, so quietly that Julia could hardly hear, 'Oh, damn, damn, damn!'

'What's the matter?'

'Why was he wearing the ring six weeks ago?'

'Habit, I suppose. He'd worn it for years until he came into the title when grandfather died. He hadn't got round to passing it on.'

'How did your grandfather die?'

'He fell off his horse. It was a bit of a surprise, since we all thought he was such a good rider, but at his age even a small fall can be deadly.'

'And he was also called Lord Bowland?'

'Of course. Why, Kit, what is this about?'

Kit started speaking rapidly and sincerely. 'Julia, I've made a terrible mistake, which I may regret till the day I die. And if things go really badly for me, that may be today. I have one chance. Will you help me?'

'Yes. With all my heart.'

'I don't need your heart, I need your horse. I've a long ride ahead of me. and I must go at once.'

'I rode Bess here. She's in Lady Fenton's stables.'

Kit raced downstairs, yelling for the horse to be saddled and brought round. She scribbled a note for her aunt:

Made a mistake. Bowland wore ring six weeks ago. Gone to his lodge.

When Bess appeared Kit mounted rapidly, pausing only to strap on her swordstick and a packet of food and water passed up by Desdemona.

'Julia, there's one more thing. I need the major's help. Get him to come to your brother's hunting lodge as soon as he can. He'll probably overtake me on the road. He must come armed, tell him that.'

'How can I do that?'

'You're a clever woman, you'll think of something. I don't care how you get him to come, but you must do it somehow. I stand a lot more chance of coming out of this alive if

Richard Lancaster is on my side.'

'Is it dangerous for him?'

'Oh, yes. But he's a hero; he won't mind.'

Julia still didn't say anything. Kit, made ruthless by her need, leaned down from the horse's back. She took Julia's hand in hers, and gazed soulfully into those grey eyes. 'Julia,' she breathed. 'I promise you. If I'm alive at the end of this I'll ask you to marry me — if you still want me.'

★   ★   ★

Kit wanted to urge Bess forward, but she knew that the mare would founder if she went too fast. So she rode through the suburbs of London at a sedate pace, at complete variance with the turmoil in her head and heart. Amid her fury at her mistake and her fear for Harry, there was joy at the knowledge that Richard Lancaster was an innocent man.

If only she'd been able to think clearly in the past few days! Of course Richard wasn't wearing the ring when George died. He wasn't the heir to the Bowland title until that point; George was. And she knew that George wasn't wearing it, because she'd have seen it. So it could only have been Bowland himself, keeping hold of it, perhaps out of reluctance to acknowledge George as his heir. That's why it was at Rundell and Bridge's — for re-sizing!

Stupid, stupid, *stupid* mistake!

I tried so hard to find a way to save both Harry and Richard, she thought, and there it was all the time. If only I'd listened to my heart — it kept on telling me that Richard wasn't a cold-blooded killer, but I ignored it.

My heart told me that Bowland was a villain, and I wouldn't listen to that either.

'Killing Lord Bowland — it's a hanging matter.' That's what George Lancaster said. He wasn't talking about what he planned to do to the new earl: he was talking about what he and Bowland had actually done to the old. She should have noticed two days ago, when Bowland had quoted the exact words, the same as Harry had told her. Not 'You want to kill Bowland,' the garbled version relayed by the constable, which was all he ought to have known had he not heard George Lancaster's last words himself.

But what could George have gained by the death of the old earl? She could see why he might have wanted to kill his brother, but why his grandfather? Then the evil of the plan hit her: it was one of mutual assistance. George had thought to gain Bowland's help in his own murder plan: after they'd killed their grandfather, to benefit Edward, they planned to kill Richard, to benefit George.

But Edward was even more of a villain than George: once he was safely Lord Bowland he had killed his accomplice.

Other pieces fell into place, little things that had puzzled her for weeks. The black cord they had found in George's bags at the Rose and Crown: now she knew what it was used for — stretching between two trees to upset the horse ridden by an old man whose sight was probably none too good.

And her drunken conversation with McTavish, when he told her about the young Edward, who hated being in debt, and would steal from servants rather than borrow.

Stealing wasn't enough now: he'd started to kill. He wasn't content with killing the old earl for his title and his cousin George to keep him quiet. He'd meant to kill Richard too. For if Richard was Bowland's heir, Bowland was also Richard's, and twenty thousand pounds a year would go far to restore the estates.

Once Richard's engagement to Julia became known, his danger increased: a wife, and children in the future, would have a prior claim on his estate. Bowland couldn't have afforded to let the marriage take place.

Perhaps there was an additional reason why

Kit Jackson had been chosen as Lucy's husband: to get the major's minion out of the way. She had saved his life once; perhaps more often, she reflected, though she hadn't realized it at the time; he had chosen to stay at home talking with her rather than going out where he would have been vulnerable to another attack. No wonder Bowland had taken such a dislike to her, which she'd put down to haughty contempt.

In the meantime he had been seeking more acceptable ways of increasing his fortune than murder: marriage. Kit wondered how long her aunt would live if she accepted his proposal. Well, at least she'd saved her aunt's life: that hurried scrawl she'd left was quite enough warning for Lady Fenton's quick brain.

Her mind went back to the time she had first met Lord Bowland. He had rushed out of the house, all attentiveness — and no surprise. He had known that he would see his cousin bleeding on the pavement. And the footpad, the one she had stabbed: Bowland had been very careful to bring him into the house, where he had conveniently died. She had wounded the man, but it had been Bowland who'd killed him.

Once Bowland had heard Harry's story by its roundabout route, he had the perfect way of killing his cousin. He just made sure that it looked like an attempt on himself that had gone wrong. So he hadn't hesitated to saw the axle of his phaeton when he knew the major was going to drive it. Even if the attempt was discovered, as had happened then, everyone would think that Bowland, not Lancaster, was the target.

At an inn outside London she stopped and gulped a glass of beer, and made sure Bess was watered. She resented every second not spent travelling, but she had to cherish the horse: they still had a long way to go. She pulled off her boot and emptied out the stones. She got odd looks from passers-by, but she didn't care. The relief from permanent discomfort and frequent pain was exquisite.

She knew she was too late to warn Harry: the meeting between him and Bowland had already taken place. She was bitterly aware that, because of her folly, the chances were that her brother was already dead. She had delivered him into the hands of a ruthless man who had killed three men: his grandfather, his cousin and a hired footpad. None of them was much loss to the world, she reflected, from all she could gather; the old earl and George Lancaster appeared to have been two of the most unpleasant men in creation. Come to think on it, the footpad may have been the best of the three.

But Bowland had planned to kill one of the two men she loved: did the other have much chance? There was always hope until she knew the worst. Perhaps Harry hadn't recognized him. Perhaps Bowland would think that the best thing to do with Harry was to hand him over to the law. Perhaps Harry had over-powered Bowland. There were a hundred perhapses, and she knew that she must do her best, however futile it might seem, to trust that one of them would save her brother.

She remounted and continued her journey. There was just one thing that still puzzled her: if Richard Lancaster was innocent, what had he meant by his anguished cry: 'The guilt! The bloody guilt'?

★   ★   ★

Kit reached the Rose and Crown in the late afternoon, heartsick that Lancaster had not caught her up. In expert hands like his, the phaeton and greys, four of the fastest horses in England, should have overtaken her long before.

What had happened to him? Had Julia failed to pass on the message? Had his carriage met with an accident? Or — dreadful thought — had he simply refused her plea for help? Could she blame him for not coming to her rescue, now he knew she was just a spy?

She left Bess at the Rose and Crown: the mare was so tired that to walk would be almost as fast as to ride, and a good deal more secret. 'Look after the horse,' she told the ostler. 'She's come a long way. And if I don't come back she belongs to Lady Julia Lancaster, Grosvenor Street.'

Like all country girls she was used to walking long distances, and three miles was little enough. Indeed, she would have enjoyed the walk in other circumstances: but not these.

When the lodge came into view she stopped and surveyed it. There was nobody in sight. She circled the house in the safety of the ruins of the cottages and the reeds that grew everywhere except immediately around the house, where there was nothing but short grass and a gravelled drive. There was no cover, and she couldn't approach unobserved unless she waited till dark.

It might have been wiser to be cautious, but Harry was in there, and for all she knew an hour might be the difference between life and death for him. There was just one hope. On one side of the house, where the chimney was, there were no windows on the ground floor. If someone was looking out of an upstairs window she would be seen, but perhaps they would all be downstairs.

She took a deep breath and stepped out into the open. She tried to appear like a country lad out for a ramble, looking around at the birds, swinging with a cane — really her swordstick — at the grass from time to time, and her mouth pursed in a soundless whistle. She couldn't give a real whistle if she'd wanted to: her mouth was far too dry.

But no cries of alarm came from the house, no blasts from a shotgun. She walked silently round the house till she reached a low window on the east, away from the light of the afternoon sun. She listened, but could hear nothing. Cautiously, she raised her head to peer in.

It was gloomy, and the panes were dirty, so at first she could see little. She was aware only that there were no shouts of discovery at her appearance at the window. Soon she made out the shapes of four men occupied in a card game: none of them Lord Bowland. Then a shaft of sunlight came through the window opposite and glowed brightly on a patch of red: Harry's hair.

He was lying on the ground. She saw with relief the ropes around his hands: nobody would tie up a dead man, would they? She studied the room as long as she dared, but could see no one else. Just four men on guard, and none of them any too watchful. She couldn't fight all of them: somehow she must deal with them one at a time. She had no gun, but the sword-stick was silent and fast. What she needed was a tactic that would get one of them out, but not all four.

She trod silently round to the stables. She would prefer to disable rather than kill, and she needed something other than a sword-stick. It didn't take long to make her favourite weapon: she took off one of her stockings and filled it with muddy sand.

There were five horses in the stables. One of them was Dan, Harry's favourite gelding, who whinnied softly and nuzzled her for the apple she'd often given him. 'Sorry to do this to you,' she said, smacking Dan hard on the rump, 'but I want you to make a noise.' Dan snorted and stamped, but he knew Kit and wouldn't protest too loudly.

She moved to another horse and whacked it sharply. A neigh rang out. There, that ought to bring someone, she thought. Nobody let their horses get upset without investigating. One whack for each horse: they whinnied at her unprovoked assault. She took up her position by the stable door, sword out, and waited for results.

She didn't have to wait long. The stable door opened and a man came in. 'What's up with you lot?' he asked. 'Come on, settle — ' He didn't finish. Not with the sharp point of a sword at his neck.

'Now, I'm quite happy to kill you,' said Kit in a voice as sinister and menacing as she could manage. 'But I've no wish to dirty my sword if I don't have to. Understand?'

'Understand,' he croaked. She recognized him: she'd last seen his face in the lamplight as she stood astride the body of Richard Lancaster. One of the footpads; Bowland had hired them then, and hired them again now.

'If you want to survive the next five minutes,' she said, 'you will do exactly what I say. Turn round.' He did exactly what she said. 'Right. Back to the house.'

'But they'll see you.'

'You'll have to hope they don't, my friend, because if that happens the first thing I do is get you out of the way.'

The man walked very, very carefully, back to the house, Kit's sword digging in his back. He didn't look round, so he didn't see her move the sword to her left hand and heft the weighted stocking in her right.

'Now call out; call just one of your friends. Not all three.'

'Bill, come out,' he croaked.

'Do better than that if you don't want those to be your last words.

'Hey, Bill,' he managed. 'Come outside!' That was enough. She brought the weighted stocking down on his head, and he slumped to the earth.

She raced over to the door of the lodge, hoping to greet the unknown Bill. But something about the man's cry must have warned the men inside, for two of them rushed out, followed by the third who carried a sword.

She recognized the two who came first: they were the other footpads who'd attacked Lancaster. The third was a stranger: an elderly man, who hung back waving his sword unimpressively.

The other two launched into the attack. Experienced street fighters, they split up fast, staying well out of range of Kit's sword. They had only long knives, but they knew how to use them, and there were two of them.

She dodged to the house where she could put a wall at her back. She held her sword lightly, ready to parry the first approach. Stalemate: she had the reach, but they had the strength and the numbers.

'It's that young shaver what turned up on the last job,' said one.

'So it is. The little bastard that killed Jacko.'

'We'll get you this time,' said the first. 'There ain't nobody gonna come when you call now.' He yelled out to the older man. 'Come 'ere, yer reverence, and bring that sticker with you.' Now they had the reach as well as the numbers, and she was about to be killed by a man in holy orders.

But then, out of the lodge, a sword gleaming in his hand, came Harry. 'Need any help?' he called.

It was no contest, for his reverence had no stomach for a fight and dropped his weapon, while the two street fighters' knives couldn't match the swords of Harry and Kit. In a few minutes the two footpads were lugging their unconscious colleague into the lodge. Four pairs of wrists, including the ordained ones of his reverence, were bound; and Harry and Kit exchanged news while they tied knots.

Kit had first to explain to the indignant Harry why she'd sent him to meet the very man he'd seen climbing out of George Lancaster's window. Then Harry told her how he'd come so opportunely to her rescue.

He had spent hours trying to loosen his bonds, and staring in frustration at a pair of swords hung on the wall of the lodge. He knew that he could use the blade to cut the ropes, given a few minutes alone. Once everyone rushed out he'd sawn the ropes on his wrist loose on the remaining sword, then come to claim his share of the fight.

The knots tied, they ran out of the door towards the stables. When they got there, Harry said, 'Just stand still a minute.'

Wondering at the delay, she did so. Then she found Harry's arms around her, hugging her close. 'Oh, Kitty,' he laughed. 'You're such a — such a right one!'

She hugged him back. 'We aren't out of danger yet. We must go!'

As they saddled two horses, Harry explained why Bowland hadn't killed him outright. 'He wants me to marry somebody. Said that if I did, he'd bribe a witness to say that I was outside the room at the Rose and Crown when the shot went off, and I'd be a free man — if you can call it free, being hitched up to a woman I've never met.'

'Did you agree, Harry?'

'There wasn't a lot of choice, when I had the point of his sword at my neck. That's why he's not here; he went to fetch her. But do you know who this female is?'

'Yes: I had a similar offer from him myself, believe it or not.'

'What's wrong with her that she needs

Bowland to find a husband for her?'

'She's a very lovely lady. There's just one small disadvantage: she's pregnant.'

'Ah! By Bowland himself. Wants someone else to make an honest woman of her, that it?'

'That's it, Harry. Charming man, isn't he?'

'He's got a bang-up rig, though,' said Harry with a touch of envy. 'Have you seen it? Four of the best looking greys I've ever seen.'

'So he's got them!' exclaimed Kit. 'They're borrowed; he sold them last week.' Was that why Major Lancaster hadn't arrived? But no; even the curricle and chestnuts should have brought him here by now.

'That takes face, borrowing someone else's team to go a-murdering.'

'They're one of the fastest teams in England,' said Kit, 'but they can't fly. That means we have plenty of time if he's got to go to London to fetch the lady and then come back again.'

'Ah, but he doesn't,' said a voice from the doorway that made them spin round in shock. They stared down the barrels of two pistols that pointed straight at their faces. 'I've always believed in planning, and Miss Maxwell was waiting at the Rose and Crown.'

Lord Bowland had returned.

12

Some hours before, while Kit was still riding through the London suburbs, Hamish McTavish answered the door of the major's house to Lady Julia. When he told her that the major was not at home, she practically had a fit of the vapours. 'Where is he? McTavish, this is desperate. Where is he?' she pleaded, but he could give her no answer.

McTavish had known her since she was a baby, and so he submitted to her demands to send the servants out looking for the major. But still there was still no sign of him. McTavish was a worried man, and Lady Julia was nearly frantic.

McTavish had a source of concern which he didn't communicate with the lady: he had seen the changes that had come over the major in the past few days.

Three days before, Hamish McTavish had opened the front door to let out a frightened young lassie in men's clothes. He had closed the door behind her, then turned to face his master, prepared for instant dismissal.

But it hadn't happened. 'You were right, McTavish, and thank God for it,' the major said slowly. 'I could not hold her against her will.' Then he added, puzzled, 'How long have you known about Mr Jackson?'

'Since I carried the lassie to her room with half a bottle of whisky inside her. I was drunk and all, but I was not stupid.' He wondered what he'd said to make the major wince.

'Do any of the other servants know?'

'Major Lancaster, have I ever blabbed aught that ye wished to keep secret?'

'No, you haven't. I don't need to ask you to keep this a secret too, do I?'

'Nae, ye dinna.'

That night the major hadn't drunk himself into a stupor. Indeed, he seemed remarkably happy considering that his young woman had literally run away from him. He was thoughtful rather than happy the next day, though he cheered up when McTavish passed on the news from the servants' hall that Mr Jackson had appeared at Lady Fenton's. 'Ah-ha! Of course! The needle!' he had exclaimed incomprehensibly.

After that, he started to lose his good humour, and the cloud became thicker and blacker with every hour. He hadn't started drinking again: McTavish almost wished he would, for at least they would have been on familiar ground. This morning he had stalked out of the house straight after breakfast, and hadn't been seen since. What with Lady Julia pacing up and down in the drawing-room, the house disrupted, and his own worries about the major's state of mind, McTavish wasn't a happy man.

At last a bellow echoed round the hallway. 'What the devil do you mean, Julia, upsetting my household like this?'

Unabashed at this brusque greeting, Julia rushed to her cousin and embraced him in relief. 'Thank goodness you're back, Richard. Where have you been?'

'If it's any concern of yours, Julia,' he said, taking her arm and ushering her up into the drawing-room, 'I was on Westminster Bridge watching the river, when I was accosted by a complete stranger who claimed the improbable name of Hamlet and asserted he was betrothed to my cook. He said you had sent everyone out looking for me. I always welcome your presence, but I hope you have something urgent to tell me.'

Julia felt the awkwardness of her position. She was about to ask a man who had proposed to her to risk his life going to the aid of another man, who had also promised to marry her. 'Um, Richard,' she said, smiling up at him as charmingly as she could. 'You know you have said that you would do anything for me?'

'Yes,' he said reluctantly.

'Would you — would you risk your life for me?'

There was a pause. 'Yes, Julia, I believe I would.'

'And would you do something for my happiness, even though it would bring you pain?'

There was an even longer pause before he answered. 'I think you had better tell me what this is about, Julia.'

The honourable thing to do would be to tell him that she wouldn't marry him before she asked him to risk his life for her, but she dared not risk it. 'There is someone who is in danger, and he needs your help.'

'Who is it?'

'Will you promise to help him if I tell you?'

'What am I letting myself in for? Very well, I promise. Now, who is it?'

'Kit Jackson.'

'What!' he exploded. 'Why the devil didn't you say so at first instead of havering about and wasting all this time? Where is he?'

'He's going to the Vicarage — Edward's lodge.'

He turned away from her and ran out into the hall. 'McTavish! John!' he yelled. 'Get the greys and the phaeton. No, damn it, Edward's borrowed 'em. It'll have to be the chestnuts and the curricle, then. Fast as you can!' He turned back to Julia. 'Tell me more: why is Edward's hunting lodge dangerous for Kit?'

'I don't know. As he ran off he said that he mightn't get out alive, and he stood a better chance if you were there. Come armed, he said.'

'Armed?' He ran to his room, returning with a brace of pistols. 'Have you no idea of the danger?' he asked urgently. 'Think, Julia, think!'

'No. Edward's there, I know that. It's not part of this business about someone killing Edward, is it?'

'I don't know. What made Kit dash off like that?'

'It was something I said. I don't under-stand it. I was talking — '

But she had no time to finish, for the curricle had been brought round. Lancaster hesitated, torn between his desire to get moving and his need to learn more from Julia. But he couldn't wait any longer: every second mattered. He raced to the curricle outside.

'Not you, John,' he told the groom, who climbed down from the seat with hardly a word of protest as he saw his master's determination.

'I'm going even if your groom is not,' said Julia, equally determined. 'You needn't worry,' she said to her own groom. 'I'm accompanying my guardian.'

'No, you're not,' said the major. 'It's dangerous.'

'I can't stay here when the man I love is in danger. And you need me to help you work out what's going on.'

Much as he hated to admit it, she spoke the truth. 'All right, I'll take you. But I'll put you down at the Rose and Crown, where you'll be safe.' He hoisted her up beside him and they were off.

He couldn't talk as they sped through the busy streets of London. But when the road opened up and they bowled along with less traffic, he turned to her and said, 'What did you mean back then, Julia, when you talked about the man you love being in danger?'

Julia was caught. She ought to tell him: she wasn't used to lying to him. But if she did, would he turn round and go straight back? No, he would not. He had promised, and never in her life had he broken a promise to her.

'Richard,' she began awkwardly. 'You remember you asked me to marry you three days ago?'

'It's not the sort of thing that slips a man's

mind,' he said drily.

'Would you be — I mean, would it hurt you terribly if — if I said no?'

She peeked shyly at him, then stared openly. It wasn't grief or anger that was written on his face: it looked very like relief. And when he said, 'No, Julia. I think I can bear the pain,' she could have sworn he was trying not to laugh.

'As your guardian, then, if not your betrothed husband,' he managed to say coolly enough after a few moments, 'may I ask who he is, the man you love?'

'Do I need to tell you?' she asked.

'I have a disconcerting suspicion that it's Kit Jackson.'

'Why disconcerting?' she stormed. 'What's wrong with him? I know he's poor and lame, but he's brave and intelligent and handsome.'

'I grant you all that and more. Nevertheless, Kit Jackson is not the man for you.'

'Oh, Richard, he is. And I'm going to marry him.'

'Don't you have to wait till he asks you?'

'But he has.'

'What? I don't believe it!'

'Well, he said he will if I still want him — if he gets out of this alive.'

'You are an unscrupulous little minx, Julia. You have brought me out, when I had proposed to you, to save the man you really want to marry!'

'You don't seem put out about not marrying me!' she retorted, nettled.

'Lucky for me, isn't it?'

'Well, why did you propose to me, then?'

'It seemed like a good idea at the time,' he answered unsatisfactorily. 'But you're right. It'd be a mistake.'

'I love you very much, Richard. But only as my big brave cousin, not as a husband. I don't think we would be happy together. We have too much in common.'

Julia had no idea why that remark provoked such a gale of laughter.

★   ★   ★

Soon they were well on the way to the Rose and Crown. The chestnuts were familiar with the road and needed little attention, so Lancaster and Julia had plenty of time to toss around ideas about Mr Jackson's odd behaviour. 'Tell me again exactly what Kit said to you before he ran off,' he asked.

'We were talking about you, in fact, and I said how well you were looking, and wasn't it nice that you could wear the Lancaster ring.'

'There's something about that ring,' he

said, to himself more than Julia. 'What happened next?'

'Then I said that it was the first time you'd worn it, and that's when he became agitated. He wanted to know who wore it six weeks ago.'

'And you told him Edward, of course.'

'Yes. And he said something about making a terrible mistake, which he'd regret for the rest of his life.'

'So the mistake is about the ring,' he said, lost in thought. 'Kit made a terrible mistake because sh — because he thought I wore the ring six weeks ago when it was really Edward. Does that sound right?'

'Yes. But why? What happened six weeks ago?'

One of the finest whips in England hauled on the reins like an utter novice, and even the good-tempered chestnuts protested. So did Julia, but he shushed her as he worked it out. 'It's what she thought,' he said. 'Her brother must have told her — and then she saw it — and she thought I was — and that's why she fainted — but it was really Edward — so then she knew — Oh, damn, damn, damn!'

'What's the matter?' Julia asked. 'Who's she? What brother? Who fainted? What was really Edward?'

He didn't answer. He turned to her and

took her hand, as tenderly as he'd ever done in her life. 'Julia, I wish to God you hadn't come. If my suspicions are right, and I very much hope they aren't, it's going to be exceedingly unpleasant.'

★   ★   ★

It was exceedingly unpleasant for Kit and Harry, sitting on the floor of the lodge, facing pistols held in the unwavering hands of two men they had tied up not twenty minutes before, who weren't going to let Kit and Harry escape again after the tongue-lashing that Bowland had dished out. Reverend Marcus Fazakerley had settled himself in one corner with a bottle, and the other footpad, the one that Kit had knocked out, was groaning as he regained consciousness.

There was a consolation: they weren't in immediate danger, for Lucy Maxwell was present. Bowland had brought her, and Kit didn't believe that Lucy, besotted though she was, would permit him to commit murder in front of her.

'I don't understand,' Lucy was saying to Bowland. 'Why are you holding Mr Jackson and the other man prisoner?'

'Lucy, will you trust me?' Bowland asked.

'Of course, Edward,' she replied with dignity.

'Just believe me when I say that these men are a danger to me — for the moment. If I don't keep guard on them, you will not be married.'

'Why not? Why should they stop our marriage?'

Poor Lucy, thought Kit. She doesn't know what's going on. He has lured her here believing that she is to marry him, not that he is to force her on a stranger.

'Lucy, my love,' Bowland continued, 'I've done you harm, serious harm. I hate being in debt: I must make amends for it in the only way I can.'

Lucy had tears in her eyes. 'You will marry me as a duty, not because you love me. You don't want to marry me.'

'No, my love. That isn't true. I love you, and I want to marry you, but you know how I am situated. You know I've no money. I cannot afford to marry you, Lucy. If my plans had gone aright, I should have had a fortune.'

Yes, thought Kit bitterly, if you'd succeeded in murdering the major.

'But now I must marry money, since I have none.'

'But what of me?' Lucy burst out passionately. 'What of the child I am carrying? Will you make your first-born child a bastard?'

'No, Lucy, I shall not — and that's why I've brought you here this evening. I misled you when I said you would be married here: you will, but not to me.'

'What?' she gasped.

'This gentleman,' he said, pointing to Harry, ' — and he is a gentleman: a squire with a comfortable estate — has agreed to marry you.'

She stared at Harry incredulously. 'Is this true, sir?' Harry blushed and nodded. 'And why, pray?' she asked.

Harry looked around in despair. The pistol was still pointing straight at him.

Lucy's face blazed. 'Edward, you must be mad if you think I would be content with a man I've never met, who is marrying me in preference to having his head blown off.'

Bowland snapped his fingers. 'I'm a fool,' he muttered. 'Excuse me, Lucy.'

He strode over to where Kit and Harry sat, and squatted down. 'Listen, Jackson,' he hissed. 'Did your brother tell you what I'd offered him to marry Miss Maxwell?'

'His life, and a witness to show he was innocent of murdering George Lancaster, is that it?' she replied.

'The offer's open to you too, Jackson. I've

the marriage licence made up, and I can write your name in rather than your brother's. Fazakerley's not the sort to quibble at that before he marries you. Lucy knows you: she likes you. I asked you before, and you refused me. I ask again. This estate will be yours and Lucy's, and you'll also gain your brother's life and freedom.'

'What if she doesn't want me?'

'Then you two are in trouble. A man wanted for murder, and his associate.'

'You daren't hand us over to the law with what we know,' she said.

'You're right, Jackson, but there are other alternatives. Let me make myself clear. Before dawn tomorrow, you will be either a married man or a dead one.'

'You're remarkably persuasive, my lord.'

'Kit!' Harry exclaimed. 'No!'

'Have you got a better idea?' she asked him. 'You were willing to marry her, but it's better in every way for me to do it. In *every* way.'

'Indeed, Faulkner,' Bowland agreed. 'If you have a fancy to see the sun rise tomorrow, you had better wish your brother success in courting Miss Maxwell.'

Kit stood up. One of the men with a pistol made to follow her.

'My lord,' she declared firmly. 'I shall do

my best, but I shall not do my wooing in front of your bully boy here. You have a hostage for my obedience: give me and Miss Maxwell some peace.'

She was allowed to take Lucy aside to an old chest which served as a seat in the corner where there was what little privacy the hall provided. She told herself that it was the best way out, far better than she could have hoped only that morning. Neither of the men she loved would hang. She would have to keep up her masquerade for a lot longer than she'd planned, but so what? And Lord Bowland would get away with murder, but was that so bad? She didn't want anyone to go to the gallows for killing George Lancaster, not even Bowland. She could find a way of warning the major about his cousin's murderous intentions — but only if she were alive.

And all she had to do for it was deceive a woman who'd already been cruelly deceived.

Lucy sat beside her looking at her warily. Where shall I begin? Kit wondered. I've never had to propose marriage before, and these aren't the most auspicious circumstances. But I can't see any better way out of it. If only Richard Lancaster had come when I asked him! 'Believe me, I understand what it is to be abandoned by the man you love, Miss Maxwell,' she began with sincerity.

'Edward hasn't abandoned me,' Lucy protested.

'I have to tell you, Miss Maxwell, that Lord Bowland has proposed marriage to Lady Fenton.'

'No! I don't believe it!' Lucy tried to cling to her happy fantasy for one last second. Kit didn't say another word: no words were necessary.

It sank home at last to Lucy that she was just another foolish girl, seduced and deserted. 'Oh, what am I to do?' She leaned against Kit's shoulder and cried.

Kit looked over to where Bowland sat unmoving. If I were a man, Kit thought, she would be much better off with me than with him. How is it that a nice woman like Lucy can love such a serpent? She remembered Dr Johnson's words: *There is no man so vile, that a woman or a dog will not love him.*

At length Lucy's tears abated. 'But what am I to do?' she cried again.

'You could marry someone else.'

'Who? That man over there with a pistol to his head? Who is he, anyway?'

'He is my brother, Miss Maxwell.'

'Your brother? What's he doing here, and why is that man of Edward's pointing a pistol at him?'

Kit realized that telling Lucy the whole

truth about the man she loved would be futile: Lucy simply wouldn't believe her. But part of the truth might help. 'You may have heard the scandal,' she began. 'His name is Harry Faulkner, and he is accused of a murder that he did not commit.'

'I remember,' said Lucy, interested for a moment in somebody else's problems. 'It was George Lancaster, Edward's cousin.'

'That's right. My brother is innocent, but he can't prove it. Lord Bowland has — er — found a witness who'll swear to Harry's innocence. That's his reward if he marries you.'

'So it isn't a pistol that Edward threatens him with, but the noose.'

'Yes.'

'I am sorry for your brother, and I would save him if I could, but I cannot marry a man I've never met.'

'Would you marry a man you had met?' asked Kit, feeling like a worm.

'You mean . . . '

'I mean me, Miss Maxwell.'

'To save your brother's life?'

'Yes.'

'And to give my child a father,' mused Lucy.

'Indeed,' said Kit, feeling lower than a worm.

'But I don't love you, and you don't love me.'

'I like you, Miss Maxwell, and you, I believe, like me.'

'Yes, I do. But that's not enough.'

Kit stood up. 'So my brother will die for a crime committed by — ' she stopped herself in time ' — someone else,' she finished feebly.

'Mr Jackson, I can see why you'd sacrifice your happiness for your brother: I have a brother too. And I'm tempted by your offer if for no other reason than to stop Charlie challenging Edward, and either killing or being killed by him.'

'It would be no sacrifice. There would be advantages for both of us.'

She could see Lucy was hesitating, so she took a step further. 'What have you to lose? I promise you, once my brother is cleared, if you wish I shall disappear in such a way that you can have me declared dead.'

'You would?'

'There will be no trace of me: you can be a widow, free to remarry. Or, if you wish, you can stay a wife, with all the advantages that brings — and none of the duties,' she added meaningfully.

'You mean — marital relations?' Lucy blushed.

'I shall make no demands on you.'

'But — would you not want to — how can I trust you?'

'You may trust me absolutely on that score.'

'No man is to be trusted on that score.'

'A man like me is. My desires do not lie in that direction.'

Lucy looked at Kit in surprise. 'Oh, you mean — like Hector Smythe?'

'Something like that,' Kit admitted.

'So, a marriage of convenience,' Lucy said thoughtfully. 'You wouldn't reproach me for being hopelessly in love with another man?'

'How could I, Miss Maxwell? For so am I.'

⋆　⋆　⋆

The curricle drew into the yard of the Rose and Crown. Lancaster leaped out and handed Julia down as the landlord bustled up, promising plenty of rooms and a woman to wait on her. 'Julia, this is where you stay. Out of harm's way.'

'Since none of our family has ever died at Edward's lodge, and George was killed in the Rose and Crown only six weeks ago, I don't entirely follow your reasoning,' she said icily.

'Don't follow my reasoning: just follow my orders.'

'Why should I?'

'First, because I am your guardian; second, because you begged me to come; and third, because we are wasting time,' he said overbearingly.

There was nothing she could do. 'Thank God I'm not marrying you!'

'I wouldn't dream of replying to that, Julia,' Lancaster called as he leaped aboard his curricle. 'Wish me luck!' And he was gone.

'If only there was a way I could follow,' she fretted. For Julia was not a country girl, and she would no more have walked the three miles to the lodge unaccompanied than she would have flown. Reluctantly, she began to make her way to the room that was ready for her, fuming at her impotence.

But suddenly it seemed as though an angel appeared. A very dirty angel, who said, 'Lady Julia Lancaster?'

'Yes?'

'Got your'orse in the stable. Gentleman said as it belonged to you.'

Bess! The answer to her prayers! She was still dressed for riding from the morning. Bess was brought out for her. The mare had had a rest and a good feed, and, though not fresh, at least wouldn't find three miles much difficulty.

Julia ordered a side-saddle, and mounted with the aid of an ostler, who looked dubiously at her as she prepared to set out alone. 'It's only to my brother's hunting lodge,' she said, declining his offer of a lad to go with her. She set off, not entirely sure what she hoped to achieve once she got to the lodge. She just knew that, whatever the danger, she wouldn't let the man she loved face it alone.

About a quarter of a mile from the lodge, she found her cousin's curricle abandoned, and a snort from Bess was answered by the chestnuts quietly munching grass in the field next to the track. There was no sign of Richard. Perhaps he's decided to go ahead on foot, she thought. She would not. She didn't believe she had anything to fear. But something gave her a feeling of unease, enough to make her stop once she turned the corner to the lodge.

Everything seemed to be normal. The lodge had never been welcoming, but it didn't appear alarming. Still, both Kit and Richard had believed there was some danger in the place. Julia wished someone was outside, even that awful man Fazakerley who kept the place up.

She rode directly to the stables, unconsciously avoiding the noisy gravel on the drive, and stabled Bess. Once outside she stood irresolutely. Away from the noise of horses she heard something that she'd missed before.

There were voices coming from the old church.

* * *

The marriage service, thought Harry. And the oddest wedding I shall ever go to. Kitty promised me never to marry a man she didn't love, but I never expected her to marry a woman she doesn't love.

Bowland had insisted that they all, captives and captors alike, go to the church and take their places as though they were a proper congregation.

Lucy and Kit stood together at the front, facing Reverend Fazakerley, who was just sober enough to stand upright and to remember the words. He began to intone the familiar phrases. 'Dearly beloved, we are gathered here . . . '

Harry was aware of a movement out of the corner of his eye. Was there someone darting past one of the windows towards the back of the church? Everyone else had their backs to the window except the vicar, and he was so drunk he could hardly see the couple before him. Harry faced the front determinedly. If there was anyone out there, it was as likely to be friend as foe, and Harry didn't want to draw attention to a possible ally.

Before the cobwebbed altar, Kit was asked to declare any impediment to a marriage between her and Lucy. She didn't declare a thing.

The vicar asked those there gathered if they knew any just and lawful impediment why this man and this woman should not be joined together in holy matrimony. Harry didn't declare a thing, either.

But then, from the back of the church, a voice rang out. 'Stop the wedding!'

Harry turned; the most beautiful woman he had ever seen stood there, the door framing her like a picture.

'Julia!' gasped Bowland. 'What are you doing here?'

'Stopping a wedding, Edward.' The beautiful woman stepped forward. 'I don't know why Kit and Lucy are getting married: I'm only sure that neither of them wants to.'

'A marriage under compulsion, is it?' said the priest, as though he hadn't seen the pistol held at Harry's back. 'Really, I cannot reconcile my conscience to that, my lord. Not, at any rate, for less than twice the fee we agreed earlier.'

'Nonsense, Julia,' said Bowland, ignoring the mutterings of the minister. 'Of course they wish to get married.'

'They surely do, Edward,' snapped Julia. 'But not to each other. Lucy wants to marry you, and Kit — ' She walked down the aisle to her betrothed and took Kit's arm. 'Kit has promised to marry me.'

'What?' her brother exploded. 'You can't be serious, Julia! A penniless cripple like Jackson?'

'A previous engagement, eh?' murmured the priest. 'Three times the fee.'

Kit said nothing.

'You promised to marry me only this morning, Kit,' Julia said. 'Why are you doing this?'

'Er — ' said Kit, wondering frantically how to get out of this. Julia's unexpected arrival would stop Bowland from killing them, at least for the moment, but it wouldn't stop him handing Harry over to the law, unprotected by a bribed witness. 'I — er — it's because — ' she stalled for time to think.

Then there came the voice that changed everything. 'I presume the gun at this young man's back might have something to do with it.'

It was, at last, Major Richard Lancaster.

★ ★ ★

298

He leaned nonchalantly against the doorpost, pointing a pistol almost idly at the man who was threatening Harry. 'Henry Faulkner, isn't it?' he asked. 'I think you may relieve the gentleman behind you of his gun.'

Harry didn't need telling twice.

Kit saw that Bowland, whose face had whitened for a second, had managed to pull himself together. 'Good evening, Richard. Do you often arrive at weddings with a pistol in your hand?'

'It is, I grant, unusual — but then, so is the wedding. You know, it's old-fashioned of me, but I do have a few scruples about waving guns around in a church. Shall we all go to the lodge?'

It wasn't a suggestion: it was a command.

Kit had to restrain herself from dancing as she helped Harry shepherd the three cut-throats back to the lodge, and then tie them up in yet another reversal of fortunes. This time, in respect of his age and his cloth, Reverend Fazakerley was not tied: he immobilized himself instead behind a bottle of brandy.

'Impressive-looking fellow, Major Lancaster, isn't he?' said Harry. 'Glad he's on our side.'

'Me too,' agreed Kit whole-heartedly. She hadn't any idea how the major would do it, but she had complete faith that he would somehow solve everything.

'How could you be such a goose as to think he was the murderer?'

Kit stared indignantly at her brother, opened her mouth, then shut it again. It would take much too long to explain. She remained silent while they finished tying the last knots.

'Richard,' cried Julia, looking about her in confusion. 'Do you know what this is about? Why was Kit marrying Lucy?'

The major, who had been watching everything from the doorway of the lodge, came forward: he dominated the room. That raw power Kit had seen in him at first, that had disappeared with familiarity, had returned. As before, it was as though he was the only living person in the room and everyone else was a shadow.

'A good question, Julia,' he said. 'What kind of man are you, Mr Jackson, that you promise marriage to two young ladies on the same day?'

'A very unusual one, Major.'

'I'll agree with you there, Mr Jackson. And you, sir,' he said to Fazakerley. 'What kind of minister are you, that you will perform a marriage ceremony here, with a couple whom you know to be unwilling?'

'A very thirsty one,' said Fazakerley, full of Dutch courage.

'What kind of man are you, I might ask, Richard,' Bowland interrupted crossly, 'that when I've gone to the considerable trouble of capturing your brother's murderer, you set him free and put a pistol in his hand?'

'On the contrary, Edward. I rather think that I am the one who has captured my brother's murderer, don't you agree?' His pistol was pointing straight at Bowland's heart.

'Richard!' Kit heard Julia's cry. 'What are you doing?'

'I told you, Julia. I wish to God you hadn't come. But now you are here you must listen to the story.'

'What story? What are you talking about?'

'Julia,' the major began, 'you haven't taken much notice of the young man with red hair who is gazing at you with such obvious admiration.' (Harry went scarlet.) 'His name is Henry Faulkner, and he has been accused of murdering George. He is also, by the bye, Mr Jackson's brother. Mr Faulkner, I've been wanting to meet you for some time. I wonder if you would cast your mind back six weeks and tell us what you heard when you were outside my brother's room at the Rose and Crown.'

Harry told how he had gone to George Lancaster's room, and what he had heard while he was outside.

'And then you entered,' Lancaster continued for him. 'You saw my brother, dead or dying on the floor, a pistol beside him. Out of the window was climbing a man — who was wearing a very unusual ring.'

There was a gasp from Julia. 'No!'

'I'm afraid so, Julia,' Lancaster continued. 'It was this ring, wasn't it?' He held out his hand for Harry to see.

'That's right,' said Harry as he looked at it. 'But I don't understand. You're not the man I saw.'

'Who is?'

'He is.' He pointed at Bowland, but he didn't need to. Julia had already withdrawn from her brother in horror; Lucy had already rushed to him in sympathy.

'I deny it, of course,' said Bowland smoothly. 'And I think you'll find that the word of an earl is worth more than that of a fugitive accused of murder.'

'You had better tell the truth, Edward,' Lancaster said, the pistol still pointed at his cousin's heart.

'Or?'

'Or I shall kill you,' said the major coolly.

The silence stretched out.

Then Bowland smiled thinly. 'No, I don't think you will, Richard. I don't think you have what it takes to shoot me down in cold blood.'

He's right, Kit thought. Richard Lancaster is not a cold-blooded killer and never has been.

Lancaster said nothing for a second. Then he acted. 'Here,' he said, handing the pistol to Harry. He picked up the swords that had been left lying on the floor, walked over to Bowland, and presented him with the choice of weapons.

'Shall we call it a wager? If I beat you, you write a signed confession.'

'What, put my head in the noose?'

'No. You hand it to Mr Faulkner here, who uses it in his own defence. Then you simply walk down the track to the river, where you may take a ship to anywhere you please.'

'A penniless exile?'

'A live exile.'

'And if I beat you?'

'I'll be out of the way and you may do what you wish.'

'What!' Bowland laughed scornfully. 'When you've given the guns to Faulkner? He'd shoot me the moment you were down.'

'He's quite right, sir,' said Harry apologetically. 'But there is someone here whom you both trust, isn't there?'

'Who?' said Bowland. 'Reverend Fazaker-ley? My cousin isn't a fool.'

Harry didn't say a word. He gathered up the pistols, and walked slowly across the room. He stopped and faced Julia. 'I've never met you before, madam,' he said formally. 'But both of these men trust you. Will you stand guard over the guns, and see fair play?'

He was right. Julia, who loved both of them, was the only person who could do it. 'Yes,' she said unhesitatingly, and took the pistols.

'What do you mean by bringing a woman into it?' Bowland exclaimed. 'They can't be trusted with weapons!'

'On the contrary,' said Lancaster, as he stripped down to his shirt and prepared to fight. 'The bravest person here is a woman. Isn't she, Kit?' Kit didn't feel at all brave, but she managed a smile.

'I can't bear it!' cried Lucy. She rushed up to Bowland and threw her arms around him.

'Don't worry, my love,' said Bowland, his voice surprising Kit with its tenderness. 'He won't kill me. He doesn't want me dead.' For a moment he held her in his arms and kissed her, then handed her to Kit. 'Look after her, Jackson.'

Who'll look after me? thought Kit, who

also wanted to be held and kissed by the man she loved before he fought a duel. She had to be content with the way he came over to her, put a hand on her shoulder, and said, 'It's nearly over, Kit. And then . . . ' He didn't say anything more to her but quietly stepped away. 'Ready, Edward?'

The sun was setting, and a shaft of light shone through one window. Lancaster and Bowland stood *en garde*. The red light from the window shone on them: the swords glinted, and their bodies were illuminated scarlet.

Lucy was trembling, her hand on Kit's arm. Harry stood beside the cut-throats, who were unable to move. Reverend Marcus Fazakerley was mumbling something to himself, conceivably a prayer. Julia was alone, one pistol in her hand, the others on the floor at her feet.

Then steel clashed on steel, and the fight began.

Kit could see they were evenly matched in strength and skill; no surprise, she thought, since they'd probably had the same fencing master.

Bowland lunged: Lancaster parried easily. Again, and again Lancaster defended himself. For a fraction of a second Bowland's guard was down — but Lancaster didn't press home. Kit realized then what an immense advantage Bowland had. Lancaster did not wish to kill him, indeed, couldn't kill him, or even disable him, since Lancaster needed his cousin to sign a confession.

But Bowland wanted Lancaster dead.

There was a pause, while both men heaved and panted. 'You really do want to kill me don't you, Edward?'

'Oh, yes, Richard. I really do want to kill you. I've always wanted to kill you, ever since we were boys.'

'But why? What had I ever done to you?'

'You were rich, and I was poor.' Bowland's handsome face was lined with hatred. 'And how you loved being generous! You'd leave your breeches with money in the pockets so I could take it. Weren't you a kind child? For years, it's been your money supporting my sister. When you joined the colours, I thought that was the answer to my prayers. But you survived, damn you!'

Lancaster stepped back, appalled. He had liked his cousin, and thought Edward liked him in return. It was as if he had opened a door into a room which he thought he knew, only to find it full of snakes and scorpions.

'The French didn't kill you, so I shall,' said Bowland as he saw his chance in his opponent's shock at his words.

He broke through the major's guard, and his sword drove straight towards the heart, ripping through the shirt, which suddenly and sickeningly turned red. Only a desperate leap sideways saved Lancaster's life.

Lancaster defended, then fought on. But they could all see that he was weakening. He was losing a lot of blood: there was a pool of it, spreading red on the floor.

In horror, Kit knew she had to face it: the unbelievable was happening. There would be no happy ending. The major was losing. He wasn't going to sort everything out.

He was going to die.

13

Lancaster's head was spinning from loss of blood and he knew he had only a few moments of consciousness left. He had to win. Not just for himself, though life was sweet now and he would hate to leave it, when he was so close to the greatest happiness of all. And he had to win in the next few seconds, or they would be the last seconds he would ever know.

Then, from years of military experience, he knew how he might do it. He gave ground slightly, and Bowland pressed forward. Again Lancaster moved back, this time sideways, and again the other man followed. Another step, and Bowland was standing in the pool of blood, his face red in the light of the sunset.

The major had his enemy exactly where he wanted.

Bowland lunged: Lancaster parried and made the riposte, with little strength left for defence. If this failed, he would die in any case.

Bowland smiled almost pleasantly as he calculated how best to deliver the death stroke. He had so many choices. He was dazzled by last of the sunlight, but it did not worry him, now he was within seconds of killing the man he had hated so long. He moved easily, contemptuously avoiding the other man's attack.

But the attack suddenly altered as Lancaster's sword struck downwards, towards his leg. Bowland stepped back rapidly; and he slipped — slipped in the blood that he'd drawn himself, where the major had lured him. He fell crashing to the ground.

'My game, I think,' said Lancaster, his sword at Bowland's throat.

'Luck, pure luck,' sneered Bowland.

'No, Edward, Napoleonic tactics. Lure the enemy onto bad ground, and launch a surprise attack.' He swayed slightly, then looked around, 'Will someone oblige my cousin with pen and paper? He has some writing to do.'

His eyes found Kit. There was a moment between them, a moment of unspoken celebration which they shared with no one else.

She saw him stagger: that was why he turned his back on his fallen enemy and reached for a chair. But as he did, Bowland jumped up, a sword in his hand and murder on his face.

'No, Edward!' cried Julia. She raised the pistol and fired.

He whirled round and stared at her incredulously. 'You shot at me!'

'I didn't hit you, did I?' Julia asked anxiously.

Then his face changed, and he laughed. 'Oh, Julia, I'm going to miss you when I'm in exile.' It was the first time Kit had seen him laugh. It transformed him, and despite everything he had done to her and the men she loved, she began to understand what Lucy saw in him.

But Kit had no more time to spare as she darted over to Lancaster, who was sitting grey-faced. She held him to keep him from falling, and he leaned his head heavily against her body. 'My God, Kit,' he gasped. 'That was close.'

She gently eased off his shirt. The wound still poured blood. She rolled the shirt into a pad, and pressed it on the wound to try to staunch the flow.

'I'll do that,' said Harry's voice behind her. 'You get some bandages.'

'You get the bandages. I don't want to let up the pressure on this pad.'

'Your brother's right,' Lancaster said quietly. 'You shouldn't be doing this.'

'Oh, stop fussing, both of you,' she said.

'I've seen blood before.'

Harry had been aware that his sister had been living in the major's household, but he hadn't realized what it meant in terms of the obvious intimacy between them. He was disturbed and a little shocked. 'You know what I mean, Kitty — er — Kit,' he whispered.

'I've seen his bare chest before, too,' Kit said, disturbing Harry even more.

'Your sister's a remarkable woman, Mr Faulkner,' said Lancaster in a voice so quiet that nobody else could hear it. 'You don't need to worry about her.'

Kit didn't understand that remark. Harry did: it reassured him immensely.

Julia settled the argument: she brought the bandages. 'You'll excuse me if I don't stay,' she said, paling at the blood. Harry took them from her before Kit had a chance, and efficiently bound up the major's wound.

Bowland finished writing his confession. Lancaster, his wound dressed, picked it up and read it aloud. ''I, Edward Lancaster, Earl of Bowland, confess that I killed my cousin George Lancaster'. Rather short, is it not?'

'It's what we agreed to. It should satisfy you.'

There was a voice from the doorway: 'It certainly satisfies me.' It was Constable Webb, who walked in holding a blunderbuss. 'I'll take that, if you please, Major Lancaster.' He put his hand out for the confession.

Lancaster, helpless in the face of the law, had no choice but to pass it over. 'I'd be interested to know what brought you here, Constable,' he said.

'I've got eyes, and I use 'em. I've kept 'em on this place for a long time, and as soon as I hear of these three bits of gallows-meat,' he said, indicating the cut-throats, 'I knew murder was in the air. Well known round these parts, ain't you?' He pointed to Reverend Fazakerley with contempt. 'D'you know what they call this villain? Fit-'em Fazakerley, the quicker vicar. Marry you to a plaster statue if you pay 'im enough.' He turned to the unfortunate priest. 'Did you believe as I didn't know what was going on here? I turn me back on christening a few bastards and marrying a few runaways, but murder's different.' He smiled grimly. 'Look a fair treat on our gallows, you will, all five of you.' He pointed his blunderbuss at Bowland. 'Come on, your lordship. You'll be the first earl I've ever had in my lock-up. I understand the nobility gets hung with a silken rope.'

All the while he was speaking, nobody twitched. They all kept their eyes firmly on

312

the constable: a considerable feat, since every one of them wanted desperately to watch Kit glide round the room, a weighted stocking in her hand.

'It seems you was telling the truth after all, Mr Faulkner,' added the constable affably. 'By the way, where's that sister of yours?'

She was right behind him. 'Sorry,' she said as she knocked him out again.

'Why did you do that, Jackson?' asked Bowland. 'It wasn't for my sake.'

'Oh, yes, it was, my lord,' she said, grinning predatorily. 'You'll be in debt to me for the rest of your life. I couldn't wish for a better revenge.'

'Edward, you must go!' cried Julia.

'I can afford a few minutes to do something I should have done long since.' He went to Lucy and took her hand gently. 'I don't know why, but you appear to love me. I can offer you nothing but disgrace and poverty-stricken exile. Will you share it with me?'

Lucy nodded, half smiling, half crying.

What some women will endure to be a countess, thought Kit cynically.

Lucy turned to her. 'You will forgive me if I prefer him to you?'

'Of course,' said Kit. 'He is, after all, the

better man. I wish you joy from the bottom of my heart.'

'I only wish you could find the joy I have, Mr Jackson.' She glanced at the major and shook her head in knowing sympathy. 'But you never will.'

Bowland too turned to Kit. 'You'll pass on my apologies to Lady Fenton, Jackson, in the circumstances.'

'Don't feel guilty about jilting her, my lord. She wasn't going to accept you anyway. Lady Fenton is a good judge of character.' She smiled at him unamiably.

Bowland ignored her and spoke to the vicar. 'Well, Reverend Fazakerley, it seems you'll earn a fee after all. You have the licence?'

Fazakerley nodded. 'Get over to the church fast,' he said. Lucy and Bowland obeyed. 'And we need witnesses,' he added to the room in general.

'Shall we, Julia?' asked Lancaster. She nodded, and they went to the church.

Fazakerley walked with great dignity to the old chest and brought out a leather bag that chinked metallically. 'I shan't be back again,' he said to Harry. 'No hard feelings, I hope?' Harry shook his head. 'And you, young sir,' he said to Kit. 'I wish you better luck next time you get married.' He staggered off.

Bowland and Lucy were already at the altar when he arrived, and Julia and Lancaster were standing near one of the pews. Fazakerley strode manfully to the front. 'I think you want my fastest ceremony, my lord?'

'Certainly, Mr Fazakerley.'

'Right,' he said, swaying gently. 'Do either of you know any reasons why you shouldn't get wed? Good. Anybody else know any? Good. Do you take her to be your wife, no matter what?'

'I do.'

'Do you take him to be your husband, no matter what?'

'I do.'

'Right, you're wed. Sign here, and that'll be twenty guineas.'

★ ★ ★

In the lodge, Kit picked up one of the swords and went over to the three tied-up men. 'Turn round,' she said.

'Don't kill us,' pleaded one.

'I won't, you fool. I'm setting you free.' She cut their bonds. 'Now, get out of here, fast, before the constable wakes up.' They didn't spare a second as they sped down the road to the Rose and Crown and the highway.

'Why did you do that?' Harry asked. Apart from the unconscious constable they were alone. 'And you didn't save Bowland's neck for revenge, either.'

'Harry, for weeks I've dreamed of men dangling on the end of a rope — you, the major, even strangers. So when he came in, the constable, and was so happy at the thought of hanging them — well, I couldn't let him. I know that Bowland deserves to die, and I know his men will probably end up on the gallows anyway, but I'll have no part in sending a man there.' She leaned heavily against the wall. 'My God, there's been enough misery, hasn't there?'

Harry saw the look of weariness on his sister's face. He went to her and took her hands in his. Without a word, she leaned her face on his shoulder and wept.

★ ★ ★

Reverend Marcus Fazakerley had had enough of being a parish priest, and he wasn't enthusiastic about meeting Constable Webb again. 'I'm sure you'll understand, my lord, why I resign from the incumbency of this parish.'

'I do,' said Bowland, handing him his last twenty guineas. He beamed, tucked his fee into his leather bag, and departed.

'Farewell, Edward,' said Lancaster, holding out his hand in friendship.

Bowland ignored it. 'I don't seem to be able to make you understand, Richard, that I really do hate you.'

Lancaster shrugged. 'Very well, Edward. So be it.' He turned to Lucy. 'Here,' he said. He pulled the rose ring from his finger and gave it to her. 'For your first-born son.'

Lucy embraced her new cousin. 'About Mr Jackson,' she said. 'You will . . . ' She realized the impossibility of putting it into words, and gave up trying.

Bowland put his arms around Julia and gave her a brotherly hug. 'You are the only person in England I shall miss, Julia. Marry that Jackson fellow if you wish; I owe him something.'

'I'm afraid you won't be able to pay off your debt to him that way, Edward,' said the major. 'Julia will not marry Kit Jackson.'

'He's right, Julia,' said Lucy. 'Kit isn't the man for you.'

'Oh, let Richard have his petty revenge, Lucy,' said Bowland. 'We must go.' He took her hand and they walked together in the light that remained after the sun had set down the path to the river.

As Julia and Lancaster stood by the church

and watched, they heard Lucy say, 'It's nothing to do with Richard's revenge. Don't you know about Mr Jackson?'

'What is it?' came Bowland's voice.

'I'll tell you later,' said Lucy firmly in the last words that Julia and Lancaster heard as Edward, Earl of Bowland and murderer, strode into exile.

★ ★ ★

'Julia, I congratulate you,' said Lancaster. 'To shoot at Edward like that took considerable resolution.'

'Thank you, Richard. That's the finest thing you've ever said to me.'

'Oh, nonsense. I've always been your greatest admirer.'

'You've told me I was beautiful, and you've treated me like an idiot. You've always tried to keep unpleasantness away from me, you and Edward.'

'Yes, we have,' he admitted.

'I think that's why I fell in love with Kit Jackson. Oh, I know he's clever and brave, but so are you. But he — well, he's always treated me as a human being, not a beautiful doll. He understands what a woman wants.'

'Yes, well, he has something of an advantage in that direction,' he said in a very odd tone. 'Oh, damn. It's not funny,' he rebuked himself. 'Julia, you've learned tonight that your brother is a murderer, and you've taken it with the best of them. I'm afraid you are in for another shock.'

'It's Kit Jackson, isn't it? You've discovered his secret.'

'Yes.'

'He's not — you know, one of those men?' she asked, alarmed.

'Whatever you mean by that, Julia, the answer is no.'

'Of course not. You wouldn't be so close to him if he were. Then what is it?'

'I'm not going to tell you, because you wouldn't believe me. You'll have to hear it from Kit.'

As they passed the stables, a horse whinnied at the sound of their voices. 'That's Bess,' said Julia, a little sadly. 'I suppose she belongs to you now.'

'Why?'

'You remember; we made a wager about who would discover Kit's secret first. You seem to have won.'

'Keep Bess. I know you're fond of her.'

'Richard, you haven't been listening! I will not be treated like a beautiful idiot. You won that horse fair and square, and I'm holding you to it. She's yours.'

'I apologize. You've been my ward and my pretty little cousin for so long, it'll take me a while to get used to treating you like a rational human being. I accept Bess with thanks.'

'You won't ride her yourself, will you? She isn't up to your weight.'

'I wish you would give me credit for knowing that,' he said, then added intrepidly, 'I'll give Bess to my wife.'

'You don't have a wife!'

'I shall have, I hope, in the very near future.'

'You're not — you aren't still hoping to marry me, are you?'

'No, Julia, you turned me down fair and square, and I'm holding you to it.'

They entered the lodge. There was still some light in the sky, but very little penetrated the few windows. Kit was lighting candles, while Harry bent over the constable trying to restore him to consciousness.

Kit's eyes were red-rimmed, and if Julia hadn't known better she'd have thought that Mr Jackson had been crying. But whatever it was, Kit's face certainly lit up when Julia entered on her cousin's arm.

'What happened?' Lancaster asked. 'Where are those gaol-birds?'

'I let them go,' Kit said calmly.

'Perhaps you're right,' he acknowledged. 'If we let their master go free, we can hardly keep them. Though we're going to have trouble with the constable when he wakes up. Why did you hit him, Kit?'

Julia thought she knew. 'Mr Jackson, from the bottom of my heart I thank you for saving my brother Edward.' She looked into Kit's eyes. 'You did it for me, didn't you?'

Kit's face paled. 'I — er — '

'I think you owe my cousin the truth, *Mr Jackson*,' came the major's command.

'But — Major — I can't!' Kit wailed.

'Kit,' Julia asked earnestly. 'What is the truth?'

Kit said nothing, but looked around the room desperately for a way out.

'Tell me,' Julia urged. 'You promised to marry me, if I still wanted to. I can't think of anything you could tell me that would make me not want to.'

There was a groan behind her. It was the constable, coming round. 'I must attend to that poor man,' Kit said hastily, and darted away. Julia was nettled that a recovering constable should prove more attractive than she was. They were all standing over the man: Kit, Harry, Richard, and so she joined them.

Kit knelt down, holding a mug of water to

the man's lips. The constable drank gratefully. 'Oh, my head.' he muttered. Then he took a look at the person holding the mug. 'Oh, no! Not you again!'

'I'm terribly, terribly sorry,' Kit said.

'I knew I'd seen you before!' he cried. 'It was you, that time at the Rose and Crown, with the major, wasn't it?' She nodded. 'It's a mercy you didn't hit me on the head that time, I suppose.' He struggled to sit up. 'Next time you want me out of the way, what about laudanum? It don't hurt so much, Miss Faulkner.'

'What?' said Julia faintly.

'I said laudanum don't hurt so much,' the constable obligingly repeated.

'What did you call him?'

'Who?'

'What did you call Kit Jackson?' she screamed.

'Please don't talk so loud, lady,' he moaned, his head in his hands.

Kit stood up. 'He called me Miss Faulkner.'

'Why, Kit?' Julia whispered.

'Because it's my name. Katherine Faulkner.'

Julia blinked. She stared at the figure before her. She blinked again, then, without a word, turned and walked over to the wall. 'Oh, Lord!' she moaned.

There was a footstep behind her, and a

voice said, 'Lady Julia.' It was Harry Faulkner.

'What an appalling thing to do!'

'Lady Julia, my sister has saved me from the gallows, and saved your brother too. She has been forced to live a life that nobody, woman or man, should lead. She has deceived you, but please, don't hate her.'

'Hate her? Oh, no, I don't hate your sister. It's me I hate, for being such a fool.'

'Pray, don't,' Harry said, distressed at her distress. 'You weren't a fool. Everyone believed in Kit Jackson.'

'Yes,' she sighed. 'But he doesn't exist.'

'Neither do unicorns,' Harry said. 'A pity, isn't it?'

She turned and studied him, the young man who'd trusted her with the pistols. He was a fairly ordinary young man, and she'd never much liked red hair, but there was something about him: something in his eyes that she'd seen in Kit's. Kit didn't exist. He'd gone the way of the unicorn. But the young man beside her was very real indeed.

'Now, then,' said the constable loudly. 'I'd like a word with you ladies and gentlemen.' He took the floor and began to declaim. 'I 'ave a problem, and it's this. What am I going to do about Miss Faulkner? I ought to charge 'er. What with helping prisoners escape, and assaulting an officer of the law — twice — I could lock 'er up and throw away the key. But I don't want to.'

'That's very kind of you, Constable,' said Miss Faulkner, abashed.

'Well, mebbe you can put it down to me not wishing to appear an idiot in court when I say a young woman got the better of me twice. But you can't keep carrying on like that. Somebody 'as to keep an eye on you. Somebody responsible.' He paused for a moment, then said ponderously, 'Somebody who's held the king's commission, f'rinstance.'

'Would a major be responsible enough, do you think?' asked Major Lancaster, smiling broadly. He glanced at Kit, wanting to share the joke, but she was staring at the floor.

'I think a major would do excellent, Major.'

'I shall endeavour to co-operate, Constable.'

'I thought you might, sir.' He prepared to go. 'I'm off to report that I've solved the murder at the Rose and Crown. Oh, I know it was none of my doing,' he acknowledged. 'But I think I deserve something for that blow on the head.'

'Are you fit to travel?' asked the major.

'Fit enough to ride, and my horse is outside.' He left.

'Mr Faulkner,' said Lancaster. 'I would be a deal happier if somebody followed him on the road. A blow on the head can be dangerous.'

'Yessir,' said Harry, unthinkingly accepting his authority.

'And I'd be obliged if you'd escort my cousin to the Rose and Crown, where she has, I trust, a room waiting for her.'

'Yessir.'

'And don't call me sir. In the circumstances, I think we may call each other by our Christian names, don't you, Harry?'

'Yes — um — Richard,' said Harry.

'But, Harry!' said his sister faintly. She waved him over to her urgently. 'You can't leave me with the major alone at night!'

'Why not?'

'But — the proprieties!'

Harry laughed. 'You aren't in a position to worry overmuch about the proprieties!'

'Harry, don't say such things.'

'Now you're being missish.'

'Me? *Missish?*'

He held her hand. 'Kitty, that man has just risked his life for us. The least I can do is give him the chance to propose in private.'

'But — he wouldn't — he doesn't — What

if he isn't going to?'

'Of course he's going to. He knows his duty. After what you two have done together he's honour-bound to marry you.'

'Oh, no!' Suddenly she realized what she'd done to Richard Lancaster, and it sickened her. The times they'd been alone together — the night they'd slept in the same room in the Rose and Crown — all unknowingly, he had compromised her, and there was no way out for an honourable man but marriage.

She had loathed the way she'd deceived and betrayed him: but this was a deception and a betrayal that she'd never thought of.

Harry saw her distress and put his arm round her. 'There's not another man in England I'd sooner have as my brother-in-law, but I won't let you be forced into a marriage against your will, proprieties or no. If we must, we'll find a way out.'

'Can you think of one?'

'We shall if we have to. Just tell me, do you want to marry him?'

'No! Not if he's forced to!'

'That's not the point. What matters to me is what you feel. You promised me that you'd never marry a man you did not love. Word of a Faulkner; do you love Major Lancaster?'

'Yes, but — '

'Well, then.' He squeezed her shoulder,

then let her go. 'Thanks, Kitty.' he said. 'You're the best sister a man ever had. I'm very proud of you.' He turned. 'Lady Julia, I'd be delighted to escort you.'

Julia was ready to leave. 'So Kit Jackson will vanish, and Katherine Faulkner will appear at Lady Fenton's, I suppose?' she said.

'That's what I hope,' replied Kit.

'And if anyone notices any similarity between the two, we can say you had the same father.'

'I'll have McTavish tell my extremely talkative groom — in strict confidence, of course — that Kit Jackson was working with me to clear his brother from the charge of killing mine, and to save his sister from disgrace,' said Lancaster. 'The story will be around town within the week.'

Julia laughed. 'Oh, yes, that will work, Miss Faulkner. Nobody will argue once they know you're marrying Richard. Very few people argue with Richard.'

'But — '

'I think I shall like Katherine,' said Julia as she accepted Harry's arm. She stood for a second, framed in the doorway and lit by the last of the twilight. 'Good-bye, Kit Jackson,' she said wistfully.

Then she and Harry left Kit alone with Richard Lancaster.

Kit stared down at the floor. She noticed idly that the pool of blood was drying. His blood, that he'd shed for her. Why hadn't she seen what she was forcing him into? Harry knew it, Julia knew it, even the constable knew it. Why had she been so blind?

'Kit — Miss Faulkner, I mean,' he began, then stopped. 'It's no use. I can't bring myself to call you Miss Faulkner, not when Kit Jackson's standing there. May I follow your brother's example and call you Kitty?'

'Yes, Major,' she said, subdued.

'I don't suppose you could call me Richard, could you? In those clothes and calling me Major, you make me feel as if I'm about to propose to a damned subaltern.'

She carried on staring at the floor, saying nothing.

'Will you marry me?'

Her lips were dry. How she wanted to say yes! But she mustn't, for her own sake as well as his. For she couldn't bear to live with him if he did not love her. He wanted to marry Julia, not her. She couldn't force the word out, but she managed to shake her head.

'Kitty?' He was very, very close to her.

She managed to drag some resolve to help her. 'No,' she whispered.

He turned on his heel in dismay. 'I'm as big a fool as Julia,' he said ruefully. 'I thought you had some affection for me. I apologize, Miss Faulkner.'

'There is no need.' She didn't feel any happier now she'd refused him, but she felt calmer and could talk. 'You have done what duty demands. You have proposed marriage, and I have declined. There let the matter rest.'

'Do you think I propose to you out of a sense of duty?' he asked incredulously, pacing up and down.

'My brother informed me that you were obliged in honour to offer marriage. I too have my honour. I am responsible for putting you in this unfortunate position. The least I can do for you is refuse.'

'And I thought your brother was a sensible man!'

'He's right.'

'Of course he's right. Yes, I do have to propose to you, and you, by the bye, have to accept. Aside from anything else, the constable has said he'll lock you up if you don't. But what call had your brother to say so? I am not, I assure you, proposing to you from duty.'

'Aren't you?'

'No, of course I'm not. Kitty, I love you.'

An hour ago she would have given the world to hear such words from him, but now it was bitter. He was a good man, and he was putting a brave face on the inevitable and wanted to reconcile her to it. 'I appreciate your saying so, Major, and I know your motives are good. But I can't bring myself to believe you.'

'Damn it, Kit, don't be a bloody fool!' he roared in un-lover-like tones. 'Why the hell shouldn't I love you?'

'Me? After what I did to you? After I lied to you and spied on you?'

'You saved my life and you saved my sanity. Six weeks ago I was drinking myself to death, and a man I liked and trusted didn't think that was fast enough, so he tried to have me murdered. You came out of the night and fought off the men who were trying to kill me. And then you came into my home, and let me talk away my nightmares until I could go to bed sober. Damn, I'm bleeding again,' he added abruptly.

'Sit down.' She knelt down beside him as he obeyed. She adjusted the pad over the wound, and retied the bandages.

'Congratulations, by the bye, on the miraculous cure of your limp.'

'Pebbles in my boot,' she said. 'They

330

stopped me walking like a woman.'

'Kitty, you're the bravest person, man or woman, I've ever met.' He saw her look of incredulity, and added, 'Oh, yes. Hot-blooded heroism, that prefers to charge the cannon rather than be a coward in front of friends, is common enough. But for sheer cold, lonely, and enduring courage, what you've done in the past six weeks is more than anything I could have believed possible.' He smiled at her. 'Especially since you're such a terrible actor.'

'What do you mean?' she asked indignantly.

'You may not realize it, but your face is highly expressive: every emotion, every feeling you have is written in your wide brown eyes.'

She jumped up and turned her face away from him.

'Kitty,' she heard him say, 'if I'm wrong, if I've misinterpreted that look in your eyes — in short, if you don't love me — then tell me so at once. I'll have no unwilling wife. But don't dare tell me that I don't love you.'

She said nothing.

'Good God, what will it take to convince you?' He stood up, grabbed her shoulder and pointed at the blood on the floor. 'Isn't that enough?'

'That wasn't only for me,' she said. 'That

was for your brother — and because you're a hero.'

'Never have I regretted my reputation more!' he cried in exasperation. 'And as for my brother! You know what I felt for George. I wouldn't have pricked my finger for him.' His giddiness returned, and he sat down again. 'By the bye: one of the unlooked-for advantages in this match is that I shall gain in Harry a brother I can like — once I've forgiven him for giving you this ridiculous misapprehension.'

'It's not ridiculous!' she cried. 'How can you love someone who betrayed you — who would have sent you to the gallows?'

'Very easily, Kitty. I can guess how hard it was for you. You were trying to save Harry, and you thought I was the murderer, didn't you? It was that damned ring on my finger. That's what made you faint, and that's what made you rush out of my house with terror written all over your face.'

'Yes.' She shuddered as she remembered her fear.

'And I — well, I'd learned you were a woman, and I guessed which woman as soon as I heard you were at Lady Fenton's. I wanted to see you and talk to you, but I could hardly press matters. For my honour was engaged to Julia.'

He had almost convinced her until he said that. She swallowed and said, 'You want to marry Julia, don't you?'

'Good heavens, no!' he said cheerfully. 'And she doesn't want to marry me, I'm delighted to say; some rascal named Kit Jackson stole her affections. I ought to call him out, shouldn't I?'

He was rewarded by a slight smile. A little wavery, but a smile nevertheless.

'Do you love her?' she asked.

'I do, in point of fact. But only as my cousin. I don't have the feelings for her a man should have for his wife — not the feelings I have for you.' He beckoned her to come to him where he sat. 'Kitty, why won't you believe that I love you?'

'Because you don't know me,' she said, not moving.

'It's only a few weeks, I agree, but in that time you and I have been intimate in a way that very few people ever achieve, men or women. We've talked together; we've met mind to mind. You know me, more than anyone else ever has. How can you say that I don't know you?'

'But that wasn't me!' she cried. 'That was Kit Jackson. You learnt I was a woman only three days ago; you've never seen me in woman's clothes; you don't even know what

Katherine Faulkner looks like. You can't possibly love me: you haven't had time!'

'So that's it,' he sighed. 'Yes, I can see why you don't believe me.' He stood up, walked slowly to the window, and stared out at the clear night sky. 'So this is what it will take.' He laughed ruefully. 'My God! I'd rather fight a dozen duels for you than say — than tell you — ' He stopped. He couldn't look at her.

'What is it?' She moved closer to him, but not close enough to touch.

'I think — ' He paused, then coughed and went on. 'I think I may have loved you from the moment I first saw you.'

'But — '

'I am certain that I've loved you since that night in the Rose and Crown,' he finished, his voice barely under control.

'But you can't have! That's absurd!'

'Those, Kitty, were precisely the words I used myself when I realized what my feelings for you were.'

'Oh,' she said in a very small voice.

'Oh, indeed. All my life I'd thought I was a normal man with normal desires. But I found myself in love with someone whom my eyes told me was another man. I'd condemned Hector Smythe and his kind; but it seemed that I *was* one of his kind. To have him smile knowingly at me — to be giggled over by girls like Julia and Lucy — ugh, I couldn't endure it! So I proposed to Julia, to try to prove to myself that I was a proper man. Didn't you realize what I was doing? Didn't you know why I was doing my damnedest to keep my distance from you?'

'I thought it was because I refused to be open with you, that night at the Rose and Crown. I saw the revulsion on your face.'

'Revulsion! For myself, certainly, but it was the last thing I felt for you.' His voice became tender. 'Do you remember the time when I went looking for you, and I found you on Westminster Bridge?'

'I remember,' she whispered.

'I knew you were troubled: I thought perhaps you were troubled for the same reason that I was. I didn't know. I thought I'd seen love in your eyes, but I'd also seen innocence. You climbed up behind me and you put your arms round me, and we rode home together. I learned then that, whatever the mockery, whatever the shame, they were nothing compared with the thought of parting from you. But then you fainted, and, when I picked you up and loosened your clothes, I discovered that my eyes had been deceived, but my heart had been telling me the truth all the time.'

'I heard you when I came round. 'The guilt! The bloody guilt!''

'The guilt was intolerable, but I couldn't escape it. I couldn't stop loving you, Kitty, even though I thought you were a man.'

She reached out to him, and put her hand on his bare shoulder. 'And I couldn't stop loving you, Richard, even though I thought you were a murderer.'

He whirled round to face her. 'You do love me!'

'Of course I do. I think I may have loved you from the moment I first saw you,' she said, looking down. She couldn't see much, only the masculine curl of the hair on his chest, matted with blood. 'And I am certain that I've loved you since that night at the Rose and Crown.'

'The time that I held you like this,' he said, gripping her shoulder, 'and I asked you if you trusted me.' His other hand held her chin, and brought her eyes up to look at his. 'Do you trust me?'

'Yes.' It was so easy to say yes.

'Will you marry me?'

'Yes.'

He didn't move for a moment, but studied her, smiling. 'You looked at me as you are doing now, with those wide eyes of yours. I suddenly realized — and the devil of a shock it was, I assure you — that what I wanted to do was this.' He stroked the soft skin of her face. 'And this.' His arm went round her waist, pulling her to him. 'But most of all, I wanted to do this,' he said, and his mouth found hers, and neither of them said anything for a very long time.

THE END

We do hope that you have enjoyed reading this large print book.

Did you know that all of our titles are available for purchase?

We publish a wide range of high quality large print books including:
Romances, Mysteries, Classics
General Fiction
Non Fiction and Westerns

Special interest titles available in large print are:
The Little Oxford Dictionary
Music Book
Song Book
Hymn Book
Service Book

Also available from us courtesy of Oxford University Press:
Young Readers' Dictionary
(large print edition)
Young Readers' Thesaurus
(large print edition)

For further information or a free brochure, please contact us at:
Ulverscroft Large Print Books Ltd.,
The Green, Bradgate Road, Anstey,
Leicester, LE7 7FU, England.
Tel: (00 44) 0116 236 4325
Fax: (00 44) 0116 234 0205

Other titles in the
Ulverscroft Large Print Series:

SLAUGHTER HORSE

Michael Maguire

The Turf Security Division is surprised and suspicious when playboy Wesley Falloway's second-rate horses develop overnight into winners. Simon Drake investigates, but suddenly there is a new twist — someone is out to steal General O'Hara, the star of British bloodstock, owned by Wesley Falloway's mother. With a few million pounds at stake, lives are cheap; Drake finds himself both hunter and quarry in a murderous chase where even his closest associates may be playing a double game.

MERMAID'S GROUND

Alice Marlow

It's been five years since Kate Williams' beloved husband died, leaving her with two young children to raise. Now she's built a good life in one of Wiltshire's prettiest villages, and she has her dream job, as gardener at Moxham Court. For the last year, Kate has had a lover, roguishly attractive Justin Spencer, but he won't commit to more than a night here and there. When she takes in a male lodger, Jem, Kate's secretly hoping his presence will provoke a jealous reaction in Justin. What she hasn't reckoned on is exactly how attractive Jem will turn out to be.

COME HOME TO DANGER

Estelle Thompson

Charles Waring has come home to Queensland to attend his mother's funeral and his remark, intended only for a family friend to hear, is inadvertently overheard by several other people. The chain of events which follows convinces Charles that his mother was murdered because she knew a terrible secret from someone's past, and he finds himself in a deadly game of cat-and-mouse as he tries to unravel the mystery. Meanwhile, he must face the certainty that someone among those he has come to care about poses a cruel threat.

SUMMER OF SECRETS

Grace Thompson

When Bettrys Hopkyns' alcoholic sister Eirlys committed suicide, Bettrys was determined that Eirlys's baby daughter Cheryl — the result of Eirlys's secretive summer love affair — would stay with her. Still yearning for Brett, her former lover, Bettrys sets herself a challenge: to find Cheryl's father. Her search takes her and Cheryl to a small seaside village in west Wales; to a close-knit community seething with secrets. Befriended by the cheerful Gordon, who falls in love with her, Bettrys is quickly drawn into a web of deceit and is forced to face the terrifying possibility that Brett might be a murderer . . .